INVITE THE WOLF

CURSED MANUSCRIPTS

BOOK EIGHT

IAIN ROB WRIGHT

ULCERATED PRESS

Super special thanks to the following people

Lisa Whitsel, Jules Banks, Andrew Callander, Lesley Pink, Tony 'Big Jacko' Jackson, Sue Jackson, Sharon Curtis, Vince Losacco, Stuart Becker, Stephanie Martin, Christina Brunskill, Emma Hawkins, Andy Callander, James McAteer, Derek Lawley, Tony Jackson, Cheryl Grimes-Sing, Anita Shell, Gareth Toon, Gray Ormond, Hilary Moreton, Sarah Ross, Sue Rowden, Samantha Scott, Margaret McAloon, Clark D. Young, Leona Huling, Joanne Dunford, Michelle Harryman, J.A. Helling, Vyxee, Naheed Naseem, Carol Hofbauer, Vanda Luty, Trący Knoblauch, Ann Harrison, Ros Howarth, Dawn Achary, Ali Nlack, Sarah Louise, Dan (from Vancouver), Trish Roberts, Lisa Burgin, Janet Wilde, Alex Cox, Stacey Crawford, Lainey Ash, Caron, Simon, Maxine Summers, Leanne Findley, Francis Keenan, Dhc, Paul, Simon Bennett, Ashley, Jack, Michelle Scholey, Anthony Wilkins, Stephen Moss, Brandi, Trudy Bryan, Lynn M, John Williams, Sue Mackenzie, Melanie Roeck, Edward Lees, Steven Pike, Barry Auerbach, Jill Hutton, David Merchant, Carl Saxon, Karen Cunningham, Jay, Helen Brisco, Rob Easthorpe, Richard Hartley, Kerry

WITH THANKS TO MY PATRONS...

Jimmy Johnson, Julian White, Emma Neil, Blanche Auxier, Wendy Daniel, Jan Willard, Fear kitty, James Cradock, Valena Smith, Renee, Lola Wayne, Sarah C, Wendy Daniel, Lisa Vaughan, Belinda Murray, Simon Longman, Lanie Evans, John Claunch, Lorraine Wilson, Fiona Thompson, Luis Roco, Terry Watson, Clark Kent, Candy, Lindsay Carter, Steve N, Rach Kinsella Chippendale, Maxons, Chris Jones, Jonathan & Tonia Cornell, Chris Hicks, Sandra Behrens, Carl Donze, Chris Nelson, Rigby Jackson, Linda Paisley, Karen Roethle, Carmen Hammond, Russell Wilson, Michael Pearse, Mark Ayre, Virginia Milway, Suzie Roush, Katrice Tuck, Adrian Shotbolt, keepsmiling, Minnis Hendricks, Kelli Herrera, Phil Brady, Steve Haessler, Darrion Mika, Karen Lewis, Suzy Tadlock, Kaarin Chadwick, mari meisel, Jayne Smith, Susanne Stohr, CJMac, Stacey, Amanda Shaw, Connie France, Gillian Moon, Robin, Stephanie Everett, Linda Heafield, Ali Black, Elizabeth Thompson, Stainedglasslee, Stacey, guitarmangrg, Diane Rushton, Stephen Moss, Jean Geill, Elizabeth Auclair, Adrianne Yang, Linda, Leslie Clutton, Sarah Chambers, Kat Miller, Sara Boe, Carole, Nigel Crabtree, Becky Wright, Claire

Taylor, Caryn Larsen, Leigh Hickey, Steve Griffith, Diesta Kaiser, Fiona Thompson, Mark Horey, Gian Spadone, Mark Stone, Rachel Stinnett, Billie Wichkan, Deborah Shelton, Pauline Stout, Angelica Maria, Katie Potter, Jordan Rasmussen, Deirdre Lydon, Bobbie Kelley, Vicky Salter, Melissa Potter, Debbi Sansom, Stewart Cuthbertson, Nicole Reid, Bruce W, Clark, carrieanne, Mark Harvey, Mark Simpson, Graeme McMechan, Jacqueline Coleman, Vanda Luty, Ruth F Phelps, Donna Twells, Katie Warburton, Susan Kay, Nick Brooks, Stewart Barnes, Nigel Jopson, Gemma Ve, Steven Barnett, Sally Jayne Dainton, Tania Buss, Lee Ballard, Emma Bailey, Clive, Robert Smith, Oscar Booker Jr, Trevor Oakley, Leona Overton, Susan Hayden, Jennifer Holston, Kelee S, Terence Smith, Michelle Chaney, Roy Oswald, Paul Weaver, Linda Robinson, Chris Aitchison, Michael Rider, Deborah Knapp, Bread, Beth Thurman, Cass Griffiths, Debbie Ivory, David Lennox, William Matthews, Kim Slater, Hazel Smith, Laurie Cook, Margaret McAloon, Paul, Neil Grey, Catherine H, Sherrie, Brian McGowan, Pam Felten, Carol Wicklund, Mary Meisel, Deborah, Lady Aliehs, Rachel Mayfield, Kerry Hocking, Maniel Le, Andre Jenkin, Lawrence Clamons, Gary Groves, Mike Prankard, Dan Garay, Rona Trout, Mark Pearson, Mary Kiefel, Emma, Karen lewis, Eddie Garcia, Tracy Putland, Laura Monaghan, Boy Stio, Emily Haynes, Pam Brown, Sharon Campbell, Scott Menzies, Deirdre Gamill-Hock, Allison Valentine, Marika Borger, Joe Wardle, William Cahill, Kristin Scearce, Lisa McGlade, Jay Evans, Janet Wilde, Mark Junk, Sarah Atherton, Phil Hope, Trudy Bryan, Joanne Wheatley, John may, Stacie Jaye, Kirsty Mills, Louise, Kenneth Mcintire, Adam Thayer, Jonathan Emmerson, Susan Rowden, Becki Sinks, Becki Battersby, Derek Titus, Phil, Rebecca Strouse, Stacie Denise, Sarah Powell, Paula Bruce, Stella, Sandra Lewis, Windi LaBounta, Stephanie Hardy, Janet Carter, Lisa Kruse, Gillian Adams, Lauren, Clare Lanes, Jacqueline Scifres, John

Best, Stacey Arkless, Nate Stephenson, Senha S., Vicki, Gary Lomax, Debi, Beth Steele, Pamela Laurence, Mandy Clark,Jane Destroyer Wick, Robin Lewis, Alfredo Borunda, Kimberly Coker, Learn Welsh Podcast, Ash, Pattie Bowen, Jeni Miller, Robin, Mary M, Dee Hancocks, Sarah Bell, PsychoWhite, Sophie Beth Conlon, Spyridon Miaris, Wendy Jones

Quotes

"Children are the world's most valuable resource."
   - **John F. Kennedy**

"The righteous anger that fuels vigilantism often masks a darker truth – the desire for personal revenge and a disregard for the principles of justice."
   - **David Wilson**

"I'm gonna chop you into 42 pieces."
   - **Max Cady, Cape Fear (1991), Universal Pictures**

ONE

The sky was overcast and grey, but Tanning Stanley Fields was a whirlwind of bright lights, and a chest-pounding beat underscored excited screams of adults and children alike. The acrid tang of fried onions battled with the mouthwatering scents of warm popcorn and hot doughnuts.

Alfie squeezed his twin sister's hand. "Come on, Lil. The candyfloss is right over there. What's the problem?"

Daisy's eyes darted towards the open-sided green van with bags of pink and blue candyfloss hanging from its awning. She fidgeted with her ponytail, which was the same white blonde as Alfie's mop. "I just don't wanna get in trouble. Mummy said ice cream later only if we're good."

Alfie bounced on his toes, practically tasting the sugar already and desperately wanting his sister to come along. "We'll be right back, Lil. It'll be fine."

She blew air through the gap in her front teeth, but finally gave in like he knew she would. "Promise we'll be quick."

"Double promise." Alfie grabbed her hand and yanked her towards the candyfloss van, dodging between the crowds. The last five-pound note remaining from his eighth birthday would be enough for two bags of candyfloss. Maybe even three, which meant Mummy could have one too. Alfie had seen her crying earlier and drinking beer. Auntie Maureen kept hugging her and saying things like, "He's a bastard. You're better off." Alfie reckoned they were talking about his dad.

Halfway to their destination, Daisy dug her heels in. "Oh, Alfie, there's a big line."

Alfie deflated like the chocolate cake Mummy took out of the oven last weekend. Behind the black-and-red spinning waltzers was a long, slow-moving line of people, all of them wanting candyfloss. Getting to the front would take forever.

I just want to do a nice thing. Why is it so hard?

After their joint birthday party last week, both Alfie and Daisy had received twenty pounds to spend. Daisy had immediately spent half of hers on him, grabbing a copy of *Cloudy with a Chance of Meatballs* on DVD when she had gone to the supermarket with their Auntie Maureen. She must have known how badly he had wanted to watch it, and had used her money to make him happy. He wanted to pay her back for being so kind. Little sisters looked up to their older brothers, and he was older by a full twenty-eight minutes.

"Why can't these people go someplace else?" he muttered, then glanced around the fair, hoping to find somewhere else to buy something delicious, but all he spotted was a burger van and a stupid hook-a-duck stand with crappy prizes. Who the hell wanted a sheriff's hat?

He stomped his foot and moaned. "This isn't fair."

Daisy tugged at his hand. "Let's go back. It'll take too long."

"Yeah, okay. Mummy might let us go on some more rides before we walk home."

"She keeps talking about Dad," Daisy said, shuffling her

feet and staring at her jelly sandals, "saying how much he's been a— Ouch!"

A tall man in a baseball cap brushed past them, knocking Daisy back a step. His sudden presence blocked out the bright lights of the waltzers.

Alfie reached out to steady his sister. "Wow, are you okay?"

She rubbed her elbow and whimpered, her bottom lip trembling.

The stranger stopped and turned to face them. His baseball cap had a picture of a howling wolf on it. "Oh, pardon me, young lady. Clumsy as an ox, I am. Plus, you're so dainty, I didn't even see you. Did I hurt you?"

Daisy shook her head.

The stranger bent forward and stared at her. "My, what beautiful blue eyes you have. Can you forgive my clumsiness?"

Daisy turned bright red, typically shy, so Alfie stepped forward and said, "Accidents happen." It was something his teacher, Mr Meadows, always told him.

The stranger chuckled, and so did Alfie. It was nice making adults laugh. Much better than making them mad.

"Accidents do happen indeed, Sonny Jim, but not everyone has manners." The tall man straightened up and folded his arms, which were covered in thick black hair. "So where's your mother?" he asked, looking around. His dark eyes were partially shadowed by the brim of his cap. "You're not lost, are you?"

Alfie shook his head. "We were just going to get some candyfloss, but..." – he flapped his arms and grunted – "there's a big queue."

"A queue? Well, that's no problem at all." The man put his hands on his hips and smiled. He had a thick black moustache, but had no hair on his chin or cheeks. His eyes seemed too far back, as if someone had pushed them into his face. "My name's Mitchell," he said. "I work here at the fair. See?" He tapped his dark blue T-shirt and pointed out a colourful sticker with a bunch of balloons and the word FUN on it.

"You work here?" Daisy asked, her eyes pointed at the ground. Her voice was little more than a whisper. "Do you get to go on all the rides?"

Another chuckle, an even bigger smile. "Why yes, miss. Although I have to admit, I get a little queasy these days so I tend to stick to the big wheel and the other gentle rides. You can see everything from up there, you know? Do you like being up high?"

Daisy nodded, and then stared across the fairground until her eyes settled on the towering Ferris wheel at the opposite end of the field. It was stopped currently, its white baskets tilting to and fro in the light breeze. "It's my favourite ride," she said.

You big fibber! Alfie rolled his eyes. *You hated it. Had your eyes closed the whole time.*

"You're not afraid of heights?" Mitchell asked.

Daisy shook her head, left then right. "Nope!"

"Then you're a very brave little lady." He reached out and pinched her cheek, causing her to giggle and grow even redder.

Alfie wanted to know more about this man. If Mitchell worked at the funfair, then he had the coolest job ever. "Can you help us skip the queue for candyfloss?"

"I can get you all the candyfloss you want, young man." He put his hands out to them both and clicked his fingers. "Take my hands and we can go grab some right now from my van. How's that sound?"

Alfie frowned. "Your van?"

"Sure. It's where we keep all the spare candyfloss and sweeties." He looked at Daisy and winked, making her blush all over again.

"My brother's looking after me," she said. "He has birthday money left to spend. I spent all mine."

Mitchell folded his arms and looked Alfie up and down. "Well, happy birthday to you both. That means extra candyfloss."

"It was last week," Alfie said, his chest swelling. "Can you not just take us to the front of the queue?"

"'Fraid not. It would make the people in line angry if they saw us bending the rules." He leaned in closer, a buttery smell coming off him. "Hey, you two are twins, aren't you? You know that makes you very, very special? Very special indeed."

Alfie rolled his eyes, believing the exact opposite. "It means we have to share everything and never get to do stuff on our own. Don't feel like we're very special."

"Shut up," Daisy said. "We *are* special. We're the only twins at our school. Mrs Danica calls us 'Double Trouble', and when we're older Alfie is going to be on TV and I'm going to do his make-up."

"A TV star, eh? Well, you've got the looks for it." He laughed out loud and then clicked his fingers again because Alfie hadn't yet taken his hand. "Oh yes, the two of you are very rare indeed. Come now, let's go get you that candyfloss. I might even throw in some popcorn, too, if you behave. I can trust you to be good children, right?"

Daisy grinned. "I love popcorn. I promise we'll be good."

Alfie turned and looked back through the crowd. He spotted his mum and Auntie Maureen still chatting away. They hadn't even noticed he and Daisy were gone. They could probably get back fast enough to avoid getting into any trouble at all.

But Alfie wasn't sure it was okay to go with a stranger, even a nice one like Mitchell. "I think we should go ask Mummy first. She'll wonder where we are."

Mitchell had a lopsided grin on his face, and for a moment he just stared at Alfie. Then he nodded. "I understand completely. Let's go talk to her right now, but I have to warn you, I could get called away at any moment. My lunch break is already over, and the only reason I'm stretching it is because I don't want to see you kids disappointed."

Alfie didn't want to miss out on candyfloss, but he also didn't want to wander off and get in trouble. "Um, how long will we be?"

"We'll be back before your mother even notices. But it's up to you, young man. If you don't want to go, tell me now so I can get back to running the dodgems."

Alfie took another glance around. People were everywhere, adults and children aplenty, all of them running around and having fun. So what was the big deal? Why shouldn't he go get candyfloss with his own money?

Alfie reached out and took Mitchell's hand – twice the size of his own – and allowed himself to be led away, his concern fading into excitement. "Let's go."

"Good lad."

They walked right past the candyfloss van with its massive, miserable-looking queue, and headed towards the outer edge of the funfair where there was only a bouncy castle and inflatable slide, used mostly by the smaller kids, and a small coffee shop/toilet block that had been opened this year. Further on lay the car park and a large playing field with bright white goalposts. Alfie walked with his head up high as they left the hustle and bustle, the blaring pop music and whooping crowds fading away behind them. He felt like one of those rich kids on the Internet who got to walk around empty toy stores and grab whatever they wanted.

I got a friend who works at the funfair.

"Thank you for helping us, Mitchell."

"Yeah," Daisy said. "You're a kind man. Do you have kids?"

Mitchell smiled at them both in turn. "Never had the pleasure, young lady, although I have two nephews. Anyway, this way. Keep up!"

"How much further?" Alfie asked, starting to wheeze. Mitchell's legs were much longer than his.

Mitchell's hand clamped around Alfie's, the grip tightening until Alfie winced. "Not much further now," he said, his voice dropping to a whisper. "But no more talking, okay? We don't want the other kids to know about this, do we?"

Alfie hissed. "You're squeezing my hand too tight. Let go."

Mitchell stopped them at the edge of the car park and bent towards Alfie, his eyes barely visible in the shadow of his cap. "I don't want you wandering off, do I? What would your mother say if I let you get hit by a car or bitten by a dog?"

He tugged at both their hands and dragged them along again, almost jogging. Alfie's new birthday trainers scuffed against the gravel as he tried to keep up, and a sickly feeling grew in his tummy as they got further and further away from the funfair.

No one in the car park noticed the three of them hurrying along, and blaring rock music coming from a small car full of teenagers made it so that nobody could hear them either.

"Just over here," Mitchell said, leading them towards the far corner of the car park. "This is my van, right here."

They came to a stop in a gap between a shiny red car with a soft roof and a dirty white van with muddy wheels. When Mitchell let go of their hands, Alfie had to make a fist to get rid of the ache in his fingers.

The white van had rusty door handles and scratches all along its side. It smelled bad too, like the oil on Alfie's bike chain.

"Y-you have candyfloss in there?"

Mitchell put his hand against the back of Alfie's head and gently stroked his hair. "I sure do. Buckets and buckets of the stuff. As much as you want." He unlocked the side door of the van and slid it open with a loud *whomp* that made Alfie flinch. "Right inside here."

Alfie saw nothing in the van except a thick, unmoving darkness. It reminded him of the understairs cupboard at home that always made him shiver whenever he passed it, fearing he might somehow get trapped inside, unable to escape and with no one to hear his cries.

"Just hop on up and get whatever you want, little miss." Mitchell winked at Daisy.

"It's high up," she said.

"Here, let me help you." He grabbed her by the armpits and hoisted her up into the back of the van, almost tossing her. "Go on now," he said. "You'll find it all right there at the back."

Alfie's heart pounded in his chest, its beat echoing in his ears. "D-Daisy, I think you should get out of there. We need to get back to Mummy."

Mitchell had a big smile on his face, but his long, crowded teeth reminded Alfie of the wolf in Red Riding Hood.

No, the wolf on his baseball cap.

"You're next, Sonny Jim."

"I don't want to." Alfie stepped back, dodging Mitchell's large hands just as they reached out to grab him. "And my name isn't Sonny Jim. Stop calling me that."

Mitchell continued smiling that wolflike grin, but it never reached his eyes. "What's the matter, lad? Don't you want some candyfloss?"

"No. No, I changed my mind. I want to go."

"Don't be silly. Come here."

Alfie stepped back again. "No."

"I said, come here!"

Alfie hurried to the rear of the van. This was wrong. Mitchell's face was mean. His arms were too hairy. He had too many teeth.

"There's no reason to be afraid, lad."

"I want to go. Daisy? Daisy, please get out of the van." He raised his voice. "Daisy, get out! Get out!"

Mitchell backed off, both hands up in front of him as if he were suddenly afraid. He didn't like Alfie shouting. "Okay, okay, just keep your voice down, won't you?" His eyes darted back and forth, seeming to scan the car park. "There's no problem here, Sonny J—"

"I said stop calling me that. It's not my name!"

"Quiet!" He lunged at Alfie, wagging a finger and baring his teeth. "You keep quiet now, do you hear?"

"I want my sister. Daisy!"

"Stop making a scene, you little shit."

Alfie gasped.

Daisy appeared in the side opening of the van, blinking as the sun hit her face. She peered at Alfie with a frown on her face. "There's no candyfloss."

Mitchell's face darkened like a horrible story-book monster who had only been pretending to be a man. He shoved Daisy in her chest and sent her tumbling back into the darkness of the van. He slid the door closed, trapping her inside, then turned to Alfie with a finger on his lips. "Shh, lad."

Daisy let out a muffled sob from inside the van.

"He's got my sister," Alfie screamed. "Help! Someone help!"

One of the teenagers listening to rock music nearby immediately took notice. He hopped out of the car and started to come over. "Hey kid, are you okay?"

"He's got my sister. He won't let her go."

The teenager stared blankly for a second, and then his face screwed up. "Come here, buddy. It's okay."

"I can't. M-my sister."

"I'm leaving, sir," Mitchell shouted back. "There's no problem here. Just a misunderstanding."

"You ain't going nowhere, mate." The teenager marched towards the van, and his friends exited the car behind him. "Step away from the kid."

"He's my son."

"I'm not," Alfie yelled. "I'm not his son."

"Get in the fucking van!" Mitchell snatched at Alfie, but quickly changed his mind. Instead, he raced around to the front of the van, yanked open the driver's side door and hopped inside.

Several adults in the car park took notice now. They hurried to help, yelling at Mitchell to stop, but he didn't listen.

All the while, Alfie stood motionless.

The sound of the van's engine grumbling to life was the worst thing he had ever heard. Like a monster waking up. A monster that had swallowed his sister.

The van lurched backwards.

Alfie's feet finally freed themselves. He leapt aside in time to narrowly avoid getting hit, but his ankle twisted as his trainer wedged in the gravel and he barely kept his balance. The pain brought tears to his eyes.

I don't know what's happening.

Mummy is going to be so mad.

The angry teenager and a pair of white-faced adults banged on the side of the van. They tried to yank open the side door, but it was locked. Daisy screamed inside – screamed for Alfie – but there was nothing he could do. He stood there, crying and begging for the adults to make everything okay.

But they couldn't make it okay.

The van's muddy tyres skidded in the gravel and threw up rocks as it spun around. It forced the teenager and the adults to turn away and shield their faces.

Alfie couldn't scream any more. He was frozen. Empty.

I'm supposed to look after her.
She's my little sister.

Mitchell glared out the side window at Alfie, the monster on full display. The teenager beat his fists against the side window, trying to get in, but the glass wouldn't break.

The van sped out of the car park and disappeared onto the busy main road.

Gone.

Daisy was gone.

Alfie tried to make sense of what had just happened, but it was like his brain had hiccups. He couldn't even start a single thought without having to restart it. Both his hands trembled at his sides and his stomach felt like a washing machine sloshing around and around, but his legs were like wood: they wouldn't move an inch.

His mummy found Alfie five minutes later in the car park, strangers fussing over him and asking him, over and over again, what had happened. When he told her about Mitchell, and what the man had done with Daisy, she made sounds he had never heard her make before.

Then she threw up and collapsed into the arms of a stranger.

Two

Alfie Everett stared at his reflection in the Nando's bathroom mirror, his blue eyes bloodshot. He rubbed at his temples, feeling the weight of exhaustion hanging off his bones. "I gotta cool it with the drinking," he said. "Or else I'm gonna be looking thirty by the time I'm twenty-two."

Someone shoved open the bathroom door and poked their head inside. It was Jaydon, his best mate and second-in-command. "You good, bro? We need to bounce."

Alfie adjusted the collar of his grey woollen overcoat and gave a thumbs up. "Better than good, mate. We're about to catch a wolf."

Jaydon returned the gesture. "Slay, bro."

Alfie took one last look in the mirror, his mind flicking back to the day this had all started, thirteen years ago – with his sister, Daisy, and the man who had snatched her away. Then he exited the bathroom with his friend, ready to go to work.

The waitress fluttered her eyelids as he strolled back through the restaurant – probably because he had tipped twenty quid on top of the bill, or possibly because she had seen him online and knew who he was.

Three million subscribers and counting.

Sadie and Ezra were waiting back at the dining booth, sipping their diet cokes and idly chit-chatting. Amassed on the table in front of them was an array of recording equipment that only Ezra fully understood. As well as being their camera-man, he was their chief tech nerd and an aspiring movie director.

"Ready to go?" Sadie asked when Alfie and Jaydon rejoined them. She put her empty glass down on the edge of the wooden table and picked up her phone, holding it out so that Alfie could see the screen. "I've got wolf number one chomping at the bit here."

"It's champing," Ezra corrected her. "*Champing* at the bit."

She pulled a face at him. "That's so not a word."

Alfie put a hand on the table and leant forward. As usual, the private chat messages she was showing him were sickening.

H: Wher r u?

S: Just leaving school 2 come meet you. Can't wait! x

H: Me erither. Gona kiss u all ovar. In your special placve. xx

"This sicko must be texting with one hand," Alfie sneered. "Typos for days."

Sadie wiggled her tawny eyebrows. "He's meeting us in twenty minutes around the back of the library. You can bring up his poor spelling then."

"I have other things I wanna talk about, trust me." He put his thumbs in the belt loops of his black jeans and leant against the side of the booth. The smell of peri-peri spice was astringent now that his belly was full, and he was looking forward to fresh air. "What about wolf number two? The whole episode hinges on him turning up as well."

"Wolf deux has gone quiet," Ezra said, adjusting the headband that held back his snake's nest of ginger braids. "Might be a no-show, dude."

Sadie shook her head. "No, no. He's eager. Probably just driving. I got him wrapped around my little finger." She batted her eyelids. "I give good bait."

Alfie delicately tapped the square tip of her nose. "You're our MVP, babe."

Jaydon shook his head with a bemused grin on his face. "Can you believe we got two of these suckers on the hook? Views are gonna go through the roof after we drop the next ep."

"I wonder how they'll react," Ezra asked around the straw in his mouth. "Will they see each other as allies when we ambush them? Or will they throw each other under the bus? We should have invited Richie Attenborough."

"Who cares how they react?" Alfie folded his arms. "All I'm interested in is exposing them for what they are. Predators."

Jaydon let out a quiet howl. It was their rallying cry, something they had done ever since filming their very first episode, where they had set up a twenty-six-year-old named Brent Busey who had been planning to meet up with a fictitious twelve-year-old at the cinema. The acts he had wanted to perform in the back row had been obscene and illegal. Now the piece of shit was in jail because of their good work.

Alfie gave a howl back and then clapped his hands together. "Let's do this."

Sadie and Ezra exited the booth and brushed themselves off. Ezra grabbed his gear, loading himself up, and then the four of them exited the restaurant. They headed down the shopping centre's escalators and headed out onto the rain-spattered high street.

As they walked towards their destination, Sadie nudged

Alfie in the ribs. "Oh, the waitress left this for you, by the way," she said.

Frowning, Alfie took the piece of paper and unfolded it. A Nando's meal receipt, and at the bottom someone had written a mobile number with a smiley face next to it. He scrunched it up and tossed it into the nearest bin. "She's barking up the wrong tree, babe. The whole Internet knows I'm a one-woman guy."

Sadie reached out and held his hand. "Who can blame her for wanting a piece of my sexy man?"

A few steps ahead of them, Jaydon groaned. "You two are gonna make me puke."

Sadie's cheeks turned bright red, bringing out the freckles on her pale skin. "Sorry," she said, and then put her fingers to her temples and closed her eyes. "Okay. Refocusing, refocusing..." She opened her eyes again. "Refocused! I've got my eye on the prize and I'm ready to roll. Wolf-hunting mode initiated."

"You're such a goof." Jaydon laughed and shook his head.

"But it's time to get serious," Alfie chided. "Because this episode is the biggest we've ever done. We need to bring our A game."

"All we have is A game, bro." Jaydon checked his Rolex. "We about that hustle."

Alfie checked his slightly more modest Tissot and saw that it was twenty to three.

Not long now. The minutes are counting down.

Today's first wolf – with the username of 'HenryLong-Shaft' – had agreed to meet with 'Stacey' at three o'clock. But instead of encountering a thirteen-year-old girl, he would find a camera shoved in his face and Sadie reeling off a shitload of incriminating messages taken from a private chat thread.

This marked the fifteenth time *Invite the Wolf* had ambushed a predator since launching as an online channel three years ago. They were now one of the top-rated accounts on both Evershare and Clip Watch, the two biggest video hosting sites in the world.

But today's episode had a little extra spice on the Dorito.

HenryLongShaft wasn't their only target.

Claypole83 had been a lot harder to hook, but Sadie had been working on him for weeks, like a dog with a bone, refusing to give in. At first, Claypole hadn't even seemed like a predator, but then, suddenly, he had taken the bait and asked to meet up with 'Lucy'. Lucy, who was a twelve-year-old horse-loving girl from Redditch, a large town south of Birmingham. Claypole83 was travelling all the way down from Nottingham just to meet with her.

And it's gonna be the worst mistake of his sorry little life.
I'll make sure of it.

Alfie and his team reached an open, red-bricked plaza opposite the town's public library and started to get set up. To keep from being prematurely spotted, they took cover inside the recessed entryway of an empty shop unit. Alfie vaguely remembered the place once having been a carpet retailer before going bust many years ago. Redditch was a place where businesses went to die, and shuttered shops rarely reopened – especially in this quiet, neglected part of town where even the pigeons didn't bother coming.

Ezra made some adjustments to his camera, a small but expensive model that Alfie knew only as 'the Canon'. They had larger equipment back at the Barn – which was where they produced and maintained their channel – but for a sting like this, they needed to stay mobile.

The plaza was quiet, but not entirely deserted, so Ezra waited until the coast was clear before he gave an 'okay' with his thumb and forefinger. "You're live, Alf."

Alfie put on his well-rehearsed, handsome smile and fixed his gaze upon the camera lens. "Hey there, wolf hunters, it's your boy, Alfie Everett, and do we have another great episode for you today! We're pulling double duty, and for the first time ever, we're going to expose not one wolf but two. You heard that right, guys. We baited two separate wolves for this special, double-edition episode, and I'm about to confront the first one right now. But first, check out the investigation that led us here." He snapped his fingers and pretended to shoot a gun at the camera. It was an editing point for Ezra, so he could insert the content the team had created during the last few weeks of chatting with HenryLongShaft and Claypole83. A typical episode was forty-five minutes long – with an additional fifteen minutes of interspliced ads to bring in the revenue. Along with merch sales, a fan club, and several links to make donations to the channel, business was good.

Better than good.

"Cut!" Ezra lowered his camera. "Nice intro, dude. I don't think we need to go again."

"Course not. I'm a pro."

Sadie checked her watch. "We need to take our positions. Five minutes, guys."

"Showtime, go time." Jaydon sauntered off towards the library, where he would take a spot nearby and pretend to be talking on his phone. As soon as the first target arrived, he would send a message to Sadie's phone and the sting would be on.

The thrill would be on.

Nothing made Alfie feel more alive than lifting rocks and exposing the filthy, writhing insects underneath. Child molesters were the lowest form of scum – human calculus – and the most infuriating part was that they failed to realise how disgusting they were. They all thought messing around with kids was harmless fun.

"A monster doesn't see a monster when it looks in the mirror."

Sadie brushed her sandy hair out of her face and looked at him. "What?"

"Nothing. Just talking to myself."

"Like a crazy person?"

"You didn't know I was mental? I thought it's why you fell in love with me."

She kissed his cheek. "Mental and brilliant."

Ezra shushed them. "Jaydon's in place. Sadie, get ready with your phone."

"I'm on it."

They crouched down in the shop's entryway. Alfie placed a flat hand against the paving slabs to keep himself from toppling over. This was the moment of electric anticipation, of swarf on the tongue; the moment where a wolf would either walk right into their trap, or fail to show and ruin everything. When the latter was true, weeks of work would be wasted.

But when it was the former...

Alfie's heart danced the calypso. His gums tingled, his tongue tasted ice and copper. Sadie put a warm hand on his back to balance herself while she stared at her phone.

Jaydon stood in a narrow thoroughfare beside the library, near where Claypole83 and HenryLongShaft had arranged to meet up with children. The only thing behind the library was an abandoned market square and some parking spaces for the nearby council offices. It was a quiet, secluded spot that few people had reason to visit. The perfect place for an ambush.

Sadie's phone pinged. She looked at Alfie. "Green light."

"Get in!" Alfie leapt up and jogged across the plaza. Ezra and Sadie went with him, Ezra pointing the Canon and Sadie reaching out to keep him going in a straight line. They always captured the run. It added excitement and urgency to the episode.

"We just got word that our first wolf has arrived," Alfie

said back to the camera as he jogged, pacing himself so as not to get out of breath. "We believe it to be HenryLongShaft, who came here to meet up with a thirteen-year-old girl for sex. Instead, he's going to get his face posted all over the Internet, along with every disgusting message and email he sent to what he thought was a child. I won't even mention the dick pics. Two words: lamb kofta."

As they got closer to the library, Jaydon started waving a hand at them in a summoning gesture. There was always the worry that a wolf might get away, but that wasn't happening today. Alfie needed this. He needed to take down a predator. Hopefully two predators, if Claypole83 kept his appointment.

Alfie raced into the alleyway and stopped in front of Jaydon. "Where is he?"

Jaydon pointed. "Man's waiting in the old market square, exactly like we told him to."

Alfie stopped and stared back at Ezra's camera. "No. A thirteen-year-old named Stacey told him to come here. But Stacey doesn't exist, and I'm about to ask HenryLongShaft some very uncomfortable questions. I'm Alfie Everett, and this is your latest episode of *Invite the Wolf*."

Barely able to contain his excitement, Alfie sped around the corner and entered the space behind the library. The market square had been constructed decades ago, but its out-of-the-way location had caused trade to die a death – until a petition had eventually forced the council to relocate the market sellers to the town's principal thoroughfare. Thus, this original paved space had lain abandoned for years.

But today it had a visitor.

HenryLongShaft was an odd-looking, gnome-like man, with a shiny bald head and an almost non-existent chin. Alfie clenched his fists at the mere sight of him.

Weak and pathetic like they all are.

Catching drug dealers and murderers was a risky business

– and Alfie didn't envy the police there one bit – but catching paedophiles was a doddle. They were inadequate losers with low IQs, and compulsions that made them blind to common sense.

Alfie hung back, not wanting to reveal himself yet. They had a routine, a way of doing things. Evidence came first. He slid his phone out of his pocket and started recording, holding the phone down by his waist where it would hopefully go unnoticed.

His senses were heightened, the smell of damp, rain-spattered concrete in his nostrils. The tickle of drizzle on the back of his hands.

"Here we go."

Alfie started forward, giving HenryLongShaft a great big smile as he approached the man. "Oh, hey mate, I know you, don't I? David Thompson, right?"

The other man flinched, clearly startled. No doubt he was as much full of adrenaline as Alfie was – but for very different reasons. He wore grey chinos and a sleeveless pale blue shirt that seemed inadequate for the damp May weather. "W-what?"

Still smiling, Alfie wagged a finger. "Yeah, yeah, we met at the Tesco Christmas party at the Duck Pond, right? That pub down in Oakenshaw? It's David? David Thompson?"

"No. No, that's not me."

"Really? I swear we've had a beer together. What's your name, then? I must have remembered it wrong."

"H-Henry." He took a big gulp, unable to make eye contact. "M-my name is Henry."

Alfie clicked his fingers. "Yes! Henry. That's it. And what was your surname? It's on the tip of my tongue."

"Um..." Henry glanced back and forth, his beady eyes like that of a bird. "Um, Stanhope. I'm positive we've never met, though. I'm not from around here."

"Henry Stanhope, is it?" Alfie put a hand over his head and made a wolf sign with his pinkie and index fingers. "You're from Coventry, right? At least, that's what it says on your profile, HenryLongShaft."

"What? I-I don't..."

Ezra, Sadie, and Jaydon arrived like the cavalry. The Canon was filming, it's red light on. Sadie had her phone out, ready to present the evidence. This was happening. Oh yes, it was happening.

I needed this.

Alfie lifted his phone and pointed it at Henry's worried face, getting close enough that he could smell the man's pound shop aftershave and minty-fresh breath. "This is *Invite the Wolf*, Henry, and you've been caught trying to meet a minor for sex. Do you have anything to say?"

"No. No, I need to go."

Henry tried to leave, but Alfie blocked him. "You can talk to me or you can talk to the police. Which one is it?"

Henry tried to back away, but found Jaydon standing there like a nightclub bouncer, ready to manhandle him if necessary. "You ain't going anywhere, bro."

"W-what do you want? Why are you doing this? I'll call for help."

Alfie shook his head in disbelief, still mystified that these predators always saw themselves as the victims. "Calm down, Henry. I just want to know why you came here to meet up with a thirteen-year-old girl. You've been exchanging explicit messages and pictures with a child named Stacey."

Henry's forehead scrunched, crisscrossing like a cattle grid. "I don't know anyone called Stacey. Please, just let me go."

Sadie lifted her phone and started reading aloud what was on the screen. The words came thick and fast, the disgust evident in her voice. "I want to strip you naked and put my tongue inside you. Will you say thank you after I take your virginity? Will you call me master?" She sneered at Henry, her green eyes like vengeful spirits. "That you, Henry?"

Alfie sneered, his amiable mask slipping away as he felt that familiar anger bubbling up inside him like gas from a sulphuric geyser. "Meet Stacey," he said, pointing to Sadie. "This is who you've been talking to these last few weeks. She's the thirteen-year-old you've been trying to have sex with."

Henry's eyes rolled back and forth like he was feeling woozy. "She... she said she was sixteen. I only came here to chat and make friends. That's all, I swear." He tried to barge past Alfie again, but Alfie was much bigger and held his ground with little effort.

"You ain't going anywhere, Henry. We've caught you red-handed."

"I didn't know she was underage. It's a misunder-standing."

Sadie went back to reading from her phone. "You can't tell anyone about me, Stacey, because they won't understand our love. They'll say it's wrong, because you're only thirteen, but you're more mature than other girls, aren't you? You're a woman. We can make love all night long and kiss and cuddle too. When you're older, you can be my wife. We can be together forever and never have to listen to your parents again."

Alfie stepped up to Henry, almost nose to nose. He wanted to deck this pathetic creature, but he knew he had to hold back and stay calm. Taking down a monster took smarts, not violence. Temper was the enemy. "You're done, Henry. We're going to post this online to millions of people. Everyone will know what you are."

Henry started shaking his head repeatedly. "Please, no. Please, don't do this. My family will be devastated. I have a son."

He's trembling like a leaf. I'm twice his size.

Am I being too hard?

No. I'm not being hard enough. *Monsters don't deserve mercy.*

"It's too late for begging, Henry. You were happy enough to come here and have sex with a child, so don't start begging now. You made a decision, and now you have to face the consequences."

"I can give you money. Anything. Just tell me what you want."

Alfie shrugged Henry's grasping hands away, unable to hide the disgust on his face any longer.

The disgust in his soul.

"The only thing I want is to keep monsters like you away from children. You're a wolf, Henry, and it's my job to defang you."

Ezra, Jaydon, and Sadie started barking. For several seconds, they howled, yipped, and growled at the snivelling creature before them.

"This is all going online tonight," Alfie said, "so prepare yourself, Henry, because you're never going to get anywhere near a child from now on."

Tears streamed down Henry's face, which only made Alfie madder. Would this horrible creature have cared about the tears on little Stacey's face if this whole thing had been real? He deserved zero sympathy.

Henry turned his attention to Sadie, begging and pleading with her to take pity on him. Did he think being a woman would make her more likely to forgive him?

Alfie's temper spiked, and he grabbed Henry by his shirt collar, pushing him back against the wall. "Don't you talk to her. You talk to me, understand?"

Henry nodded, snot dripping from his nose and a wheeze coming from his sallow chest.

"Good. Now, do you have anything to say to all the people

who'll be watching this? Do you have any defence at all? What are your family going to think?"

Henry slumped against the wall and sobbed. "It's not my fault. You tricked me. You're the bad ones, not me." He dropped to his knees, shiny bald head in his hands as he blubbered. "It was a mistake. An accident. Accidents happen."

Accidents do happen indeed, Sonny Jim.

Alfie pictured the face he spent so much of his time trying to not see. The black moustache. The sunken eyes and wolflike teeth.

The rusty white van that swallowed up his sister.

Daisy...

"Alfie? Alfie, are you all right?" He blinked twice. Sadie was standing right in front of him, tilting her head and frowning. "Alfie, are you okay?"

"I... I'm fine."

She didn't seem convinced, her eyes narrowed almost into a squint. "Shall we wrap this up? We've got what we need."

"Y-yeah. We're done." He glared at HenryLongShaft, his anger replaced by a cold, emotionless breeze. "Henry Stanhope from Coventry, you have been found guilty of attempting to solicit sex with a minor. Say fucking cheese!"

Ezra pulled out a compact camera he kept attached to a pouch on his hip and pointed it. Henry looked directly into the lens as the shutter clicked, snot and tears covering his gnomish face.

"That's a wrap," Alfie said, unable to tolerate this lowlife and his self-pity a moment longer. They were all the same. They always ended up begging.

It's not my fault. I thought she was older.

Alfie's anger came back.

The chill breeze turned hot.

Jaydon gave Alfie a gentle shove that prompted him to turn around. "Yo, Alf. Check it out."

"What is it?" He craned his neck to see what Jaydon was pointing at. "Oh? Oh, wow."

A shadowy figure stood on the far side of the abandoned market square. They were watching intently, a witness to all that had just happened.

"Who *is* that?" Jaydon asked.

"It's Claypole83," Alfie said, sneering. "It's wolf number two."

Alfie studied the stranger, still standing motionless on the other side of the market square. He wore a wide-brimmed hat and knee-length overcoat.

"Bro's dressed like the frikkin' Undertaker," Jaydon said as he hurried to catch up with Alfie. "Maybe it's just a homeless guy."

"No, it's him," Alfie said. "It's Claypole83."

"How can you be sure?"

"Because there's no reason for anyone else to be here. It's got to be him."

Jaydon folded his arms and nodded. "How long you think bro has been standing there?"

"Long enough to see what we did to Henry." Alfie glanced back over his shoulder. "Hey, Ezra? You filming?"

"Camera's on, dude."

"Then follow me."

"Be careful," Sadie said. "We haven't got the jump on this guy like we usually do. He's seen us coming."

Alfie started towards the stranger, laser-focused. He must have come from the nearby underpass that allowed passage through the large council building that loomed over three sides of the old market square.

Why isn't he moving? Why isn't he attempting to run?

Doesn't he get it? Doesn't he know he's been set up?

"Hey?" Alfie yelled, his voice echoing across the empty square. "What's your name, buddy? I could really use your help. We've had a problem with that guy over there. What's your name?"

The stranger said nothing, didn't even flinch or show recognition that he'd been spoken to. His arms remained pinned to his side, appearing slightly too long, fingers like a crone's talons.

Alfie slowed his approach, unease creeping in at the fringes of his mind. "D-did you catch me, bud? I asked your name."

The stranger still gave no response. His face was a black shadow beneath the brim of his hat. Shoulders so square it looked like he had a coat hanger tucked inside his coat.

Alfie stopped short, a timid voice in his head pleading with him to be cautious. In all the episodes of *Invite the Wolf*, no target had ever behaved this way. Where was the fear and panic? The realisation that their perverted desires had been exposed?

"That's, um, quite the outfit you're wearing," he said casually, hoping to lower the stranger's defences, as usual, by acting friendly. "You work in a graveyard or something? Ha! Just kidding, mate. How you doing?"

Jaydon moved up beside Alfie, standing shoulder to shoulder and pointing a finger excitedly. "Or do you not want people to see your face, bro? You came here for a reason, right? Came here for a little hook up?"

Alfie didn't mind Jaydon butting in – they often shared on-camera duties – but he questioned his friend's choice to escalate things so quickly. He was clearly amped up after their success with Henry, but there was something off about this stranger. Did they have the wrong guy?

"Do you not have anything to say at all?" Alfie asked, trying to disguise his confusion. Every episode, they followed a set path, but things had deviated this time, and he was unsure how to proceed.

Finally, the stranger moved; only the slightest tilt of his

head, but enough to allow a slither of sunlight to hit the bottom of his face. It revealed an angular chin covered in inky-black stubble.

Jaydon jabbed his finger in the air again. "You're Clay-pole83. Just admit it, bro. We got you." He turned and pointed back towards where they had left Henry Stanhope covered in his own snot, but the sorry creature had already crawled away. "We got *him* and now we got *you*."

"Yeah," Alfie said. "Game's up. We know all about you, so just play ball and things will go easier for you."

"We are *Invite the Wolf*," Jaydon said, "and we expose predators like you on the regular."

Sadie and Ezra stood ten feet behind Alfie and Jaydon, both of them filming – Ez with his camera and Sadie with her phone. Veteran wolf hunters. Professionals.

Fifteen episodes and counting.

The stranger continued to give no reaction. If he was innocent, then he would speak, surely? Which meant this must be Claypole. They had the right guy.

So why isn't he concerned? Is he crazy?

The abandoned market square suddenly seemed *too* abandoned. A quiet breeze floated above the concrete, carrying the damp, but all was as silent as a graveyard at midnight. The windows of the council building were grey and empty, or covered by blinds. To be heard, you would have to bellow real loud. Or scream.

"Last chance," Alfie said. "If we've got the wrong guy, then now is the time to say so." He waited... waited... and when there was still no response, he let out an exasperated sigh. "Fine, then you leave me no choice."

He lifted his phone, and when he noticed his hand shaking, he had to grab his wrist to keep it still. Using his thumb, he opened up the thread pinned to the top of his chat app.

He read the messages aloud. "I-I will come to see you soon, Lucy. It will be a ride you'll never forget. Claypole83." When the stranger still gave no response, he read another snippet from the chat. "I'm coming for you. We're finally going to meet."

Jaydon folded his arms and scowled. "That you, bro? That you, sending messages to what you thought was a twelve-year-old girl?"

Calm down, Jay. Don't you see this guy isn't afraid of us?

The stranger tilted his head forwards, returning his chin to the shadow of his wide-brimmed hat.

Alfie's mouth turned dry. A lump filled his throat. He tried to push his anxiety away, but it was like feeding a stray – it kept coming back. But, knowing it would be a disaster to show fear, Alfie forced himself to close the distance between himself and the stranger. The other man was at least a foot taller than him, but that meant nothing. They had him outnumbered. They had him on film. He was just another wolf that needed to be taken down.

"It's over, Claypole. You're not getting away with what you came here to do. So say something, will you? Come on, what are you waiting for? Come on. Come on, you goddamn freak. Speak!"

Sadie, standing behind Alfie, urged him to relax. The success of *Invite the Wolf* relied on everyone staying calm and maintaining the higher ground. If things escalated, they could end up with legal trouble, or turn away their more sensitive subscribers.

But this guy isn't playing ball.

Is he expecting us to turn around and walk away?

Not gonna happen. I won't stand by and do nothing.

Alfie clenched his fists and puffed out his chest, feigning confidence. Sadie called out to him again, but he ignored her. He allowed his temper to take over, pushing aside his uncertainty and transfixing him on the deviant standing before him. Nothing else existed.

"It's time to take responsibility," he said. "Time to admit what you are – a monster who snatches children and does terrible things to them. Admit it!"

"Alfie, leave it," Sadie urged. "This isn't working out."

"Yeah," Ezra agreed. "It's a wrap, dude. Can't win 'em all."

Alfie turned to his friends and sneered. "What? We should leave this piece of shit to go off and hurt a kid? No way. No way will I let that happen."

"Me either," Jaydon said confidently. "Ride or die, bro."

Alfie nodded appreciatively, then glared at the man beneath the wide-brimmed hat.

If I can't get your name, I'll at least get your fucking face on camera.

"Take that stupid thing off." Alfie reached out a hand.

Claypole moved.

Something sliced through Alfie's vision, a streak of silver cutting from left to right. It kissed his cheek with cold, wet lips.

Sadie squeaked like a mouse.

Alfie felt like a curling iron was pressed against his face, scorching hot and radiating. He tumbled backwards as adrenaline gushed out of a pipe buried somewhere in his guts. His anger turned to panic in an instant.

He cut me? Did he cut me?

"Yo, what the fuck?" Jaydon grabbed Alfie and pulled him aside. "You okay, bro?"

"I-I think so." He put his face in his hands, searching for the source of the searing hot pain. "It hurts."

"Goddamn it." Jaydon moved Alfie aside, then rushed headlong at the stranger. "Crazy motherfucker. What the hell did you just do to my fr— Ah!" There was a scuffle followed by a scream. "Shit! My leg, my leg. He bust my leg."

Alfie glanced through his fingers and saw Jay collapse to the ground, clutching his knee and gritting his teeth.

Claypole had changed his stance, as if he had just thrown a kick or a punch. He wore thick-soled black boots with silver buckles. And he clutched a glinting, blood-tinged machete.

Sadie stumbled into the fray, crying out for help. "Somebody! Somebody call the police. Help!"

Alfie reached out and grabbed her. "Sadie, stay back."

"I-I got it all on film," Ezra said, almost screeching it. "I got everything. Shit. Shit-shit-shit."

Claypole remained standing before them, so calm one might have mistaken him for a statue.

"Get the fuck out of here, you psycho!" Alfie yelled at him. He brought his hand away from his face and found his palm soaked with blood. "You maniac!"

With the spiteful-looking blade still extended from his hand, Claypole turned and walked back towards the underpass where he must have first entered the market square. He made no effort to quicken his pace or run. No one had heard a thing, not even the ghosts of the market's past.

Alfie groaned. He wanted to scream out obscenities at his attacker, but truthfully he was relieved to see him walk away. For this first time since starting the channel, he had met a wolf who truly frightened him. The first one since...

Daisy.

Once the danger had passed, Sadie rushed over to Alfie and started fussing over him. A wave of nausea crashed against his insides as he slumped to the damp pavement. His mouth tasted of metal.

Jaydon was still down, clutching his wounded knee and breathing rapidly. Ezra placed his Canon carefully on the concrete and knelt down beside his friend, trying impotently to help. "Fuck, dude, this is messed up. So messed up."

"You're telling me, bro. I think my leg is broken."

"W-what the hell happened?" Alfie clutched his stomach as it expanded and deflated, trying to keep himself from puking. His face was numb. "What the *hell* just happened?"

Sadie enveloped him in her arms, cradling him like an infant. He didn't resist, didn't resist at all. "That maniac cut you, babe. He cut your face."

"H-how bad is it?"

Sadie eased him back to examine him. She had tears in her eyes and her pale skin was even whiter than usual. "I can't tell. There's too much blood."

"I need to see it, Sadie. I need to..." He looked around for his phone and realised he had dropped it several feet away. "Let me see a selfie. Let me look."

Her hands were shaking, which meant she almost dropped her phone as she pulled it out of her jeans pocket. As requested, she opened up her front-facing camera and handed it to Alfie.

Jesus Christ.

Alfie's face was a crimson mask, like the wrestlers he'd watched as a kid – John Cena, Edge, Randy Orton, Bautista. But unlike those brutal performers, his injuries were not part of the show.

With his right hand, he tried to wipe away enough blood that he could inspect the damage. A crescent-shaped gash dissected his cheek, destined to leave a scar for sure. The sudden realisation that he'd been maimed sent a shiver up his spine, but he tried to reframe it in his mind and keep from freaking out.

It's not that bad. Only a cut.

"Alfie, you've gone really pale? Is it shock?"

"Quite possibly." He studied himself a while longer, hardly recognising himself. He looked like a barbarian, fresh out of battle. It should have caused his pulse to quicken, but the sight of his own blood had the opposite effect. Oddly calming. Primal. Basic.

Sadie reached out and grabbed his hand. "Babe, you're freaking me out. Are you okay?"

He nodded, breathing in and out slowly. "It's not that bad."

"It *is* bad. What if he comes back?"

"Babe, it's okay. This whole thing is gonna go viral."

"So? That's not why we do this, Alfie. I told you to back off, but you ignored me. Now look. Was it worth getting your face slashed just to get some good content?"

"Of course not, but don't you get it?" He wiped blood off his hands onto his jeans and took a moment to swallow back a wave of nausea before continuing. "After millions of people watch the video, Claypole83 is finished. Someone will identify him, and when they do, he'll pay for this. We got everything on film. The police will get him and lock him up. This is all gonna work out for the best. We can turn this into a positive. As long as we get another wolf off the street, then it's all worth it."

Sadie gave a weary sigh, while Alfie went back to examining his war wound on camera, and trying his very best to look on the bright side. Nothing drove clicks quite like a bit of unexpected violence.

"It's not that bad," he muttered. "Everything is fine. All fine."

I let him get away. Like a coward, I watched him leave. Forgive me, Daisy. I'll make this right.

Three

I t had been one week since Alfie's encounter with Claypole83, and the wound on his face – drawn tight with five stitches – had scabbed over. As predicted, it gave his face a rugged slice of character, and the inevitable scar would look totally badass.

Gotta keep moving forward. Dragging the past around does nothing except give you a bad back.

Invite the Wolf's most recent episode had been its best. Two targets, and an ending which had resulted in Alfie needing stitches. The reward was worth the pain.

I'm gonna get you, Claypole83. You can't hide from my Internet army.

Invite the Wolf now had almost four million subscribers, and the views of its most recent episode had exceeded twenty million – with more than a quarter of those originating in the UK. That meant a lot of eyeballs searching for the man who had sliced Alfie's face. Thousands of comments hit the fan page every day, which Alfie and his friends had been diligently working their way through.

—*He's a fireman in Luton.*

—Seen this guy around Leeds a few times.

—Scumbag is part of a grooming gang in Rochdale. Muslim, as you might have guessed.

—Far-left paedo.

—This is my ex-husband. One hundred per cent.

—Cliff Richard.

—Don't mess with this guy. He's dangerous.

—Far-right paedo.

No doubt Claypole83 was a different animal than the usual wolves they exposed via the channel, but Alfie refused to back down or move on to fresh prey. The scar on his cheek was not going to be a reminder of failure, but instead a trophy of success.

Claypole won the last battle, but he's going to lose the war.

Alfie got up from his desk in the Barn's office area – a large, rectangular space at the back of a converted farm building, which had once housed hundreds of cattle before its owners had converted it into a luxury residence. Alfie now owned the place, mortgage-free, along with several acres of surrounding land. Sometimes he had to stop and pinch himself. It was hard not to lose sight of how fortunate he was, and how quickly his fortunes had changed.

I made it, Mum. I didn't let anything stop me.

Three years ago, *Invite the Wolf* had been little more than a hobby. Even in his wildest dreams, he'd never expected to become a millionaire at twenty-one. Auntie Maureen had accused him of being a drug dealer at first – especially when he had turned up to her bungalow in a brand-new Alfa Romeo Stelvio Quadrifoglio. Nowadays, she was proud of him, and told everyone who would listen that her nephew was a famous online celebrity.

It was a high that never wore off.

If only Mum was around to see how successful I've become. She never thought I would ever fix myself.

But I did.

Out in the Barn's main living space – which consisted of a large, open-plan kitchen, adjacent dining area, and a wide sitting area with several armchairs and a sofa – the others were all chilling. The black-and-gold wall clock in the kitchen read five thirty, which was when they usually knocked off for the evening.

Sadie perched on a bar stool with her elbows on the black granite worktop. She was reading a magazine and swinging her socked feet back and forth. When she saw Alfie, she smiled. "Thought you were never gonna come out of there. You need to take a break once in a while, babe."

"Yeah, don't be a workaholic, dude," Ezra said, sitting in an armchair in front of the wall-mounted television. His face was almost as red as his hair, and he had slumped down so low that he was almost lying flat. "You ain't no shark that needs to keep moving constantly to stay alive and be free, and like that movie with Samuel L and the parrot with the oven. You seen that film, right? It's real? Or did I imagine it?"

Alfie took the stool next to Sadie and raised an eyebrow at her. "He been on the wacky?"

"Since about noon." She rolled her eyes. "He's still celebrating the latest episode."

"Aren't we all?"

"Twenty-five per cent subscriber uplift," Ezra said, followed by a dozy *whoop*! "And still rising, yo. Most popular episode since the first one we did when we caught that saddo Brent Busey."

Alfie studied Ezra for a moment, a worried whisper echoing in the back of his mind that all was not well. Was he really celebrating? Or was he trying to medicate the fear and anxiety he'd been dealing with since the scenes in the marketplace? Ezra had never been good at dealing with his feelings, probably thanks to his RAF officer father who considered saying *excuse me* after a sneeze a sign of weakness.

Wanting to stay focused on the positive, Alfie grinned. "You see? It's all been a massive success."

Sadie let out a sigh as she ran a fingertip along the lengthy scab on his cheek. "You could've been killed for those extra subscribers, babe. When is enough enough? How successful do any of us need to be?"

Alfie frowned, taken a little by surprise. "Dunno. Haven't really thought about it."

"Don't you ever get tired of plugging the channel? The fan club? The merch? It's twenty-four seven."

"I don't see you turning down the pay cheques."

She rubbed at her forehead. "You're right. I don't want to be a hypocrite. I just feel like this might be a good place to end it, you know? Ride off into the sunset, or something."

"End it? We're only just getting started. Sadie, if we keep this up, we can all retire by the time we're thirty."

"Not if you get killed by some psycho we back into a corner. Last week was terrifying, Alfie. We haven't even spoken about it properly, but I never want to go through anything like that ever again."

"Me either," Ezra said. "I almost pissed my pants."

Alfie grunted. "Hey, it was me who got hurt. It's me and Jay who take the risks confronting these monsters face to face." *It's me who's been disfigured!* He grunted again. "You two have nothing to worry about."

Sadie punched his arm. "I have *you* to worry about, you jerk. And Jaydon got hurt too. His knee is still bugging him."

Alfie softened, the fight in him momentarily batted away. "You're right. We need to be more careful in the future. I'll figure something out, okay? Change the way we do things. But we need to keep the channel growing. What we do here... it's not even about the money, babe. We're protecting children. *Children*. We've helped put bad people in prison."

She sighed. "Back when the police used to work with us. Now they'd rather see us shut down."

"Or put in jail ourselves," Ezra muttered.

"Because the world has gone insane," Alfie said. He reached out and took both of Sadie's hands. "We're a force for good, babe. We do what the police refuse to do. I mean, how easy is it? Catching a predator is like fishing. All it takes is patience and the right bait."

"Yeah, Alfie, I know that, because I'm usually the bait. It's me who has to talk to these monsters. It makes my soul feel dirty. Some of the things they say... the pictures they send..." She shook her head, revolted. "Men are so gross."

"Hey, we catch female wolves too, babe."

"One," Ezra said from the couch. "We caught one woman in more than a dozen ambushes. The bipolar chick, remember?"

"You see?" A hint of a smirk spread across Sadie's lips. "Men. Gross."

Alfie squeezed her thigh. "What we do is rough, babe, but does that mean we shouldn't do it? If not us, then who?"

She brushed back her hair and offered a weak smile. Her lips were red, as if she'd been pressing them together. "I know children need protecting, babe, but I wonder sometimes how we ended up being the ones in this position. We could have been accountants or photographers – anything, really – but instead we chose this... this crazy existence."

He put a finger beneath her chin and made her look at him. "Can you imagine the utter, banal misery of being ordinary? You're meant for better things than accountancy, babe. We all are. The world tried to tell us we were worthless, but we refused to accept it. You and I helped each other, and now we help others."

Sadie looked into his eyes, breathing slowly. Her expensive perfume wafted into his nose, like gin-infused rose petals.

A door opened. Jaydon came limping into the living area from the other end of the Barn where three large bedrooms were located. "Yo, check this shit out," he said. "Someone reckons they have our man."

Alfie hopped off his stool and hurried to meet him. "Someone knows who Claypole is?"

"They reckon so. Not checked it out yet, but there's a link to a video."

"Then let's load it up."

The two of them met in the centre of the living area and halted behind the armchair that Ezra remained sprawled out in. Sadie came to join them, and the three huddled around Jaydon's phone as he clicked on the video link.

The video started with a typical English high street. It was unclear which part of the country it was, but the number of paving flags and scruffy shop facades suggested it was somewhere run-down. It reminded Alfie of his hometown, Kidderminster, a place famous for carpets and little else.

Whoever was filming didn't speak, but they could be heard sniggering and whispering to someone else also unseen. They passed over a pelican crossing while several cars waited for the lights to turn green. On the opposite pavement, a man in woolly overcoat and wearing a stiff black hat with a red feather in it pushed a small two-wheeled tartan shopping trolley along the path.

Words appeared onscreen, and an AI-generated female voice recited them aloud. *'When you find the violent pdf that attacked your favourite Internet star.'*

"That ain't the guy," Alfie said. "It's just an old man with a similar coat and a black hat."

"You sure?" Jaydon tilted his head. "Looks like the same guy to me."

"It's not him," Alfie snapped. "Claypole's hat was wider, and it didn't have a feather in it. He wasn't old either."

"How do you know? We barely got a look at him."

Sadie put a hand on Alfie's lower back and leant in. "No, Alfie's right. That isn't Claypole. It's just a harmless old—"

They all gasped as the person filming suddenly yelled obscenities at the stranger with the shopping cart. Once they had his attention, they hurried over to confront him. "Oi, Claypole? You meeting any kids today?"

The old man stopped and turned, clearly confused. "I-I beg your pardon, young man?"

"Yeah, you better beg, you fucking nonce!"

Sadie put a hand to her mouth and turned away as soon as the first punch landed. Alfie wanted to do the same, but he was transfixed by the meaty thumps of fist hitting flesh. The old man's screams sounded like lambs bleating.

"Jesus, Jaydon." Sadie covered her eyes. "Turn it off. Turn it off. That poor old man."

Alfie held his stomach and turned away. *Did this happen because of us? Are we responsible?*

"They attacked an innocent person and filmed it," Sadie said, still hiding her face.

"Because they thought he was Claypole," Jaydon said with a shrug.

Sadie shook her head, opening her eyes and wincing. "People like that just want an excuse to be violent. We should report them to the police. They knew they had the wrong man. They knew it!"

"It's posted on Evershare," Jaydon said. "All anonymous on there. The site's hosted in Laos."

"Maybe we should post it on our channel, then, so other people can figure out who they are and report them."

Ezra was sucking on his vape, full of God knows what, but he pulled it out of his mouth and turned around in his armchair to look up at them. "Isn't that the reason the old boy got it in the first place? We posted about Claypole and it started a witch hunt. You think doing it again might turn out differently?"

Jaydon pulled a face. "We didn't start a witch hunt, Ez. We just wanted engagement."

"Well, you got it. Old guy got engaged."

Alfie frowned. "You already seen this video, Ez?"

"Yeah, dude." He held his phone over his head. "Came through on an email twenty minutes ago. I might be stoned, but I still got my nose on the pulse. We've had half a dozen videos like that. People been wildin' since the Claypole video. We unleashed the beast, dude. Like *Psycho Goreman* or that moth thing Godzilla is always scrapping with."

"Don't be dramatic, bro." Jaydon slid his phone back into his pocket and shrugged again. "It's not our fault what other people do. They would go around attacking each other regardless of what we do."

Ezra shrugged. "Who am I to question the human condition?"

"It's sick." Sadie rubbed at her forehead, which was now clammy with sweat. "And I think we *are* to blame. If our channel is going to continue growing, then we need to take responsibility for what we're putting out there. We're not producing ten-minute shorts to an audience of thirty any more."

Alfie put a hand up. "All right, babe. Stop. I agree with you. *Invite the Wolf* has grown more than any of us expected. We need to take a few days to restrategise. None of us wants to see innocent people get hurt."

"For sure," Jaydon said. "We'll put a disclaimer at the start of every episode or something, yeah? Tell people not to take justice into their own hands. We can do that, right, Ezra?"

Ezra put a hand in the air and gave a thumbs up. "I'll get to it as soon as I wake up tomorrow."

Sadie rolled her eyes. "That'll be about noon, then."

"Ease up, Say." Jaydon patted her on the shoulder and then left his hand there. "The video was bad, for sure, but we can't control what other people do. Try it and you'll go insane."

She sighed and walked back into the kitchen. "I just don't want us to lose sight of who we are. When we started this, we were a bunch of kids with time on our hands. Now, suddenly, we have all this money and fame and..." She sighed again. "It just frightens me. Especially after what happened last week."

Alfie went over and grabbed her hips, pulling her into a hug. "We'll figure this all out, babe. Just try to relax, okay?"

She tensed up, refusing to relax into him. "I just don't want us to change, Alfie."

"We won't."

"You can't promise that."

He kissed her forehead. "Nothing will ever ruin what we have. I won't let it."

She nodded, seeming to think it over. Eventually, she looked him in the eye and offered a weary smile. "I need a drink. How much wine do we have?"

Alfie went over to the fridge. "Not sure. Let me check." He opened the door, letting out a chilly blast, and revealed a dozen bottles of white wine lined up inside. "Think we're good."

Sadie nodded, deadpan. "That should last us a day or two. What should we have for dinner?"

"Chinese," Ezra mumbled. "Gotta be Chinese."

Alfie looked back and forth between Jaydon and Sadie. Both of them shrugged, so the decision was made. "Chinese it is, then."

"Great," Sadie said, pouring herself a glass. "That should solve everything."

Alfie reached out to her. "Babe..."

She turned her back and headed for the bedrooms. "Let me know when it's here."

Jaydon watched her leave and then looked back at Alfie. The two of them shared a shrug.

———

Alfie felt like he'd swallowed an inflated balloon. His mouth was awash with salt and garlic.

Man, those salt-and-pepper chicken wings slayed. I musta killed a dozen, at least.

Everyone was chilling on the sofas in the sitting area, surrounded by empty takeaway containers and dirty plates, taking turns playing *Stardew Valley* on the PS5. Ezra called the cute farming simulator his 'zen fix', and Sadie liked it too. Jaydon, however, only ever played sports games, so he watched – slumped into his leather armchair as he drank his fourth glass of wine.

Alfie needed some fresh air – and a stretch to ease his bloated belly – so he dragged himself to his feet and announced he was going for a vape. He received a trinity of drunken murmurs in reply.

Heading into the kitchen, he passed through the small laundry nook at the rear of the Barn and opened up the back door. A rush of crisp, late evening air wafted inside.

Stepping down onto the small sandstone patio outside the door, Alfie surveyed his kingdom beneath the silvery light of a half-moon. While Sadie had voiced her doubts about the future, it enlivened him for the most part. Their current success was likely a fleeting moment in the sun, but the longer their success continued, the easier it would be to pivot – or even change lanes completely if the channel lost popularity or got demonetised for some reason. Besides, it was him – Alfie Everett – that people bought into, not specifically the channel itself.

The fans will follow me anywhere because they know I'm the real deal. I don't fake it. Sadie shouldn't feel guilty about what we do. The world needs heroes like us.

Alfie sucked on his Chilli-Lime Blast. Unseen in the dark was a flat, grassy field dissected on one side by a natural, rocky stream. Beyond the field was a grassy hill that hid the entire property from the main road and surrounding Worcestershire countryside. Alfie owned ten acres in total. His own domain.

Yes, the future is indeed bright.

We can't let what happened last week make us doubt ourselves. I won't let it. Sadie will come around... We just need to move forward. Never back.

The very best thing about concentrating on the future was that it pushed the past further and further behind – a past he would rather see swallowed up entirely. A past where his dad had walked out on Alfie when he was just twelve, and his mother had died a month before his sixteenth birthday. The past was a smog-shrouded nightmare, haunted by a tall stranger with a wolf on his hat.

Get in the fucking van, kid.

Alfie shuddered and asked the night a question. "Who would you be now, Daisy? Would you still look like me?" He realised the absurdity of it and laughed ruefully. If Daisy had been alive now, she would look nothing like him. He had dyed his light blonde hair black and covered his arms with tattoos. The only part of him he could not change were his steely blue eyes.

Daisy's eyes.

He still saw his sister every time he faced himself in a mirror. There was no way to disguise the guilt lines etched into his face; they had been there ever since that terrible day when he had failed to protect his little sister. The day when candyfloss had been more important than his common sense.

Alfie rubbed at his arms, pulling up his sleeves and tracing the ridged scar tissue hiding beneath the ink of his colourful flower tattoos, wounds he had inflicted upon himself after his mother's suicide.

Death stalked his past. He had to outrun it.

Sadie and the guys were Alfie's salvation. Each of them had their own reasons for being part of *Invite the Wolf*, but their individual traumas had bonded them. They were a family. They held each other up.

He took another drag on his vape, blowing lime-scented mist into the night air. Peering up at the moon and stars, he felt at peace. Content. Merry even.

"I'm king of the world."

And I've had too much food and wine.

Alfie was about to go back inside, maybe even to bed, when something caught his eye.

A tiny red light.

Such a thing would have been insignificant in most places, but out here in the countryside, it had no reason to be there. Had Ezra or Jaydon left something out in the field?

Unable to explain it, Alfie shuffled his feet into the black Crocs he always left outside the back door and went to investigate. He hesitated for a moment, considering that there might be some kind of danger, but no plausible threat presented itself in his mind. In fact, he pictured a harmless drone, lost by a careless owner sending it out of range, or even a fan, trying to get intimate footage of *Invite the Wolf*'s headquarters. Alfie was careful about guarding his privacy, but doxing was an ever-present threat.

The thought of someone trying to spy on the Barn caused Alfie to make a fist. As much as he loved his viewers, his home was his sanctuary, and anyone who tried to invade it would be sorry.

Calm down and don't make assumptions. It's just a little red light.

The red dot didn't move at all as he headed towards it, a stationary pinpoint in the darkness, halfway up the hill. By day, it was a bright and open expanse, a space where you could see a mile in every direction, but by night it was impossible to see beyond your nose. Nighttime in the countryside was a pure and unrelenting thing – a velvet sheet broken only by the merest slither of moonlight reflecting off the nearby stream. The silence was also absolute. Usually, you could hear the water trickling down the stream, but not tonight.

"Hello?" Alfie was sure no one could be out there with him, but he wanted to dispel the unrelenting quiet. "Hello?"

No answer.

And yet...

There was a muted, snuffling sound like a dog snoring.

Some kind of animal?

"Hello?"

More silence.

"Oh, screw this for a game of cards." Alfie picked up speed, wanting to put an end to this mystery and get back inside his nice, warm house. The red light was right up ahead, growing larger in his vision as he got closer, but it still failed to move.

Something else moved instead.

The meagre illumination given off by the small red light and the half-built moon provided the merest hint of a thing hiding in the darkness.

Alfie's steps faltered a few feet from the bottom of the hill. "I-Is someone there? This is private property, okay? You need to leave."

No answer.

That soft snuffling sound came again.

"Get the hell out of here, Mr Fox, or whatever the fuck is out here. Go away. Get!"

What the hell is that red light? It shouldn't be out here.

Alfie trudged up the hill, growing impatient and apprehensive in equal measure.

The red light finally made sense.

"What the fuck?"

A video camera sat upon a tripod, its lens pointed towards the Barn. Someone was filming Alfie's home.

Who? And where the fuck were they now?

"You invited the wolf," came a soft, raspy voice that seemed to flow through the air all around him.

Alfie's heart thudded in his chest. "Who the fuck is out here?"

The snuffling got louder, interrupted by a sudden, ear-piercing squeal. Alfie sensed something – or *someone* – rushing down the hill towards him. Something coming fast.

Terror took hold. Alfie turned and ran, sprinting back towards the Barn and screaming at the top of his lungs. Gravity, along with the sloping ground, almost caused him to break a leg, but he wouldn't slow down. He was freaked to shit.

The hellish squealing continued, catching up on Alfie. Right behind him now. He screamed louder, his vocal cords like overstretched elastic bands.

"Jay! Ez! Help me! I need your hel—"

Alfie yelped as something barrelled into the back of his legs and sent him crashing to the ground. The air exploded from his lungs as his chest hit the dirt and he struggled to take another breath inwards to replace it.

The manic squealing continued, right in his ear, a needle driven into his brain. He kicked out and wailed in horror, unable to see his attacker in the darkness. Movement to his left. A flash of pale skin rushing by. Then stars exploded in his vision as something collided with his face, knocking his jaw sideways.

"Wha... hum... la." He reached out blindly, his temples closing in on his skull like a vice. "Don up. La."

He tried to keep his eyes from rolling; tried to keep the fuzzy warmth of unconsciousness at bay. *Need to get back up. Need to get away.*

"Alfie?" Sadie called out to him, and then Ez and Jaydon did the same. He tried to yell back at them, to tell them he was here on the ground, but he was too winded from the fall, too dazed from the collision.

That same pale flesh flashed in and out of the darkness, the squealing growing quieter.

Alfie realised he was soaking wet, but the grass beneath him was merely damp.

He tried to get up, but his arms shook so much that he collapsed back onto his front, his face hitting the dirt. He coughed and spluttered to clear the grass from his mouth.

"Alfie, hold on," Ezra yelled out, sounding both near and far away at the same time. "We're coming, dude."

The night lit up – not with anything approaching daylight – and several shafts of light whipped back and forth through the darkness. Mobile phone torches. One shaft shone directly in Alfie's face, causing him to shield his eyes.

"Babe, where are you?"

He finally found his breath enough to voice a reply. "I-it's a monster," he said. "There's a goddamn monster out here."

Sadie appeared a few feet to his left. She skidded to a halt, staring at him in horror. "A-Alfie? You're covered in blood."

"What?"

Jaydon and Ezra arrived beside her, their torches combining to illuminate a circle of grass around Alfie.

Ezra gasped. "Dude, what happened?"

Alfie fought with his limbs, trying to raise himself up on his elbows so he could see something – anything.

The mad squealing stopped.

It soon became apparent why.

A dead pig lay on its side, its bloated belly skewered by a knife. It must have barged into him in a blind panic as it bled out all over the place. Bled out all over Alfie.

Who did this? Who planned for this?

Why would they do this to me?

Something was wrapped around the knife's handle.

Sadie warned Alfie not to move, but he ignored her and reached out to grab what appeared to be a scrap of paper secured with a pink hairband – a crumpled note, folded up and stained with blood. When he opened it, the words were barely legible, but he made them out still.

They were the same words a stranger had whispered to him up on the hill.

You invited the wolf.

Alfie glanced back into the distance, but the little red light was gone.

FOUR

Sobering up while awake always sucked. Alfie's head throbbed and throbbed and his mouth tasted like a camel's arsehole. It was three in the morning and everyone was exhausted.

What a freakin' night.

Alfie hadn't wanted to call the police, but Sadie had insisted, growing hysterical when he had attempted to argue.

So here they were, sitting in his kitchen and drinking his coffee when all he wanted to do was go to bed.

The male officer had introduced himself as PC Colman. He was a muscly dude with sleeve tattoos on both his swollen forearms, while his colleague was a wide-hipped lady named Kilmani, who had a frizzy brown afro parted in the middle that was actually pretty fire.

Colman glanced up from his notepad and focused on Alfie, his stubbly cheek twitching as if he had an itch. "So you think this intruder might have been a crazed fan? Someone who watches your online channel? Have you had any issues like that in the past?"

Alfie shrugged. "Sure. We try to keep our lives private off-camera, but there's no shortage of loonies in the world."

Colman nodded. "And you say this stranger was out on the hill, filming you, and that they said..."

"You invited the wolf." Alfie sighed, annoyed at having to repeat himself. "They whispered it to me."

Colman wrote it down on his pad, then glanced upwards. "What exactly does that mean?"

"It's a reference to our online channel," Sadie said, leaning over Alfie's shoulder, her hands on his chest. "It's called *Invite the Wolf*."

Officer Kilmani laced her fingers together in her lap and looked up at the Barn's high-vaulted ceilings and around at the large, open living space. "What exactly is your channel about? It must be very successful."

Jaydon and Ezra were in the kitchen, perched on stools and sipping water. They both groaned, probably because they knew how the conversation would go.

Alfie licked his lips and stared at the dried pig's blood on his hands. It was cold and tacky, almost like a second skin. "We catch wolves."

Kilmani frowned. "What does that mean, exactly?"

Alfie looked her in the eye. "We bait child molesters online and expose them to the public. We protect kids from Internet predators, because no one else is doing anything to keep them safe."

Both officers sat with that for a moment, likely wondering if it had been a dig at them, which of course it had been. Alfie cared little for the police. After his sister was abducted all those years ago, they had questioned him for seven hours, refusing to let him go home, yet they had failed completely to find the monster who had taken Daisy.

Officer Kilmani cleared her throat and leant forward. "So

you're one of these vigilante groups who hang around chat-rooms and pretend to be children?"

Alfie didn't appreciate the slightly derisory way she had said it. "I wouldn't have to chase down child molesters," he said, "if you did your jobs properly."

Jaydon hissed. "Jesus, bro. Chill out."

Colman put a hand out. "You're being rather reductive about a very complex issue. What you're doing is extremely dangerous. Do you not think it likely that someone you previously targeted is behind what happened tonight? What happened to your face, by the way? Looks like it's going to leave a nasty scar."

Alfie's hand rose towards his face. The wound was wet, part of the scab torn away by the pig crashing into him. It felt like a cube of ice being pressed against his cheek, painful and numbing. "It's nothing. Just a—"

"Claypole83," Sadie said, followed by a long, drawn-out sigh. "We tried to expose a man last week who was using the online name Claypole83."

Colman wrote it on his pad and looked at Alfie. "And he's the one who cut you?"

Alfie shrugged. He didn't want the police interfering in his business, but Sadie had put him on the spot. "Claypole's a degenerate loser, same as them all. He got away from us, but I'm dealing with it."

"I suggest you do not deal with it, Mr Everett. If this indi-vidual is dangerous, we will handle it."

Kilmani put a hand on the counter. "I understand that you're trying to a good thing – a brave thing – but do you not realise the risk to yourself? If this person had a knife, you could have been killed."

"But I wasn't. Did you cross the road this morning? You could have been killed too."

Kilmani sighed.

Colman was shaking his head. "You obviously don't want us here, Mr Everett, so why don't you describe what happened with this Claypole individual and we'll leave you in peace."

"Fine, but I'm only saying it once. I'm tired and I want to go to bed."

"Very well. I'll make sure I take notes." He tapped his pad with his pencil. "I'm all ears."

Alfie reluctantly told the police officers everything that had happened last week in the old market square, about how they had exposed HenryLongShaft and had attempted to expose Claypole83 too. Sadie then took over and described the knife attack, as well as the clip of the old man being wrongly accused and beaten in the street. Alfie would have withheld that part of the story, and both officers grew visibly dissatisfied when they learned about the brutal assault.

Officer Colman put his notepad in his breast pocket and placed his hands on his knees. "I could arrest you all. For breach of the peace, if nothing else. What you are doing is incredibly irresponsible and risky. You are not are law enforcement. Any evidence you collect—"

"Is compromised and of no use in court," Alfie said. "We've heard it all before. You talk about arresting us, but what about the lunatic who killed a pig tonight?"

"Do you think you can catch him?" Sadie asked.

"We'll conduct a search and make enquiries," Kilmani said. "The person in question is guilty of animal cruelty, so we have grounds to arrest them."

Alfie sighed. "Why am I not filled with confidence?"

Sadie tapped his arm. "Alfie, stop it."

"Yeah, dude," Ezra added. "They're just doing their jobs."

"Sure, whatever."

Kilmani stood and straightened her shirt. "Look, try to get some sleep" – she glanced around at the empty Chinese containers and wine bottles – "and maybe tidy up a little bit. In the meantime, let us do our jobs and keep you safe, okay?"

Colman stood up and joined her. "And consider getting some better security. Big place like this, out in the countryside, you should have cameras."

Sadie nodded. "It's been on the to-do list for a while. We'll get on it ASAP."

Both officers gave Sadie a polite nod but didn't bother turning to Alfie. If not for how tired he was, he might have had something to say about that, but he just yawned instead.

Useless idiots. How dare they blame me.

It's not my fault.

The words echoed in his mind, the same words he had said, over and over again when the police had asked about the man who had taken his sister. *It's not my fault, it's not my fault.*

Sadie showed the officers out. Alfie stood at the window and watched them go, refusing to look away until their headlights disappeared behind the hill.

Sadie came over and squeezed his hand. "You okay, babe?"

"I don't like police officers."

"I know you don't, but I was talking more about what happened with the pig. You're angry."

"No shit. Why don't I cover you in pig's blood and see how you feel."

"Alfie..."

He let out a sigh and nodded. "I'm all right. Just give me a while to calm down. My head is banging."

She stroked his arm and then stepped away.

"It's still out there," Ezra said. "The pig. It'll start rotting soon. We should bury it, do a funeral."

"Sod that," Jaydon said. "I'll call someone to come take it away."

"In the morning," Alfie said, rubbing at his eyes. "I need to sleep."

Sadie pulled a face. "What, here? Aren't we going to a hotel?"

"I'm covered in blood and knackered, babe. Whoever was here tonight is long gone, and even if they aren't, the doors and windows are locked and there are four of us. Let's just go to bed."

"I don't want to stay here."

"Well, I'm not leaving. Not now, at this time of night."

I was safe until I left the house. We shouldn't leave.

Jaydon came over and placed a hand on the back of Sadie's neck. "Don't worry. We got each other, yeah? The monsters fear *us*."

She nodded, although she couldn't keep her lower lip from trembling. "Fine, but I want to push the furniture up against the doors."

Alfie moved away from the window. "Whatever you want. I just need to wash this blood off me."

"Go shower," Jaydon said. "I'll sort everything out."

"Thanks." He went into the bedroom he shared with Sadie and stepped inside the en suite bathroom. He stood in front of the mirror to observe the state he was in. His cheek bled from the reopened cut that now resembled a pair of pink puckering lips, and his neck was awash with dark, sticky pig's blood.

I look like I've just walked off the set of a horror movie.

Could it really have been Claypole83 who had done this? How would the man even know where to find Alfie? And why come after him in the first place? Did he feel entitled to some kind of revenge for being targeted?

"They always think they're the innocent party," Alfie muttered to his own reflection. "They never understand that they're the monsters."

Throat swelling with a dull, tasteless rage, Alfie reached into his bloodstained jeans and yanked out his phone.

I can't do nothing about this. Whoever's responsible needs to know that Alfie Everett is not to be messed with.

He opened up the video app and hit LIVE BROADCAST.

The red light came on and Alfie saw his own scowling, bloody face captured on the screen. "Hey, wolf hunters," he said in a croaky voice, "do I have another freaky twist for you? It's three in the morning, so I guess this is going out to my viewers across the pond. Well, guess what? I was just attacked, on my own goddamn property, by a—"

The feed went wild, messages popping up on screen like machine gun fire. *Ping! Ping! Ping!*

—*Dude! You're ok. Thought u might b dead.*

—*How's the pig? Is it okay?*

—*Can't believe what I just saw. Was it real?*

—*Bruh, Claypole is gonna kill you! Rofl.*

—*Alfie? What the hell! We need an update.*

—*Are you ok?*

—*Far-left activists.*

—*U got schooled by a pig.*

—*Call cops.*

—*Claypole got you proper, m8.*

—*Cliff Richard.*

—*Far-right extremists.*

—*This is sooo fake. Obvious set-up. Do better.*

—*Yeah, this is all a prank.*

—*For real.*

—*Major fail.*

Alfie stared at his phone, speechless. His hand started to tremble. His mind spun, confused and disorientated.

Then someone posted a web link.

He tapped it and a video began to play.

"Oh, you motherfucker!" Alfie shook his head, a vein throbbing in his temple. "You goddamn motherfucker!"

———

"I feel sick," Sadie said as she buried her face in the crook of her arm. "I'm seriously going to throw up."

"It's fucking gross," Jaydon said, spitting into the kitchen sink.

Alfie stood, looking out of the window in the lounge area and watching the sky outside change from onyx to indigo. The sun would wake up soon, but none of them had slept a wink.

Claypole83 had claimed responsibility for the video that was now circulating online like a goddamn virus. It showed the events of the previous evening – Alfie stumbling towards the red light in the darkness before being tackled by a dying pig – but it also showed several other disturbing things.

Claypole had been watching and filming them all week. The video contained footage of them chilling in the garden and relaxing inside, as well as several minutes of Alfie and Sadie making love in their bedroom. Ezra had been caught masturbating in his.

Worst of all was the incident that had happened in the kitchen while everyone had been sleeping.

Alfie shuddered, violated and humiliated.

His privacy. His home.

My life.

Jaydon smashed his fist into his hand, his jaw bulging with tension. Ezra hung out a window in the kitchen, smoking cannabis and blowing the fumes out into the fresh morning air while birds chirped and whistled. He had barely spoken since viewing the video.

Alfie dumped himself onto a kitchen stool, his head heavy

like a bowling ball. He couldn't believe what had happened, couldn't believe what Claypole83 had done.

The last clip of the video posted online had been taken from *inside* the Barn. Claypole crept through their bedrooms, one by one, filming each of them as they slept. Then he had gone into the kitchen, opened the fridge...

And pissed in several of the wine bottles.

Wine they had all drank the following evening.

Alfie groaned. Sadie wasn't the only one who felt sick.

"It must have been the night before last," Jaydon said, both hands forming fists. "Man, I wish I had woken up. I would've killed that fucker."

"We were all wasted," Ezra said. "He could have brought an elephant into our rooms and we wouldn't have woken up."

Sadie put her hands to her cheeks and started pacing. "He could have murdered us in our sleep. Oh God, oh God."

"Instead, he just made us drink his piss," Ezra said. "We should count ourselves lucky."

"Lucky?" Alfie leapt up from his stool. "Lucky? This son of a bitch needs to pay. He's humiliated us. People are laughing at us."

Sadie stopped pacing and put her hands on her hips, and then clasped them in front of herself. It was as though she didn't quite know how to stand. "I don't care what a bunch of strangers think, Alfie. This man was in our house, in our bedroom. We need to get those police officers back here right now."

Alfie dug his fingernails into his palms, his temples thudding with rage. "The police are useless. We need to find out who Claypole83 is ourselves."

"No way," Sadie said. "We need to report this. This isn't just animal cruelty now. It's... it's..." She shrugged. "Breaking and entering... trespassing... I dunno."

"Biological terrorism," Ezra said, twisting one of his ginger braids around his finger as he continued to blow smoke out of the window. "A breach of the piss?"

Alfie gawped at him. "How are you making jokes about this? You drank another man's urine."

"I did worse in college. Besides, laughing is the best way to deal with shit like this. If we let it get to us, we'll make a bad decision and things will get worse. Let's just keep our heads and deal with this rationally."

"I say we find the guy and break his knees," Jaydon said, thumping the meat of his palm again. "Give him some payback and send him packing."

Sadie threw her head back and exhaled. "God, I'm going to have to go stay with my dad."

"Are you kidding?" Alfie turned to her, his fists clenched at the mention of the beast who had beaten Sadie for most of her childhood. "You want to go stay with the man who made your life a living hell?"

"It's safer than staying here."

"Is it? I mean, if Claypole found us here, then he can find your dad's place too. At least here we can stick together and make a plan."

"Have you've lost your mind? Babe, this guy is unhinged. He could have stabbed us in our sleep. Don't you get that?"

Alfie closed his eyes and took a breath. The space behind his eyes vibrated painfully. If he didn't sleep soon, he might just pass out where he stood. To keep that from happening, he went and sat back down on his stool, rubbing the fuzziness from his eyelids. "We're not going to be frightened out of our own home, Sadie. If Claypole wants to come after us, then nowhere is any safer than this. Our best defence is to find out who he is and *then* go to the police. We don't even have proof yet that it was him who made the video."

"He claimed responsibility," Sadie argued.

"Claimed it from an untraceable account."

"He's right," Ezra said. "It could have been anyone."

Alfie raised an eyebrow. "You see? We need to stick together and find something incriminating on this guy – and the best place to do that is right here where we have all of our equipment. Ezra, can you call someone to put up cameras and install an alarm? Pay whatever you have to, but get them here today. Jaydon, can you take care of the dead pig outside?"

"And what about me?" Sadie asked. "If we're staying, then I need to keep busy or I'll freak out."

"See if you can reach out to Claypole on the messaging app and agree a truce? He's probably not planning anything else, but just in case, it might buy us some time while we try to find out who he is."

"Okay. I'll try, but I really don't like this, Alfie. Can't we go someplace else? I feel like I'm in prison here, trapped inside."

He summoned her over and wrapped his arms around her. "It's just a bad day at work, babe. Claypole messed with us and got his revenge. He'd be stupid to try something else now that we're on our guard."

"Do you really think so?"

"I do."

"Yeah," Jaydon nodded. "Don't sweat it, Say. Ain't nobody gonna hurt you, I swear down."

Alfie nodded a thanks to his friend for helping assuage her fears. "You see? We stick together and everything will be fine."

There was a *ding*. It came from Ezra. He moved away from the window and pulled out his phone. The bags beneath his eyes were battleship grey, his pupils the size of dinner plates, but despite that, he appeared focused as he tapped away for a moment.

Twenty seconds later, he looked over at Alfie with a dour expression on his face. "You ain't gonna like this, dude."

Alfie marched over, his stomach groaning. "What? What is it now?"

Ezra turned his phone around to show another video playing. This one had been recorded only a couple of hours ago. It showed the police car leaving the Barn, and Alfie watching them through the window.

"He was out there the whole time?" Sadie said, and she started to cry. "What the hell?"

Jaydon took a step and faltered. He had to grab the back of an armchair for balance. "W-who the hell does this guy think he is?"

Alfie froze for a moment, an operating kernel in his brain failing momentarily. When he eventually rebooted, he did so with a sense of dread that caused him to stiffen up, a feeling he could not allow to take root, a feeling he had only truly ever felt once before.

A victim. I feel like a victim.

I refuse.

"Enough of this," he said, slipping off his stool and marching over to the front door. He unlocked it and yanked it open, then stormed out into the misty dawn.

The sky had turned the same turquoise as a robin's egg. The silhouette of the grassy hill faded into view beyond the field.

He was out here the entire time, watching us and filming us. As if we're here for his goddamn amusement.

"Babe, get back inside," Sadie called out to him through the open door. "Don't leave."

"Yeah, man," Jaydon said. "We need to keep our heads."

But Alfie wasn't in the mood to keep his head. This had to stop. He would not be intimidated. Fear was not an emotion he would ever give space to.

He marched out across the garden, stepping up onto a small raised deck area that was due a strip and paint. Glaring off towards the hill – to the spot where he imagined Claypole was skulking around and watching them – he cupped his mouth and bellowed. "You're fucking toast. Do you hear me? You have no clue who you're messing with. Not a clue. There'll be nothing left of you by the time I'm done. Do you hear me, you sick fucking loser?"

Sadie called him back inside again, and this time he listened. He just hoped he'd got his point across.

Because I'm coming for you, Claypole83. You're just another wolf to be put down.

FIVE

Ezra came into the Barn's long rectangular office at the back of the building, shielding his eyes beneath the bright skylight window. He'd spent the entire morning napping in the living room, but he appeared better for it. Alfie, on the other hand, had been tapping away at his laptop for hours, chasing down every lead he could dig up on Claypole83. His eyeballs throbbed after focusing for so long, and the crusted wound on his face itched relentlessly.

"I made some calls," Ezra said, stifling a yawn. "No luck with CCTV installation for the next day or two, but Jay got someone to handle the dead pig situation. That, um, was a tough one to explain."

Alfie lifted his fingers from the keyboard and gripped the edge of his height-adjustable glass desk. "We need eyes, Ez. If Claypole comes anywhere near us, I want his ass on camera."

"You reckon he'll be back, then?"

"I don't know. We need to be prepared either way."

Ezra leant against his own desk, a black wooden slab covered in camera lenses and memory cards. He seemed troubled by something, unable to look Alfie in the eye as he spoke. "So, um, what are you up to right now?"

"Damage control. People are taking the piss out of us non-stop, but thankfully no one is unsubscribing. I've put our superfans to work trying to find Claypole, checking on missing pigs, animal cruelty convictions, stuff like that. It's only a matter of time until someone finds out who he is."

"So take a break and see what happens, dude. The rest of us caught some winks, but you haven't slept at all. It's bad for the mind."

Alfie waved a hand. "I'll catch a nap soon as I finish up here."

"All right, just don't drive yourself loopy."

Alfie turned in his chair to face his friend. His vision tilted for a moment, but the dizziness soon passed. "I'm fine, Ez. It's business as usual. Claypole's just another degenerate begging to be caught."

"But what if he's not, dude? What if we bit off more than we can chew this time? Claypole was able to find out where we live and set up a camera without us noticing. He isn't like the others. You see that, right? Alf?"

"What are you saying? That we should back off and hope he leaves us alone? What message would that send to our viewers? How can we continue our mission if every wolf we go after knows they can intimidate us? I refuse to be frightened by a prank."

"Killing a pig is a hell of a prank, dude. Not sure I see the funny side."

"We have to hold our heads high, Ez. We have to be better than the people we expose – or else the whole thing falls apart."

Ezra put his hands in his jeans pockets and gave a lopsided shrug. "I feel you, dude. Whatever you wanna do, I'm all in, you know that. But don't let the past push you into making a mistake. Claypole isn't the man who took your sister."

"Don't you think I know that. This isn't about Daisy."

"Then think about letting this one go. It might be for the best."

Alfie paused a moment. "Fine, I'll give it some thought."

"Good. We love you, dude. Come and be with the rest of us."

Alfie felt a sudden tickle at the back of his eyes, followed by an upswell of emotion. He didn't like the off-kilter sensation, so he got up out of his seat and tried to shake it off by pulling Ezra into a hug and patting his friend's back. "I appreciate you, man, but don't worry, okay? Claypole's going to get what's coming to him and everything will go right back to normal."

"Yeah. Yeah, okay, mate." Ezra broke away from the hug and exited the office in silence. It left behind an atmosphere, as if his lack of parting words was some kind of condemnation.

A condemnation of what? I'm doing what has to be done to keep us safe.

Alfie let out a sigh and considered whether Ezra was right about him needing a break. While he wasn't ready to clock off and take a nap, he could probably do with some fresh air and a quick mental reset. So, grabbing his vape pen, he exited through the office's separate entrance and stepped outside, standing on the same raised deck area he had stood on earlier when he had vented his fury at the dawn. In the early afternoon sunlight, the trickling stream shone like a streak of silver. Its gentle movement breathed life into the otherwise static green field. But it was only a matter of time before Alfie's mood darkened as he glowered at the hill.

Unlike the field, which Alfie kept neatly mown, the hill was thick with dandelions, daisies, and other weed-cum-wild-flowers. In the spring, white-tail rabbits often streaked back and forth across it.

What's your deal, Claypole? Do you have a family? Kids?

There was no sign of anyone on the hill – no camera or tripod either – but there were plenty of other places to hide. Alfie couldn't shake the sensation that he was being watched.

Ezra's right. Claypole isn't like the others. He's dangerous.

Which means I have to stop him. I need to stop him before he hurts anyone else.

"Hey?" Sadie came up behind Alfie and rubbed his lower back. Her familiar rose-scented perfume instantly put him at ease. "You finally taking a break? You must be exhausted."

His focus remained on the hill. "I wish everyone would stop worrying about me. We should all be worrying about Claypole."

"We *are* worried about him." She closed her eyes. "I don't even want to be here after what that creep did. But if I go stay with my dad..."

She didn't have to finish. Alfie knew all about the kicks and punches she'd endured from her drunken piece-of-shit father.

He wrapped an arm around her shoulders and pulled her close. "I know you're scared, but you don't need to be. Ez is working on getting a security company out here pronto, and if Claypole turns up again, we'll call the police and have him arrested. You don't need to go stay with your dad; I'll never let that happen."

"You can't promise everything will be okay, Alfie. You had your face slashed, our home was invaded..." She pulled at her earlobe, breathing rapidly through her nose. "It's like a bad dream."

He squeezed her more tightly. "Hey, babe, I'm here, okay?"

She took a few shallow breaths, and when she looked at him, tears filled her eyes. "Can we go for a walk?"

Alfie glanced towards the hill. "You want to?"

"Only to the stream and back."

She took Alfie's arm, prompting him to start walking. They stepped down off the deck and headed towards the stream, Sadie's favourite place on the property. Sometimes you could spot tiny fish swimming downstream.

"I've been a bit obsessive lately, huh?" Alfie admitted.

"A tad."

"Perhaps we should book a holiday soon, eh? Hit Disney World again?"

She shrugged.

"What is it? Is it Claypole? Because I—"

"It's not just Claypole, Alfie."

"What do you mean?"

She rubbed her hands together, as if washing them in an invisible sink. "What about the next freak carrying a knife? Or the one after that? What if the next person we expose is even more deranged than Claypole? I'm proud of what we've all done here, babe – I really am – but I'm scared that this can only end badly. I think... I think we should quit while we're ahead."

"And do what?"

She lifted an arm and did a quarter turn, gesturing to the undulating fields, hedgerows, and dense woodland surrounding them. "We have all of this and enough money to enjoy it. Hell, let's turn the place back into a working farm and live the simple life."

Alfie smirked. "A farm? You want to spend your life waking up at the crack of dawn to feed the sheep?"

"Don't the sheep just eat the grass?"

"Pigs then."

"Whatever. I just want to do something safe and normal, Alfie."

"Farmers get injured too, Sadie. Life is full of risks no matter what you do."

"Look, I know how much the channel means to you, babe, because of what happened to your sister—"

"Please, I don't want to think about that right now. I already had it from—"

"—but you're never going to heal that wound, Alfie. No matter how many wolves we catch, it'll never be enough. I... I worry about the toll it's taking on you."

He wanted to argue. In fact, he wanted to yell in her face for being so naïve and unambitious. Didn't she see that everything they had was because of *Invite the Wolf*? And yet, when he looked at her – at the face that had brought him so much comfort during the last few years – he couldn't hold on to his anger. It slipped through his fingers like fine sand and left him questioning himself.

Is this one of those moments I'll look back on and wonder if I did the right thing? Said the right thing?

"You really want to end the channel?" He looked her in the eye. "Seriously?"

"I'm not sure what I want, only that we should give it some thought. What's the point of being successful if we spend all of our time being afraid? And after what's happened this week, babe, I *am* afraid."

"Sadie, this is just—"

"Listen to what I'm saying." She raised her voice. "The channel can't be the only fucking thing in my life, babe. I won't let it be."

He flinched, taken aback by her venom. The only thing he could think to say was: "Okay."

She frowned. "Really?"

He nodded slowly. "I accept that I've been burning the

candle at both ends. I'll try to ease up a gear and touch grass a little more often."

"Wow, that was a lot of metaphors all in a row."

He smirked, glad to see her make a joke. He reached out and repositioned a strand of blonde hair out of her face. "I'm just trying to bite the bullet and step up to the plate, you know?"

Chuckling, they reached the stream and came to a stop. The water was crystalline – the chalky gravel and submerged branches visible beneath its rippling surface. Alfie watched as a disembodied magpie feather floated by.

Sadie put her hands on Alfie's chest. Her hair was so blonde in the bright sunlight – even her lashes – that she seemed to glow. Her brows were delicate gold threads. "You should get some sleep," she said. "I got a few hours in and I'm still a zombie."

"Nah. Think I'll chill in the house for a bit, watch a movie and have an early night."

"Okay, I'll join you," she said, "but please, I beg you, make it a comedy."

"A comedy it is then." He leant forward and kissed her satin lips, then pinched her cheek and said: "I love you, Sadie."

"I love you too," she replied, but she sounded tired and didn't look at him when she said it.

As they walked back towards the house, Alfie had a feeling it would be a while before things returned to normal. He just hoped they didn't get any worse in the meantime.

———

Alfie endured thirty minutes of a ninety-minute Disney merchandise ad before falling asleep in Sadie's lap. Some time later, he found his way to bed and slept straight through until morning. Now, in the light of a new day, he felt partly renewed

– a battery three-quarters full. The chaos of the last week was distant, and the clatter in his head had quieted down. He realised now how much pressure he'd been under.

Sadie's right. I need to ease up.

Sadie had awoken earlier than him, so he was lying in bed alone. He could hear her and the boys chatting out in the kitchen.

Alfie got dressed and headed out the bedroom. He found Ezra, Sadie, and Jaydon sitting around the kitchen island having breakfast. When Jaydon saw him, he nudged over a stool. "Plenty to go around, bud."

The smell of eggs and bacon made Alfie's stomach gurgle. The last time he'd eaten properly was that fateful Chinese meal before Claypole had ruined their evening with a knife and a pig.

Sadie grabbed a plate, piled it full of food, and slid it over to him. "Eat up."

"God, this looks good." Alfie licked his lips. "Sorry I wasn't awake to help make it."

Not that any of you woke me up...

"No worries, bro." Jaydon winked at him. "Sadie and I teamed up. You and Ez are on clean-up duty, though."

Alfie grumbled – he hated loading the dishwasher – but he couldn't argue. "Fair enough."

For the next ten minutes, the clink of cutlery and the smacking of lips were the only sounds. Nothing put the world right quite like a hearty meal. They all needed it.

Alfie finished first, dropping his knife and fork down with a clank and letting out a satisfied moan. "I feel like a new man." He put a fist to his mouth and stifled a burp. "That was fire."

Sadie rubbed his back. "You seem brighter today. I thought you were going to have a stroke with how tired you looked yesterday."

"I was in a bad headspace, but the sleep has done me good. You were right about me needing to ease up. I'm gonna take a couple of days to myself."

"Wow," Ezra said. He was sitting the furthest away at the opposite end of the granite-topped island. "Who are you, and what have you done with Alfie?"

He forced a grin. "Don't worry, he's still here. Just taking a break."

Sadie stared into space for a moment, then slid off her stool. "I'll stack the dishwasher," she said glumly.

Alfie stood to go after her. "No, I'll do it. I'm on clean-up duty, remember?"

"I don't mind. You go sit down."

"Really?"

Why do I feel like you do mind?

"It's all good. You can relax."

"Thanks, babe. You're okay, yeah?"

"Uh-huh."

"Right..."

"I'm gonna clear out the fridge," Jaydon said, standing up as well. "I don't trust anything in there after... you know."

Alfie groaned. "How have the comments online been this morning? People still dragging us?"

"We're the goddamn meme of the week, bro. Doing my best to laugh it off, but it's a tough ask."

Ezra pushed his plate away. He'd eaten less than everyone else and an entire juicy sausage lay unclaimed. "Claypole's video has gone more viral than anything we've ever put out. But the upside is that it's driving a tonne of new traffic to our channel."

"Can't we get it taken down?" Alfie asked. "It's footage of a crime taking place."

Which is why I can't believe we're not getting to work and doing something about it. Claypole is getting away with it while we 'take a break'.

Chill out, Alfie. You promised to take a breather and relax. Sadie clearly needs it, even if you don't.

Ezra answered his question. "The original upload has already been struck down for content violations, but it'll never stop circulating. I'll do what I can to suppress it, but I can't wipe it from people's hard drives."

The hairs on the back of Alfie's neck stood up. Being humiliated online was about the worst thing he could imagine, and yet...

"Nothing stays relevant on the Internet for long," he said. "In a couple of months it'll be forgotten about and people will move on to the next thing. In the grand scheme of things, who gives a shit?"

Sadie frowned at him from over by the sink. "You really did get a good sleep, didn't you? You're honestly okay about everything? What about Claypole?"

He looked at Ezra, exchanging glances. "Maybe he's not worth the hassle. For today, at least, I'm off work. Everything else can wait."

"You still want the CCTV installed?" Jaydon asked.

"Yeah. It's still worth getting. It's 2024, after all. Who knows what crazy reality is lurking round the corner?"

Ezra put a hand up. "I pick alien invasion. That or Portugal declares war on Tonga."

"I would laugh at you," Alfie chuckled, "but after the last few years, who can rule anything out?"

Jaydon rummaged in the kitchen cabinets and produced an orange tennis ball. "Anybody fancy some fresh air?"

"Not me, dude." Ezra went and sat down in the lounge area, proceeding to pull out his tobacco tin and to roll a joint. "I ain't moving from this seat today. Need to find my zen."

"I'll join you," Alfie said, putting up a hand and motioning for the ball. Jaydon tossed it and he caught it.

"I want you back before dark," Sadie yelled after them.

"Promise, Mum." Alfie said, smirking.

Outside, the two of them took a space and started tossing the tennis ball back and forth. The simple distraction, the act of throwing and catching a fuzzy orange ball, lifted both their spirits, and within moments they were chatting and laughing.

"How's your war wound?" Jaydon asked. "Looks like it's healing all right."

"It *was*," Alfie replied, touching his the dry, cracked skin on his damaged cheek. "Until that sodding pig ran into me. Poor thing. How do you do that to an innocent animal?"

"I'm still trying to wrap my head around it, bro."

"We all are. Hey, can I ask you a question, man?"

Jaydon caught the ball and then tossed it around his back in a well-aimed trick shot. "Shoot!"

"Do you think everything is okay with Sadie? She's really down on the channel after what happened, and I'm worried she's keeping things inside. Has she said anything to you?"

Jaydon caught the ball again, but this time he didn't return it. Instead, he rolled it in his hands as if it were a crystal ball. "She and Ezra, they ain't as invested in things as we are, bro. What happened to your sister, and what happened to me in the kid's home, gave us a perspective most people don't have. We understand first-hand what some people are capable of."

Alfie nodded at the truth of it. "But she's been fully onboard until now. Ezra too."

"People change, bro. Just because Say's spent the last few years luring wolves for the channel don't mean she wants to spend the rest of her life doing it. She has other dreams."

"What we do is important, Jay."

"Hell, yes it is. But it's also dark as shit, bro – and Say's the one who's been dealing with the targets directly, chatting with them for hours on end and having to pretend to be a child. It's gotta wear thin, man. Proper thin."

Alfie gestured for the ball and caught it, but instead of tossing it back, he studied it for a moment. "I guess I never thought about that. I've only ever focused on the innocent kids we're saving, and that helps me sleep at night. Sadie should do the same and think about the positives. She's looking at it the wrong way."

Jaydon folded his arms and shook his head. "You want my advice, bro?"

"Of course."

"If Sadie wants out, let her go. She can still be your girl-friend, but not everyone is built to face this kind of darkness day in, day out. You and me? Our minds are already twisted, but Say still has some innocence left in hers. Let her keep it."

"I agreed to take a break. Why is she still in a mood?"

Jaydon shrugged. "Maybe she wants more than a break."

"You really think she wants to be done? Like *completely* done?"

"Maybe. Hey, did I ever tell you about Jordan Harris? Kid I was in the care home with?"

"No, I don't think so."

"Well, he was a similar age to me, nine or ten, but smaller, you know? Like chronically underfed small. He never grew like he was supposed to. Anyway, kid was cute and quiet and friendly, which is exactly what foster parents go for – especially the ones who are planning to later adopt. He was only in the home ten minutes before a nice family with an SUV and a house in the country took him home. We were all happy for him, and he seemed happy too. He even wrote me letters for a while afterwards, telling me how he had his own room and a television, and how his new folks took him on holiday twice a year. They spoilt him rotten."

"That's good. He must have got a raw deal to end up in the home, right?"

"All kinds of abuse, bro. Parents were druggies who did all kinds of sketchy shit to him. So it seemed like a happy ending when he found a new home with a nice family, right?"

Alfie nodded. "Sure. But why do I get the feeling it wasn't a happy ending?"

"Jordan drank bleach a year later. Left a letter for me explaining how the nightmare he went through as a kid made it too painful to be happy. Every time his foster parents showed him love or kindness, it sent him spiralling. The darkness inside him wouldn't allow him to enjoy anything good or decent. Or even normal."

"Fuck, that's rough. You don't think that's us, though, do you? We're happy, right? Things are good."

"My point is that dark and twisted shit is like radiation. Expose yourself to too much of it and you get sick. Sometimes you get better, but if the dose is too big, it eats away at you until there's nothing left. If Sadie is sick, then you should let her step away before shit becomes terminal."

Alfie tossed the ball again. Jaydon caught it, but instead of throwing it back, he walked towards Alfie and looked him in the eye. "Don't lose sight of what's important, bro – and it ain't the wolves we hunt down."

"Then what is it, Jay?"

Jaydon smiled, but instead of answering, he headed back towards the Barn. Alfie stood a while longer, staring off towards the grassy hill where Claypole had ruined everything.

He's to blame. Not radiation sickness.

Claypole is to blame.

Staring off towards the hill, Alfie wondered if the psycho was still out here somewhere, watching. Waiting. Planning.

You don't scare me.

Six

The following day, Alfie was still willing to take an extended break, but a nagging piece of him was itching to restart his pursuit of Claypole83. But he'd given his word, and that was enough to keep him away from his computer for at least a couple of days.

So, he and the others had spent the day zooming around on the pair of quad bikes taken from the Barn's triple garage. Jaydon rode on one, with Ezra clutching his back like a baby monkey, and Sadie held onto Alfie while he steered the other. By the time they came to a halt in the far field, all of them were laughing and picking bugs out of their teeth.

The security of Sadie's arms around his waist made Alfie think of Jaydon's words yesterday. Was he truly losing sight of what was important? Simple things like spending time with his friends and having fun, the wind in his face and laughter in his ears.

"I think I swallowed a bee," Ezra said, coughing and spluttering into his fist. "I hope I don't get hives."

Jaydon switched off his bike's ignition. "I've seen you put worse in your mouth, bro. Wotsits and mayonnaise, for one."

"I've been trying to cut down on that."

Alfie cackled, so hard that everyone paused to look at him. Sadie squeezed his waist. "What's so funny, babe?"

"Not funny. Just... nice. This is nice. The four of us having fun together.

"Like I said: no point having all of this if we don't enjoy it."

"Damn straight," Jaydon said. "You know, if we move away from *Invite the Wolf*, we could move our audience over to a vlog channel. We could just film ourselves doing wild shit right here at home."

Ezra made a *nuh* sound. "Vlogs are on a downswing, but we could potentially make something work. There's a big audience for sustainable living and surviving off the grid. That could work."

"Whoa." Alfie put a hand up. "We're taking a break, but we're not seriously thinking about ending *Invite the Wolf*, are we? It's one of the most popular channels on Evershare. Why would we start all over doing something else?"

"I'm just chatting shit," Jaydon said. "Nothing wrong with having a plan B, is there?"

Alfie shrugged. *As long as it remains plan B. Plan A is still working out quite fine.*

Sadie released his waist. "I would feel better knowing we have an exit strategy. We don't know what the future holds."

Jaydon's words echoed in Alfie's head. *If Sadie is sick, then you should let her step away before shit becomes terminal.*

"You were right about needing a break," he said. "Can we not just put everything else aside for now?"

He heard her sigh in his ear. "You say you're going to take a break, Alfie, but I can hear the gears whirring in your head. You haven't let go. Work is still on your mind. Admit it."

"What? No. I'm all yours. Work can wait."

"Prove it."

He turned back to try to look at her, but it was too difficult to see directly behind him. "How? How can I prove it?"

"Put out a video," Ezra said.

"What?"

Sadie wrapped her arms back around his waist and leaned against him. "Ez is right. Put out a video announcing the channel is taking a hiatus. Tell all of your fans that you won't be back for a little while."

"No way. What if we lose all our momentum? Our subscribers expect regular content."

What if they move on to something else? Someone else.

"Who cares?" Sadie said. "What matters most? Them, or us?"

Jaydon gave him a look. "Come on, bro. Let go of the reins for a while. We all need a break."

"Are you serious? You all want me to put out a video?"

Jaydon shrugged. So did Ezra.

"Yes," Sadie said. "If we're going to continue with the channel, then you need to show that you can take a step back when required. You're obsessed, Alfie."

"I'm not!"

"Then prove it."

"Fine." He pulled out his phone and switched on the selfie camera.

He hesitated, staring at his mud-flecked face reflected back at him.

This is a bad idea. What if it tanks the channel?

What choice do I have? It's three against one. Traitors.

With a sigh, Alfie hit *record* with his thumb. "Hey... Um, hey there, wolf hunters, this is Alfie E. It's been a busy week for the channel, no doubt, but it's led me to realise a few things. The daily uploads and weekly episodes have been amazing, right? We love doing them, but... Well, it's hard to keep up with that kind of pace on a long-term basis, and I hope you can appreciate that, from time to time, we all need to take a break. I promise you all that *Invite the Wolf* is not going anywhere at all, but the team and I will be taking a well-deserved break. I can't say when we'll be back, but in the meantime you can still enjoy all previous uploaded content, so be sure to check you haven't missed anything. Um, take care out there, okay? We'll be back soon."

He ended the video and lowered his phone, wanting to check out his friends' reaction. Ezra was nodding appreciatively, while Jaydon was smiling. Sadie, still sitting behind him, squeezed his waist tightly. They all looked relieved.

They're totally burnt out, and I didn't even see it.

"You sounded a bit like a hostage being forced to read out a message," Sadie said. "But thank you."

He chuckled. "All right, I get it. I'm sorry for working us so hard, guys." He slid his phone back into his pocket and then put his hands on his thighs. "I'll upload the video as soon as we get back, okay?"

Jaydon waved a hand. "Bro, we've all been grinding. It's addictive, what we do, so don't sweat it. It's done now, so just relax."

"I'm proud of you," Sadie whispered in Alfie's ear. It caused his stomach to swell.

He looked back and forth between everyone. "Are we really going to sit around and do nothing every day? Won't it drive us insane?"

"Eh, nothing wrong with a little boredom-induced insanity," Ezra said.

Sadie agreed. "I'm all for a boring week or two. These last few days have traumatised me."

"A little break will do us good. Maybe I'll finally get around to tinting the windows on my Range."

Alfie pulled his phone back out and sat for a moment, taking in the brief silence that seemed to wait on him to act. He couldn't deny that the thought of shutting off for a while was tempting – if nothing else, he was exhausted – but at the same time, every day off was a day where they weren't chasing down predators. Taking a break might result in a kid getting hurt. It felt wrong to ignore that.

But I can't save everyone. No matter how much I wish I could.

"I hope we don't regret this," he said, pulling a face at his friends. "But screw it, I'll upload the video right now. Before I lose my nerve."

Sadie stroked his back. "Babe, stop panicking. It's just a short break. We're not robbing a bank."

She's right. Why am I making such a big deal of this? Maybe I am obsessed.

No maybe.

He opened up the channel's social media page and prepared to post the update, but then he noticed an influx of follower activity and wondered if he had already done so by accident. People were posting comments, dozens and dozens of them.

—*Hypocrite!*

—*Can't believe this sicko.*

—*Alfie should be in prison.*

—*He's no better than the wolves.*

—*Always knew Sadie was a dirty girl ;-)*

—*Can't believe he preaches to the rest of us after he's done this.*

—*Alfie is a nonce!*

—*And a far-right thug!*

—*Cliff Richard.*

—*Alfie needs unaliving.*

—*Thumbs up to that.*

—I'm blocking him. Right. Now.

Alfie's stomach turned. He had no idea what was going on, but it was clearly bad. Had he drunk too much last night and posted something stupid?

No, these messages are hateful.

Why are people so mad at me?

He shook his head in confusion and glanced over at Ezra, a burning sensation in his throat. "Dude, have you been checking the feed today? Something's happened. Something bad."

Ezra pulled a face. "Huh? What do you mean? I checked the pages an hour ago and everything was fine. Just a few people chatting shit and posting memes."

Alfie's hand shook as he flicked through more and more hate-filled messages. Hundreds of them. Approaching the thousands.

Then it suddenly all made sense.

Claypole had posted a new video.

As usual, the wide brim of the man's hat cloaked his entire face in shadow. His voice was like glass shards on an iron skillet. "Alfie Everett was a juvenile menace, prosecuted for multiple assaults, drug possession, and various other pettier offences. He claims to be an agent of justice, a protector of the innocent, yet he is a remorseless criminal."

Alfie gasped, his hand trembling as he held his phone.

"What is it?" Jaydon asked.

Alfie ignored him, unable to form words.

The camera zoomed in on a five-year-old newspaper article. It described the teenage rampage of a troubled young man who had assaulted several youths and smashed up a neighbour's car. It had been Alfie's third conviction, resulting in him receiving six months in a juvenile detention centre, with leniency shown because his mother had died one year prior.

His friends didn't know about his past – at least not this part of it.

What are they going to think of me? Sadie hates violence. She can't even watch a boxing match. What will she think when I know I have so much aggression deep down inside me?

"Dude, what's going on?" Ezra asked.

Alfie shushed him. Claypole wasn't done. The son of a bitch continued talking. "Furthermore, this so-called vigilante specifically targets those who wish to fornicate with minors – those he labels *wolves* – but he is guilty of the very same crime."

No. What is he talking about? Lies.

An image flashed up onscreen: a selfie taken from a mobile phone. Alfie didn't remember the exact moment the photograph had been taken, but it was an image of him and Sadie kissing. Sadie was wearing her high school uniform.

"Sadie Wilson is three years younger than Alfie Everett, meaning he was eighteen in this picture. She was only *fifteen*. An adult and a minor."

Alfie hissed at the screen. It was true, Sadie was only fifteen in the picture, but they hadn't had sex until fourteen months into their relationship, after she had turned seventeen. Things had developed slowly, the two of them both damaged in their own ways. Trust had not come easily. Nor had physical intimacy.

People don't understand. There's nothing wrong with our relationship. We love each other.

Claypole had nothing further to say. The video ended on a still frame of the previous newspaper article, shining a renewed spotlight on Alfie's past carnage.

He swiped at his phone and opened up the live video function to record a new message. His intentions had changed. No more talk of 'taking a break'.

"Claypole83, if you're listening to this, I just want you to know that this means war. You're the monster here, not me. I'm going to expose you. I'm gonna make you pay, motherfucker."

Unable to contain his rage any longer, Alfie hurled his phone into the air. His friends all looked at him, but they said nothing.

————

Alfie tried his best to stay off social media during the days that followed. The hatred spewed in his direction was shocking. It was hard to fathom that people could hate him so much. Two weeks ago, he'd been adored. Claypole had ruined everything.

He can't get away with this. What right does he have to expose my past? I've changed. I'm not that person any more.

After the revelations, Sadie had delicately probed Alfie about his former criminal behaviour, and reluctantly, he had told her everything in graphic detail; about how angry he had been after his sister's abduction and his mother's suicide, and how his teenage years had only fertilised that rage inside him until it had exploded in a whirlwind of muggings and robberies, all attempts to make him feel alive.

Or pass on my misery to others so I didn't feel so alone.

One incident in particular stuck with him more than any other, and he struggled to describe it to Sadie.

Drinking underaged at a pub in town one night, Alfie had made friends with a quiet lad named Solomon, who had been stood up by his mates. Alfie had bought the lad drinks and laughed the night away with him, genuinely liking the kid. Wanting to continue the growing friendship, Solomon had invited Alfie back to his place to grab a few more drinks. Walking home, Alfie had stopped them about halfway – and had proceeded to beat Solomon until he was screaming and begging and crying. The kid had been utterly bewildered by the sudden betrayal and the brutal violence. Alfie hadn't even understood it himself.

It was because I trusted him, and every person I ever trusted up until that point had let me down. The anger and the pain of it all came out, directed at an innocent kid who just wanted to make a new friend.

Fighting hard to stay calm and detached – not wanting to wear his past or accept that it was a part of him – Alfie had gone on to recount how his Auntie Maureen had gone on to adopt him to keep him from being taken away by the state, but she had never intended on becoming a mother, and her discipline was non-existent. Sex, drugs, and violence soon wrapped a chummy arm around Alfie and gathered him in – a tale as old as time – and before he knew it, he was drowning in a bleak, hopeless pool with no hope of reaching the sides.

But things changed when Alfie was sent to a young offender's home. There, he finally found the discipline he was so sorely lacking. A mandatory IT course had taught him the basics of website design and content production, while the prison chaplain helped him to finally process his cancerous grief.

When he regained his freedom six months later, Alfie was a different person, dedicated to making something out of his life and making up for the sins of his past. Not long after, he had met Sadie at an open-air festival in the park, and the rest was history. Ezra and Jaydon he met at college while taking media studies.

Now his twisted past threatened the life he had worked so hard to build.

Starting a new day, Alfie went out into the kitchen to make a cup of coffee and wake himself up. Ezra was in the lounge area, a laptop balanced on his knees. Alfie asked if he wanted a drink.

"Just a tea for me, dude."

"Coming right up."

Once he'd made the drinks, he went and sat on the white leather sofa underneath the window. He handed Ezra his tea before leaning back against the seat cushions.

"Weber-Cooks Security is due any time to install the cameras," Ezra said. "You want me to deal with them?"

"Nah, I'll sort it. You found anything useful on Claypole yet?"

Ezra sipped his tea before placing it down on the glass coffee table. "Can't find a thing. He's just a hat and a username at this point. Sorry, dude."

Alfie grunted, his stomach taut with frustration. His plan to suspend the channel had gone to pot when Claypole had released his 'exposé', but Alfie could see the strain it was putting everyone under. But what choice did they have other than to retaliate? If they did nothing, the accusations would stick and they would all be cancelled.

Alfie was going to find out who Claypole was and bring him into the excoriating light where everyone could see that he was the only one at fault here.

"Someone must know who the guy is," he said. "He dresses like a mortician, for God's sake."

"That's the funny thing," Ezra said. "I've had loads of people claiming to have seen him, but they're all over the place. One person here says they spotted him in Newcastle. Another swears they've seen him in Gloucester. If it really is Claypole, the guy moves about a lot."

Alfie scratched at his chin. He needed a shave, his blonde stubble several days old. His black hair was also growing out, exposing his natural roots. "Maybe he's a truck driver or something."

"I considered that, and it's definitely a possibility. I'm checking each sighting location for similarities. Maybe he's tried to meet up with a minor before. I'll look through the police reports and see what comes up."

"Good." Alfie nodded. "Good."

Ez put his laptop on the table and picked up his tea again. He held it in both hands and squinted at Alfie. "You okay, dude?"

"Me? Yeah, I'm fine."

"You've had a rough few days."

"Internet noise. People think they know the truth, but they don't."

Ezra scooped his braids back and rubbed at the back of his neck. He hadn't smoked weed today, which was unusual for him. "It'll blow over, but it's okay to wig out if you need to. No one would blame you."

"Appreciate it, but I'm really okay. I'm just sorry so many people have unsubscribed from the channel because of my past."

"Not 'cos of you, dude. Claypole. The guy has it in for us."

"Doesn't that piss you off? All we're guilty of is trying to stop him from hurting children. Where does he get off coming after us, like we're the ones who deserve punishment?"

"Guess it should have occurred to us that a child predator could actually be dangerous. Clearly, they're not all betas like HenryLongShaft."

"Do we know what happened to him after our episode? With everything that's happened, I've forgotten to do a follow-up."

Ezra put his tea back down. "From what people have been saying, he got fired from his accountancy job and his wife kicked him out of the house. No police investigation, though, even after Jay sent them all the evidence we put together."

"Useless. It's almost like they refuse to prosecute out of spite. What do they have against us?"

"Dunno, dude."

Movement in the corner of Alfie's eye caused him to turn his head. Through the window, he saw a blue-and-white liveried van arriving down the gravel driveway. "Looks like the CCTV people are here," he said, standing up. "I'll go out and meet them."

"All right, boss. Shout if you need me."

"Just find out who the hell Claypole is and I'll be happy."

"Roger that."

Alfie headed outside.

Sadie and Jaydon were sitting on a couple of chairs on the deck. They waved when they saw him, but quickly returned to chatting. Alfie had hardly spoken to either of them all day. Sadie, in particular, had been distant with him since the online attack on their relationship and the revelation of his violent past.

A man in a blue baseball cap climbed out of the van and approached Alfie with a clipboard. They greeted each other with a handshake and the other man said: "Got a big order here. Six cameras. Alarm. Spotlights. Backup battery supply and secure data storage."

Alfie gave a single nod. "The works."

"You been having problems? Or is it peace of mind you're after?"

"A little from column A and a little from column B. How long will it take, buddy?"

"The battery backup isn't in stock until tomorrow morning, but I'll get the majority done today, hopefully. Got a colleague on his way to come help, which should speed things along."

"Okay great. What do you need from me?"

"Just show me where your main fuse box is and I'll get started."

"No problem. Follow me." Alfie approached the garages and keyed a six-digit code into the wall panel. The triple roller doors slid upwards, revealing the quad bikes, ride-on mower, and the two cars parked inside. Alfie pointed. "Fuse box is in the back, mate."

The security guy whistled and walked over to the car parked in the garage's first section. Alfie's emerald-green Alfa Romeo. "That is one pretty car. I've always loved Alfas. A car lover's car, you know?"

"That's what they tell me. Honestly, I just liked the colour."

"What model is it?"

"Stelvio Quadrifoglio. Got it a couple years back. Drives like a demon."

"I'll bet." He ran his hand over the sleek round bonnet as if he were caressing a woman's breast. He seemed entirely uninterested in Jaydon's black Range Rover Sport parked in the next bay. "Would you mind if I had a little sit inside?"

Usually, such a request would irritate Alfie, but after all the abuse online, it was nice to talk to someone friendly. "Let me unlock it for you." He reached into his pocket and pressed the key fob. The car beeped, and the security guy opened the driver's door with a satisfying *thunk*.

"My name's Michael, by the way."

"Pleased to meet you. Alfie."

"You're obviously doing pretty well for yourself, huh? What is it that you do, Alfie?"

"Just... um, online stuff. Websites and that."

"Huh, I'm in the wrong business." He slid into the driver's seat and ran his hands over the leather steering wheel, then twiddled with the various sleek black knobs and dials. After a minute, he got out and closed the door. "Right, thanks for that. I'll get to work. Hopefully, I won't be too much in your way."

"Don't worry about it. Just do what you need to do."

Alfie stepped out of the garage and felt a light drizzle on

his face. The sky was grey, matching his mood. It looked to only get darker.

Sadie and Jaydon were still chatting away on the deck. Alfie went and joined them. "Looks like it's gonna start pissing it down," he said, glancing upwards.

"Yeah, bro." Jaydon stood up. "I was heading in, anyway, but I don't fancy getting soaked. Everything sorted with the CCTV guy?"

"Michael. He said to just leave him to it."

"All right, cool. See you inside, bro." Jaydon walked back to the Barn, hands in the pockets of his Aston Villa shorts.

Sadie stood up to leave as well, but Alfie stopped her by putting his hands on her hips. "Everything okay?"

"Sure. Taking a break. You?"

"I'm good. We haven't spoken much these last few days. Not since we talked about my past."

She looked over his shoulder, her blonde eyelashes flickering. "I'm just processing everything. It's a lot. Plus, the things people have been saying about our relationship..."

"We'll get through it, babe. Soon as we get some new episodes posted, people will move on. Ezra is working on an update about HenryLongShaft. We just need to put our narrative out there."

"I'm not sure I want to do this any more, Alfie."

The statement hit him like a punch in the guts. "Don't want to do *what?* Us?"

"No, not us, the channel. I don't want to live my life online. I don't want to be leered at and insulted by strangers or have to deal with horrible, perverted men. It's not fun any more."

"You're being rash." He didn't know what else to say, still shocked by what she was saying, but relieved that she didn't want out of their relationship. "This time last month, everything was great. You enjoyed what we did."

She finally looked him in the eye. "I had my doubts then, but I always told myself the channel was a temporary thing that wouldn't last forever. Now feels like the right time to move on."

Alfie took his hands off her hips, realising that she was rigid and unreceptive to his touch. "How is that going to help us, Say? People are calling me a nonce and making threats. The channel is the only way I can fix my reputation."

"Your *online* reputation. Who cares what a bunch of strangers think about you?"

"I care! This could follow me the rest of my life. Don't you want to tell our side of the story?"

"To who? Everyone I care about is right here."

He understood what she was saying – people on the Internet didn't matter and their opinions were nothing but bits of code – yet he couldn't bear the thought of simply running away with his tail between his legs. That would mean Claypole had won. It would mean a wolf had taken everything from him for the second time.

I lost Daisy, and now it feels like I'm losing Sadie.

"Just think about it a while longer, babe," he said. "Please. We don't have to make any big decisions right away, do we?"

"*You* think about it, Alfie. Think about whether this is all worth it." She turned away. "I'm going inside before I get wet."

"Wait. Are you one hundred per cent about this? You really want out?"

She shook her head, rain droplets beading on her hair. "No. I'm only ninety per cent, but isn't that enough for you to take me seriously?"

He nodded.

She left him there, the rain falling heavier and heavier on his face.

Could he really walk away from the channel? Three years of work?

He wasn't sure who he would be without *Invite the Wolf*, didn't even know what his future looked like. Things had made so much sense, but now it was all a great big mess.

It's all Claypole's fault.

Everything will go back to normal once I deal with him. Sadie will come around. She will.

SEVEN

The rain had mostly stopped and the smell of damp soil filled the air.

Sadie left the house shortly after Alfie came in. She wanted some time to herself, but she also wanted to leave him to think. To think about what she had said. Fortunately, he hadn't followed her outside.

What has happened to us? I feel so stressed when he's around lately.

Just relax. Don't overthink things.

Sadie's favourite place on the property was out by the stream, so that was where she went now. A rocky incline on the far side made it feel hidden, and the thick trees thirty metres away obscured the roads and wilderness beyond. Today, however, the spot felt even more isolated and quiet, like the trees were creeping closer and the grey sky getting lower. The light drizzle still threatened to become a downpour, but right now, getting wet seemed better than being trapped inside the house.

Claypole had invaded their sanctuary, making home feel like a prison.

How did everything change so suddenly?

"You spoke to Alfie about how you're feeling?" Jaydon asked her. He was standing close, his athletic arms folded and his weight mostly on one leg.

She nodded. "I told him we should think about shutting down the channel, that we should at least think about it. You agree, right?"

He rubbed at his mouth and then the back of his neck. His shaven head was growing out, his thick black curls emerging. "I agree something needs to change. We got swept up in this thing of ours – the money, the fame – but it hasn't all been bad, Say."

"I know that. But I don't like what it's doing to Alfie. He's getting more and more obsessed. This Claypole thing has only sped things up; the problems were there before. It's like he doesn't even see me any more. It reminds me of my dad."

"Your dad? Shit, Say."

She rubbed at her arms, damp with drizzle. It sent up a spray of mist as her arm hairs rebounded. "My dad never made me feel like I mattered, that I was a human being with feelings. I was just a thing that was there in his house. That's how Alfie is starting to make me feel. And now that I've learned about his past, about the violence..."

"Hey, hey, that ain't worth thinking about. Alfie isn't that guy. He would never hurt you like your dad did. He might be a lot of things, but he's not a monster."

Sadie sighed, wishing her head wasn't such a mess. She knew she was getting carried away, seeing demons beneath her bed instead of harmless shadows, but she couldn't help who she was. Anxiety was a part of her, wedged into her chest by the years spent with her unpredictable father. Even now, as she stared off towards the nearby treeline, she couldn't shake the feeling that they were watched. Stalked.

Jaydon reached out and took her hand. "We need to get

Alfie to back off with the Claypole thing. Ez can't find a thing on the guy, and every time we prod him, he hits back twice as hard. Gotta just accept the loss on this one."

Still holding his hand, she turned towards the stream. "Not sure Alfie can do that. He has to win, especially when it comes to catching wolves."

He squeezed her hand, his palm a little clammy and cold against hers. "We both know why that is, Say. This shit is personal to him."

She put a hand against his stubbly cheek. "To you too, Jay, but you don't let it consume you like Alfie does. Why are you able to keep your feet on the ground but he can't?"

"Because of his sister, Say. The bad stuff that happened to me happened to *me*. It's something I came to terms with, and I can even forget about it altogether sometimes, but Alfie lost someone he loved. He failed his sister, and there's no way he can ever get closure on that. He doesn't target wolves for revenge; it's about saving Daisy."

She put both hands against his chest and allowed him to take her weight. "There's this hole inside him, Jay. I don't think he'll ever be at peace. No matter how much we build together, he'll always be restless. It's exhausting. Jay, I feel like I'm cracking up."

"I got you. I'll hold you together." He put a hand on the back of her neck and pulled her in. Their lips met and they were kissing.

This is wrong.

But it keeps on happening. And it feels right.

Sadie broke away, but not soon enough – not before enjoying it. "We can't keep doing this. It's cruel."

Jaydon's head dropped and he stared at the ground. "I know, but we didn't choose it, did we? It just is what it is. You and me... We make sen—"

"I love Alfie, Jay. I can't hurt him."

But I already am by doing this. I'm a terrible person.

Jaydon looked her in the eye. "You love me too, Say. And the way you love me makes you happy. Admit it. Admit that Alfie makes you sad." He placed his hand flat against her chest. She shuddered against his touch. "Admit you've already moved on in here."

"You were just defending him, and now you want me to leave him?"

"I love Alfie like a brother, but that doesn't change how I feel about you. Every time I look at you..." He reached out to grab her again.

She moved away from him. "I can't do this right now, Jay. There's too much to figure out without making it even more complicated."

"Say..." Jay reached out to take her hand, but she moved away a second time.

"Please don't put pressure on me. I have no idea what I want, so just let me figure it out."

He put his hands on his hip and blew air out of his cheeks. "All right. I'll back off."

She was relieved to hear it, but like with Alfie, she wasn't sure Jaydon could stick to his word. While he was more stable than Alfie, he was emotional and could act without thinking. It left her worried, in the same way she had been worried as a child whenever her father had held a can of beer in his hand. Just like then, she couldn't shake the feeling that things could turn bad at any moment.

Claypole was still out there.

And Alfie would never let that rest.

And right or wrong, this thing with Jay isn't going to go away. It's like a zit waiting to be popped, throbbing in the background.

Jaydon called out to Sadie as she walked away. She ignored him, not wanting to continue the discussion.

"Sadie, stop!"

She spun around to face him. "What? What is it, Jay? I need to go back to the house. If Alfie catches us out he—"

He was facing away from her and pointing.

She followed the tip of his finger. "Is that...?"

Jay nodded. "Someone's coming out of the trees. Were they watching us?"

"Who is it? Where the hell did they come from?"

The man exited the trees, shambling towards them.

"Oh snap!" Jaydon said.

"On no," Sadie echoed, realising that the she knew the man hurrying towards them. In fact, she recognised him right away.

———

Alfie and Ezra were out in the far field chipping a football back and forth. The security guys – Michael and the young lad who had turned up an hour or so ago – were drilling and banging away, which made it necessary to escape the house and the noise. The din continued in the distance but was no longer loud enough to cause a headache. The drizzle was coming to an end, despite that dark grey sky that threatened worse.

"That guy is the real-life Dracula, dude," Ezra said as he hoofed the ball wide of Alfie and forced him to chase it. "Tommy Wiseau is a certified vampire. That's why they used a green screen for the rooftop scenes. Real sunlight would have killed him."

"Nah." Alfie hoofed the ball back, putting a little spin on it. "He only made the film so he could do a bunch of sex scenes with the blonde. Guy has no rizz, so he needed to pay to get a girl in bed."

Ezra trapped the ball as it landed and did an absolutely

superfluous three-sixty with it, almost falling down. "Hahaha! What a story, Alfie. Anyway, how's your sex life?"

They shared a chuckle and continued playing for a while until Alfie brought something up that had been on his mind for a while – and was now right at the forefront. "You know, Ez, the double episode with Claypole and HenryLongShaft wasn't just about raising the channel's profile. It was supposed to be a landmark for us all. I wanted it to be special. Something to celebrate."

Ezra put his foot on the ball and frowned. "Special? What do you mean?"

"Sadie reckons we should end the channel. What do you think?"

"Dunno. It's hard work, but I enjoy it. At the same time, I can appreciate how rough things must be on you and Sadie. She has to deal with some real dark stuff, and you put yourself in danger every time we confront a wolf. Jay too. Guess I've got the easy part, so I shouldn't get a vote. I just like us all working together."

Alfie gave that some consideration, crossing his arms and stepping back and forth. "I was planning to ask Sadie to marry me."

And now the ring is burning a hole in my pocket instead,

"Shit, dude. That's... awesome. Happy for you."

Alfie nodded, glad that Ezra didn't react negatively to the notion. "After the last episode, I thought we would all be on top of the world. Capping it off with a proposal would have been perfect."

Ez rolled his foot off the ball and let it roll away. "I'm sorry it didn't go that way. You really want to get married? You've thought about it?"

"I have. I want to spend my life with her, man. Until recently, I was certain she felt the same way. Now, I'm not so sure. My past has upset her, but I think it's more than that."

And I'm worried I'm losing her. Without her... I don't even want to think about it. I've never felt this way about anyone else. It would kill me.

"With all that's going on, she's probably just worried. Talk to her. Figure it out."

"I've tried talking to her, but something's changed, Ez. I don't think she's being honest with me."

"Honest about what?"

"I don't know. Something just feels off."

"We're all just stressed out, dude. Leads to paranoia."

"So does weed," Alfie said, smiling, "but that never stopped you."

"I have an elevated brain. I feel none of the negative effects of weed." Ez went and retrieved the ball, then kicked it back over to Alfie. "You and Sadie are forever, dude. Give her a little time to get over things and you'll be sound. Must be difficult, finding out she's been sleeping with a hardened criminal."

Alfie controlled the ball with his left and knocked it to his right side, ready to lob it back. "Not funny, Ez. People change."

"Did you ever shank anyone?"

"Stop! It was a young offender's home, not Shawshank. I spent most my time playing pool and watching TV. It did me good. Gave me a break from the chaos I was living."

"I'm glad you sorted yourself out, dude. You're a decent bloke, Alfie. I wouldn't be here if you weren't."

"I've got good people around me. Makes a big difference."

"So let's see the ring then?"

"Huh?"

"The ring, dude. I assume you have it on you so Sadie doesn't find it."

Alfie reached into his jeans pocket and pulled out the small black box. He walked over to Ezra and flipped it open. "Diamond and morganite. What you think?"

Ezra squinted at the gem and whistled appreciatively. "I like it. Blingy, but not too much. Sadie will love it, dude."

"You reckon."

"Uh-huh."

Alfie put the ring back in his pocket, smiling. He went over to where they had left the ball and knocked it a short distance away before turning and lobbing it into the air. Ezra leapt up to head it but missed. The ball bounced off towards the stream.

Ez raced over to retrieve the ball, but he stopped short, his run faltering until he came to a stop. Frowning, Alfie asked him what was wrong. When he failed to answer, he headed after him. "Ez, what are you..."

Alfie saw what Ezra had seen.

He saw Sadie and Jaydon marching over from the direction of the stream. He also saw the man walking behind them with a shotgun.

"Oh shit!" Alfie stumbled, his heart skipping a beat and his morning breakfast leaping up into his throat. "Oh fucking shit!"

EIGHT

The blood in Alfie's face drained into his feet, making him feel upside down. He could smell the oil on Henry's gun, could tell that it was real. In the distance, the security guys continued making a racket with their power tools, unaware of what was transpiring two hundred metres away.

"Please," Alfie said, his hands in the air. He moved in front of Ezra, trying to give his friend a chance of creeping away unseen. "Don't do anything, okay? We can talk about this. Stay calm."

Henry Stanhope looked different from before, battle-hardened and weary. Back in the market square, he had been a trembling wreck of a man. Now he was wild-eyed and twitchy, almost feral-looking. In his shaky hands, he wielded a short-barrelled shotgun, waving it back and forth as Jaydon and Sadie stood ahead of him with their hands on top of their heads.

Sadie was the colour of chalk. Jaydon's warm brown skin had turned ashen.

"I told him we can figure something out," Jaydon said, his

voice quivering. "We can upload a video saying we made everything up, right? Whatever he wants."

"Yeah," Alfie said, nodding enthusiastically. "Whatever you want, Henry. We can make it right."

"Make it right?" Henry's puggish face contorted. "How can you possibly make it right? You kids have ruined my life. My family is gone. My job is gone. I have nothing. Why? Why did you do this to me?"

"Put the gun down and we can talk about it." Alfie took a step forward, wanting to get closer to Sadie, to somehow pull her away from this danger. "I know you don't want to hurt anyone, Henry."

"You're right, I don't want to hurt anyone." Tears formed in his beady black eyes. "But... but I can't help myself sometimes."

Alfie tried to remain impassive, not wanting to push Henry into any kind of reaction. "You mean children?"

"I know it's wrong, but I-I just love kids. They're so innocent, and they never do anything bad. Being with them makes me happy, but... but I do things I don't mean to."

"It's all right, man," Jaydon said, his hands wavering as he tried to keep them raised. "We understand."

"No!" Henry speared him in the back with the shotgun, causing him to arch painfully and let out a hiss. "You don't understand. You don't know what it's like. If you did, you wouldn't have ruined my life. I just needed some help, that's all. I'm unwell. It's an illness. You people, though, you hurt others on purpose. My family is destroyed. My wife, my son..."

Alfie couldn't stop himself. "And how many little kids are now safe because we exposed you, Henry? You think we do what we do for fun? My twin sister was snatched right in front of my eyes by a guy who couldn't help himself just like you. What we do, Henry, is necessary. We do what we do because there's no other fucking choice."

"You have a choice." Henry's lips curled spitefully. "We all have a choice about what we do. For instance, do I blow your brains out right now? Or do I not?"

Alfie held his breath.

Why can't I back down even a little? Is being right worth getting shot in the face?

Sadie was trembling, her eyes pleading as she looked at Alfie. "Babe? Please?"

She needs me to keep my cool.

Alfie recomposed himself and started again. "Look, I'm sorry Henry. You've got us all scared. It's a tense situation. So why don't you put the gun down and we'll listen to everything you have to say, okay? We want to help you."

Henry lowered the shotgun a little and glanced aside, scanning the distant Barn and its surrounding acres. "All of this in return for ruining the lives of others. It's not fair. You don't deserve it. You don't deserve to get rich by causing misery."

"Maybe you're right." Alfie took another step forward, both hands out in supplication. "But if you think we have it easy, you're wrong. Things have been falling apart. We've realised it's time to take a look at how we've been doing things. You could help us with that, Henry. You can tell us our mistakes and show us how to put them right."

Henry refocused on Alfie. The tears in his eyes had dried up and he seemed less feral. Whatever madness had led him here had abandoned him, and now there was nothing left except a man with nothing to lose.

Am I getting through to him?

Is he buying it?

Does he believe, for one second, that we would ever work with a degenerate like him? He's going straight to jail after this. Where he belongs.

Alfie took another step forward, the thrum of distant power tools vibrating in his skull. Did Michael and the kid helping him not have any idea what was going on? Had they not seen Jaydon and Sadie being frogmarched across the field at gunpoint?

"Come on, Henry. Let's figure this out together."

Ezra stepped up beside Alfie, his whole body shaking. "Y-yeah, dude. Let's be civilised and work this out."

"Does that sound good, Henry? Better than this, right?"

A creepy smile crept onto Henry's face. He lifted the shotgun towards Alfie. "You're full of shit, Alfie Everett. You're a monster just like me. At least *I'm* able to realise it."

Alfie realised then that Henry had come here intending to pull the trigger. This was his ending. He saw no other way forward.

The only thing he has left is vengeance.
There's no going back for him now.

Alfie felt his past self overlap with his present, experiencing the old familiar rage and bitterness that had taken hold of him after losing his mother, his father, and his sister. The emptiness of their loss had been a sucking vacuum inside him, demanding to be filled by chaos and destruction. He knew how Henry Stanhope felt.

Henry wasn't here to make threats.

Knowing he had mere seconds before his world disintegrated in a blast of shotgun fire, Alfie leapt for Sadie. He got a split-second head start on Henry, enough to duck his head and charge into Sadie, barging into her hard enough that she went staggering a dozen feet.

With Sadie out of harm's way, Alfie turned around to Henry. Then, both arms outstretched, he lunged at the smaller man.

You're going the fuck down, buddy.

The butt of the shotgun hammered against Alfie's sternum, instantly dropping him to his knees, his chest imploding like someone had popped both lungs with a pin. He wheezed and gasped like a fish on a beach.

"Oh hell," Ezra shouted, standing ineffectually with his hands over his face. "Oh hell. This is bad. This is so bad. Please stop."

"I'll kill you all," Henry yelled.

"Get back." Jaydon lowered his arms and rushed at Sadie, shoving her away and shielding her with his body. She screamed out for Alfie, and begged Henry not to shoot.

Henry pointed the shotgun squarely at Alfie's chest. Struggling to breathe, Alfie put his hands out in front of his face. "H-Henry... please."

I don't want to die.

I want to ask Sadie to marry me and be happy. This isn't right. The bad guy isn't supposed to win.

Henry placed the shotgun's barrel right up against Alfie's heart, looking him in the eye with utter and complete hatred. "You'll get what you deserve. In the end, you will. Then maybe you'll understand."

Henry Stanhope turned the shotgun on himself and blew his brains out.

Alfie fell backwards onto the grass, his ears ringing like saucepans on metal bars. His silent screams turned inwards, blocking his throat. His face was wet with another man's blood, and the smokey tang of destruction wafted up his nose.

W-what the hell? What the hell did you do that for, Henry?

Sadie began to howl. Jaydon wrapped his arms around her and tried to calm her down. But she would not be calmed.

―――――

Officers Kilmani and Colman returned to the Barn while a forensics team dealt with Henry Stanhope's corpse out in the field. The man's puggish face was an open wound the size of a dinner plate. His nose and mouth were gone, along with any tendrils of his sorry existence.

Alfie couldn't keep his hands still; they danced atop his bopping knees as bile burnt the back of his throat. Several times, he had doubled over, certain he was going to be sick, but each time he managed to breathe through it.

His head exploded right in front of me. His blood got in my eyes.

Sitting, once again, on a kitchen stool, Officer Colman rubbed his hands together in his lap. His long face was red, and his stubbly upper lip twitched periodically. Some time passed before he spoke. "I understand what you kids are trying to do here – I might even say I admire it – but a man is dead because of your actions. Put aside whatever Henry Stanhope may or may not have been guilty of, he has a family who will now have to mourn him."

Alfie considered arguing, but what would be the point? Colman was correct in what he was saying – Henry Stanhope was dead because of *Invite the Wolf* – but at the same time, that wasn't really their fault.

It's a win, at the end of the day, another wolf dealt with. Now Henry Stanhope will never get to hurt a kid ever again.

It was his own guilt that led him to do what he did. He got what he deserved.

"You all need to stop this," Colman said as he looked around the kitchen at their glum, shell-shocked faces. Sadie had her eyes closed, as if she couldn't bear to look at the world any more. "This has gone too far now, and you need to think about the dangers. You're young, all of you, and this isn't how you should be spending your time."

Jaydon nodded, leaning over the counter and staring at the worktop's patterned surface. "We hear you, man. None of us wanted anyone to get hurt. This isn't us."

"And yet a man is dead." Colman adjusted his shirt cuff

where it had folded beneath his cheap digital watch. "Right out there on your property."

"I tried to stop him," Alfie said. "I told Henry to put down the gun and talk, but he wouldn't listen."

Kilmani was standing to one side, making notes on a pad, but she came over now, licking her lips before speaking. "Henry had likely made his mind up about what he was going to do before he ever got here. Consider yourselves lucky he directed the violence only at himself."

Jaydon nodded.

Alfie considered it too, feeling sick at the notion that Henry could have chosen to murder Sadie right in front of him. In fact, he didn't understand what had stopped the man from shooting them. If he was set on killing himself, then why not take his enemies with him?

"So what happens now?" Alfie asked.

Officer Kilmani placed an elbow on the counter, leaning instead of sitting. "We've taken your preliminary statements and now there'll be an investigation. We're also going to have to confiscate any footage you took regarding Henry Stanhope. It's all evidence now."

"Everything's online," Jaydon said. "On the channel."

"We need the original footage," Colman said. "The unedited film, along with transcripts of any conversations you had directly with Mr Stanhope."

Ezra was in the lounge, sitting on the sofa, but he was listening closely. "I can get everything for you," he said. "No problem, officers."

Sadie opened her eyes but immediately placed her face in her hands. "This is really bad, isn't it? Are we in trouble?"

Kilmani smiled at her, not unkindly. "I think that should be clear by now, Miss Chase. Whether you're guilty of a crime, however, is yet to be determined. You also need to consider

Henry Stanhope's family. They might pursue civil action against you all."

"We've done nothing wrong," Alfie said, slapping a palm against the counter. "Henry Stanhope came onto *our* property and killed a goddamn pig. He filmed us while we slept. And then, to finally end things, he shot *himself* in the face. Why is any of that our fault? Because we exposed him for what he was? He was planning to meet up with a child, for God's sake."

Colman cleared his throat. "Like I said, whatever he may or may not have been guilty of, this has gone too far. My suggestion is that you retire this channel of yours and consider making money some other way."

"It's not about making money," Alfie hissed. "And what if we *don't* stop? Are we breaking any laws?"

Sadie groaned. "Alfie. Seriously, give it a rest. Officer Colman is right; this has got out of hand. A man committed suicide on our property."

Alfie turned on his stool, brooding.

Kilmani's lapel radio beeped and a snippet of garbled speech came through. Somehow, she seemed to understand what was being said and responded with: "Ten-Four." Then she looked at Alfie. "They're done with the body. The coroner is coming to take it away, but forensics might be here a while longer, so please keep the area clear for them."

Alfie sighed. "So, is that it for now? Or do you need anything else?"

"We're done." Kilmani tilted her head. "Unless you need anything from *us*?"

"Like what?"

"Well, we can arrange for someone to come and talk with you about what happened. You've all been through a nasty ordeal. It may be an emotionally difficult time for you over the next few days."

"We're fine," Alfie said.

"No. We're *not* fine," Sadie argued. "I would like to talk to someone, please, officer."

"Of course."

Ezra tittered. "I need to talk to someone, too – my weed guy. This is too much to deal with."

A silence fell upon the room.

Colman put a hand against his forehead and rubbed as if he was having a migraine. "I'm going to pretend I didn't hear that."

Ezra pulled a face. "Yeah, um, it was just a joke. I'm more of a chamomile tea kind of dude, I swear."

"Uh-huh. Very well."

Kilmani reached into her jacket and pulled out a business card. She handed it to Sadie and looked at her earnestly. "If you need anything, you can call me directly on this number, okay?"

Sadie took the card and thanked her.

"And I'll have someone contact you in the next few days from victim support, okay?"

"Okay, thank you."

Alfie rolled his eyes. The last thing he wanted to do was talk to some do-gooder working for the police. After Daisy had been taken, social services had spoken with him once a week for over a year. Nothing they said helped him – not even a little bit. For the most part, they left him confused and distracted, constantly probing him about his parents and asking if they had ever hurt Daisy.

Colman and Kilmani headed for the door, their hats tucked beneath their arms. Before leaving, Kilmani turned back and gave Sadie a tight smile. "A hot bath and a good book always helps me get over a bad day. Take care of yourself."

"We'll be okay," Jaydon said, and he gave Sadie a brief hug around the shoulders. "It's just been a bit of a shock."

Colman nodded. "Of course. We'll be in touch."

The officers left. Alfie checked his watch and was astonished to see it was almost five o'clock in the evening. He hadn't eaten all day, and an emptiness suddenly filled him. It wasn't hunger, though.

Henry used Claypole's name so we wouldn't know it was him all along stalking us. Smart.

So smart he killed himself.

Guy still managed to cause some damage on his way out, though. Gonna take a while to fix my reputation after the things he put online. Asshole.

"Will someone take me to my dad's?" Sadie asked. "I'm not staying here."

"What?" Alfie blinked at her. "What are you talking about?"

"I can't be around this place after what happened."

"You mean your home? It's over. Henry Stanhope is dead."

"Exactly. His blood is still out there staining the grass."

"I'll drive you," Jaydon said. "Just give me an hour. My nerves are too fried to drive right this second."

"Okay, that's fine. I'll put the kettle on. I'm sure we could all use a cup of tea."

Alfie chuckled, trying to right his mind by being positive. "And that's just a start. I can't believe what happened today. I thought... I thought Henry was going to shoot you both."

"You pushed Sadie out of the way," Ezra said. "If Henry had pulled the trigger, you would've been toast."

Sadie was moving towards the kettle on the back counter, but she stopped and went over to Alfie instead, wrapping her arms around him and placing her cheek against his chest. "Ez is right. You put yourself in harm's way. If I'd lost you..."

He kissed the top of her head. "I'm not going anywhere."

She turned her head towards Jaydon who was still

standing on the far side of the kitchen counter, almost seeming to glare at them. "Are you okay, Jay? He hit you in the back really hard."

Jaydon reached behind himself and rubbed his spine where Henry had speared him with the shotgun. "Bruised the shit out of me, but I'll live. My brain got the worst of it. I keep seeing Henry's face when he…" Shuddering, he closed his eyes. "It's stuck on pause in my head."

"I don't think I'll ever get it out of my mind either," Sadie said, going over and switching on the kettle. She shook her head. "How do you even start to forget?"

"There are ways," Ezra said, reaching into his hip pocket and pulling out his weed tin. "Anyone care to join me?"

"Not if I've got to drive later," Jaydon said.

"I'll have a drag," Alfie said, not usually one for smoking, but he needed something to take the edge off. "I'm just going to get some air first. Anyone want to join me?"

Sadie shook her head. "I don't want to risk seeing them move the body. I'll stay here and make that tea. Maybe it will stop me from shaking."

"Okay. Love you."

She nodded wearily.

He went out front, taking a deep lungful of air that seemed to fill his entire body. Had he really come close to losing one of his friends today? Even his own life?

Is this the part where the flowers smell better and the trees look greener?

So why don't I feel anything?

Two police vans sat in the far field where Henry Stanhope had killed himself. Alfie couldn't see what the forensic officers were doing, but the tent they had erected earlier was now gone. Hopefully they were wrapping up and would leave soon.

If I upload a video about this, the views will be sky high.

But then where will it end? How do you top an episode about someone killing themselves on your property?

Alfie's mind turned to other things, such as how Henry Stanhope had managed to take both Jaydon and Sadie hostage at the same time. Where had they been when he had arrived with his shotgun?

"Excuse me, sir? Mr Everett, is it?"

Alfie flinched. The last thing he needed right now was someone sneaking up on him, but a stranger approached from the direction of the garages – a slender, middle-aged man, wearing a Weber-Cooks Security uniform that clung tightly to his wiry biceps. His bald head had a triangular dent in it like an axe had once bounced off his skull.

Alfie relaxed. "I thought the police asked you guys to leave. Is Michael still here?"

"No, sir. He got most of the cameras installed, but there're a few things left to finish up. I was in the area on another job, so he asked me to pop by and double-check everything is safe to be left overnight. He was working on the main fuse board, right?"

"I dunno, mate. It's been a hell of a fucking day."

"Someone died, I heard. I'm sorry for your loss."

"It wasn't like that, but thanks."

The man clapped his hands together, the seams at his biceps threatening to burst. His arms weren't particularly big, but the top was very tight. "Well, my name's Brent, and I'll be out of your hair in just a few minutes, if that's okay, boss?"

"Sure thing."

He headed back off towards the garages, but Alfie turned and called after him. "Hey, can I ask you something?"

"Of course."

Alfie looked up at the Barn's roof. He saw several CCTV cameras, but one in particular caught his attention. It was right at the end of the garages, looking down at the driveway.

"That camera there?" He pointed. "Could you redirect it? I want it pointing off towards the stream."

That's where Henry, Jay, and Sadie came from. If there's an entry to the property via the treeline, then maybe it should be monitored.

"You mean you want it pointing away from the driveway?"

Alfie pointed at the next nearest camera. "That one covers the approach to the house as well, doesn't it? No point having two pointed in more or less the same direction." He motioned towards the stream. "There's a dip on the other side of that stream where my girlfriend likes to sit and meditate. I want to make sure it's safe, so can we raise the camera up higher and point it over there?"

"I guess so." The man cupped a hand over his eyes and stared off towards the stream. "Yeah, that shouldn't be a problem. I'll get right on it for you."

"Thanks. What did you say your name was again?"

"Brent." He offered a hand and Alfie shook it. "This is a lovely little slice of heaven you have here. What is it you do, exactly?"

Alfie gave a weak smile. "I used to run a video channel online."

NINE

Jaydon had grown too tired last night, so Sadie had been convinced to stay at the house and reassess in the morning.

Things had felt a little different with a new dawn.

The fields outside showed no sign that there had ever been a police investigation or a body, and the dark sky and pervasive drizzle had been replaced by a clear, sunny morning. That didn't mean things were okay, but the atmosphere had become less oppressive. It felt like the bad things were all behind them now.

Sadie had still wanted out of the house, though, and she wouldn't take no for an answer, so Alfie had agreed to take her out for lunch in the Alfa, hitting the highway and doing an easy eighty until they arrived in posh Solihull. Now they were sitting in a lovely little place called the Crystal Lotus, waited on by a funky young waitress named Lily with a pink streak in her blonde hair and a piercing in her lip.

"One lamb shawarma and one chicken arrabbiata," she said, a plate in each hand.

"Shawarma right here," Alfie said, mouth watering at the

peppery smell of spiced lamb wafting over. The waitress set the plate down in front of him. She eyeballed him suspiciously.

"I know you," she said. "*Invite the Wolf*, right?"

Sadie groaned.

Alfie managed a smile. "Are you a fan?"

"My dad left last year, and me and my mum didn't really know what to do with ourselves. We ended up binge-watching your channel from start to finish every evening. Can't believe the sickos you have to deal with. The world is a scary place, full of vampires looking to feed."

Alfie frowned, finding the expression a tad dramatic – but not necessarily incorrect. "It's a tough gig, that's for sure."

The waitress smiled at him, and then at Sadie. "Least there's good guys like you, huh? Anyway, enjoy your meals."

They both said thank you and then ate without speaking. Conversation during the car ride had been sparse, but it was non-existent now. Sadie stared off into the distance, seeming to study the flowery wallpaper as she chewed her tomatoey pasta tubes. Alfie wanted to break the silence, but he struggled to know exactly what to say. He knew she wouldn't want to discuss what had happened with Henry Stanhope, nor would she want to discuss the future of *Invite the Wolf*, which left very little else to talk about.

I could ask her to marry me right now. I have the ring in my jacket pocket. But what if she says no?

He decided not to risk it, at least not until things were a little closer to normal. "Are you feeling better today, about what happened?"

"I guess. It all feels a bit blurry now, like it was a bad dream. I can't believe I had a shotgun pointed at me."

"You *and* Jaydon."

She sat back slightly and looked at him. "Huh?"

Alfie shrugged. "Henry Stanhope had both of you at gunpoint. Were you together when he showed up?"

She looked down at her food, prodding at a soft pasta tube with her fork. "We were hanging out by the stream. The security guys were making so much noise back at the house."

"Yeah, me and Ez were outside for the same reason."

It makes complete sense. What am I even getting at?

"Alfie?" Sadie looked up at him, her right hand still occupied with rolling pasta around her plate.

He was strangely relieved to hear her speak his name. "Yeah? What's wrong?"

"I need to tell you something."

The waitress, Lily, came rushing over, bashing her hip on a vacant table and making the cutlery jump. "Um, do you guys own a fancy green car?"

Alfie nodded. "An Alfa Romeo?"

"A green car?"

"Yeah, it's green. What's the matter? Have I blocked someone in?"

She shook her head, a pained expression on her pretty young face. "Someone's just vandalised it. Our chef was on a fag break and saw a weirdo legging it."

Alfie slammed a fist on the table and leapt up out of his seat. "You've got to be kidding me? I swear, I can't deal with much more."

The waitress winced as if she felt his pain. "Sorry, dude."

He moved past her and hurried through the restaurant. Outside, in the car park, he found his car exactly as the waitress had described. Graffiti covered the bodywork on all sides, words scrawled in black paint across both driver's side doors. Names. Names that meant nothing to him.

CoNNeR. Ivy. MiLLie. AMiRa.

Is it the names of the people who did this? A gang of graffiti shitheads targeting sports cars?

Sadie gasped beside him. "Why would someone do this?"

Alfie stumbled forward, trying to understand why the universe hated him so much. After everything that had happened with Henry Stanhope, it was beyond unfair that someone had now randomly defaced his car.

But then he saw what was scrawled across his bonnet and realised it wasn't random at all. His blood turned cold as he studied the black-painted words.

The WoLf is HUNgRy.

Alfie put his hands on his thighs to keep himself from falling. *It's not over*, he told himself. *It's not finished.*

Sadie put a hand on his back, but it wasn't enough to keep him from shuddering.

———

A short while after leaving the restaurant, Alfie stormed back into the Barn, leaving Sadie behind on the driveway to catch up with him. He didn't know if his name had been blacklisted, but the police didn't even bother to turn up and take his report about the vandalism to his car. They gave him a crime number over the phone and promised to pass on the information to Officers Colman and Kilmani, but he lacked confidence that it would happen. For once, he actually wanted the police around. Enough was enough. They needed to do something about Claypole.

The maniac needs locking up. He's stalking me.

Ezra and Jaydon were inside playing football on the PlayStation. He needed their full attention, so he marched over and switched off the console and TV at the wall.

"Yo!" Jaydon kicked his legs out and used the momentum to sit himself up. "We were in the middle of a game, bro!"

"Games over. This crazy bastard isn't gonna stop unless we make him."

Ezra straightened up, his fuzzy red eyebrows making a downward V. "Whoa? What are you talking about, dude?"

Alfie told them about his car and the graffiti, and about the strange names and obvious threat scrawled across his bonnet. "He's coming for us. It isn't over."

Ezra grimaced. "Shit, dude, that's heavy. So what happened with Henry had nothing to do with the other stuff that's been happening? It really was all Claypole?"

"For all we know, Claypole and Henry were working together, but it results in the same thing – the guy is still messing with us." Alfie turned a circle, wanting to find something to kick, but when he saw Sadie standing anxiously by the door, it caused him to take a calming breath. His speed on the highway had frightened her, and her attempts to get him to calm down had failed.

"We don't know if he'll try anything else," Ezra said. "Maybe your car was a parting shot."

Alfie sneered. "Claypole slashed my face with a knife, cut open a pig, accused me of being a paedophile, and now this. He ain't gonna stop, man."

"We should bolt for a while," Jaydon said, placing his wireless game controller down by his feet. "Lie low some place and let shit blow over."

"That won't work, Jay." Alfie marched over to the window and stared out at the fields, wondering if Claypole was out there again after fleeing the restaurant. "Something dawned on me driving back home," he said. "That day in the old market square, Claypole was coming to meet up with a child, right? Tina."

"Lucy," Sadie said, still standing by the door. "The bait was named Lucy."

"Whatever the name, he was meeting up with a child, wasn't he? So why the hell did he bring a goddamn machete with him?"

Nobody said anything for a moment, but Ezra turned pale. "Shit, dude, you're right. Why the hell would he be carrying that? Do you... do you reckon he was planning to do something? I mean, besides the usual?"

"We had no idea who we were messing with when we went after Claypole. We lured an *actual* wolf this time, with big fucking teeth."

"A goddamn alpha," Jaydon said. "He's not scared of us at all. I don't think he even cares about being exposed or arrested... or anything at all."

"All the more reason we should get out of here," Sadie said, her fingers going to her mouth. "Let the police find Claypole. We never should have tried to do their jobs in the first place. It was only a matter of time before something like this happened."

Alfie moved over to her, wishing she would close the door and come inside. Was she worried to be near him?

That's ridiculous. She has no reason to fear me.

"Look," he said. "I agree that we've been naïve. Success made us cocky, and we took too many risks, but what's done is done. Claypole is still after us, and the only way to stop him is by doing what we do best."

"Which is what?" Ezra asked, leaning forward across the arm of his chair.

"We trap wolves and defang them. We need to find out who Claypole really is. If we don't, then who knows where this ends?"

Sadie finally stepped away from the door. "Alfie, for God's sake. Will you listen to yourself? This isn't a game. Claypole is dangerous."

Jaydon folded his arms and pulled a face. "I hate to sound like a pussy, Alf, but Say is right. As much as I would love to give this guy what he deserves, I honestly just wish we could go back and never have met him."

"Amen," Ezra said. "We should try to make peace with him, not prod him even more."

"Make peace with a child predator?" Alfie blinked. "Are you for real?"

Ezra looked away sheepishly. "If it means we can go back to normal, then yeah. Like you said, this guy slashed your face and slaughtered a pig. What else is he capable of? The guy is unhinged."

"Which is why we need to protect ourselves."

Sadie glared at Alfie. "What will it take for you to back down, Alfie? Is it ego, or are you just pig-headed?"

"Babe, come on."

"Don't 'come on' me, Alfie. You're obsessed, and I don't know if I can..."

"Don't know if you can what?"

She paused, her lips moving but no words coming out for a moment. Her hands went to her face and she rubbed her cheeks. "Jesus, I don't know. I guess I would need to think about things. About us."

Ezra groaned. "Guys, let's not fall out. We're on the same side.

"I'm not sure we are," Alfie said, shaking his head. "I didn't ask for any of this, Sadie, so making threats isn't fair. And as far as being obsessed, do you expect me to just ignore everything that's happened? You forget that I know better than any of you the consequences of doing nothing and hoping for the best. People get hurt. People get snatched away right in front of you and you never see them again."

"This ain't about Daisy, bro,' Jaydon said.

"You're right," Sadie said, blinking slowly. "You didn't ask for any of what's happened, Alfie. That's true. But what happens *next* is up to you. The consequences from this point forward will be because of what you choose to do right now."

Alfie couldn't believe what he was hearing. She was

turning this around on *him*? Claypole was a sadistic maniac who had tried to ruin their lives. Was he supposed to just let that go?

None of them have my back. I can't believe I thought Sadie would want to marry me when I can't even count on her to take my side.

"So what is everyone saying?" he asked. "I get on my knees and beg Claypole for peace, or you'll all abandon me?"

"No one is saying that, bro," Jaydon said.

"We just don't want to carry this on," Ezra said. "You're in a bad place because of all this and we're worried about you, dude."

"Why is this all about me? Am I alone? It fucking feels like it. My car, my face... Maybe it's easy for you guys to forget everything because it hasn't happened to *you*."

"You got it all wrong, bro. What happens to you happens to us all. That's why we want to see a peaceful end to this."

Ezra was nodding in agreement. "Maybe trying to make a truce is the right way to go, Alfie. Claypole might back off if we put an apology out on the channel."

"And what if he doesn't back off? What if this guy keeps on stalking us and messing with our lives? Will you keep on blaming me then?"

"No one is blaming you now," Sadie said in a huff. "We just want you to be safe, don't you see that? The best thing to do is give up and move on with our lives."

"And let Claypole get away with it?"

The silence in the room gave all the answer he needed.

Letting out a sigh, he slowly nodded. "Okay, fine."

Obviously, I have no choice here. I either do what's right, or I lose my friends?

Some fucking friends.

Alfie took out his phone and released a seething breath.

Sadie's eyes narrowed. "Alfie, what are you doing?"

"Giving you all what you want. I can't argue with three against one, can I?"

"We're not ganging up on you."

"Sure." He opened up the live-streaming app on his phone. His thumb hovered over the *record* button.

Fuck it. Just get it over with.

He hit *record* and proceeded to post a short video directly to the channel, asking Claypole83 for one thing and one thing only: a truce. A plea to agree that what was done was done, and that they should leave each other alone before things got truly out of hand. It made Alfie feel sick.

This is wrong. We're letting evil win.

Once the video was uploaded, Alfie put his phone back in his pocket and sighed. "Thanks for having my back, guys. Really appreciate it."

Jaydon flapped his arms. "Bro, seriously?"

"We love you, dude," Ezra said.

"Really?"

Sadie tutted and stormed off into the bedroom. She slammed the door and didn't come back out again. At least, not until an hour later when Ezra started yelling for everyone to come quickly into the kitchen. "We got a response," he said. "From Claypole."

———

Claypole had replied to Alfie's message within thirty minutes. He didn't do so publicly; he sent a private message.

"He wants to meet," Ezra said, reading from his laptop, which he had placed on the kitchen counter for all of them to see. "He says if we want a truce, Alfie has to meet with him face to face and do an interview."

Alfie's blood went cold. "Why would he agree to an interview? To help our channel? Or help himself in some way?"

"It's a trap," Sadie said, reaching out to grab Alfie's wrist. "You can't meet with him. It would be insane."

The knot in his stomach agreed with her, but...

It might be the only way to put a stop to this.

I want to look the son of a bitch in the eye.

"It's risky," Ezra said. "He might pull a knife on you again."

Alfie read the message on screen over and over again.

Alfie Everett. If you want a truce, we should meet for an official interview. Tanning Stanley Fields. Tonight. Eight PM. Be there, or things will continue to get worse for you. Call the police and you'll regret it. Claypole83.

"Where the hell is Tanning Stanley Fields?" Jaydon asked, his sleeves rolled up and his arms folded.

Alfie knew the answer all too well. "Tanning Stanley is where my sister was taken. The last place I ever saw Daisy."

Sadie put a hand on top of his. Her eyes bulged. "The funfair? He knows about your past?"

Alfie nodded, his breathing coming slowly. "If I don't meet with him, he's not going to stop. What other choice is there? Maybe I really can make peace with him."

Either that or he guts me like that pig.

"Alfie, he's a lunatic."

"Lunatic or not, he's beaten us at every turn." Alfie clutched the edge of the granite worktop and ground his teeth together so tightly that his molars creaked. "Just look at what he's done to us. You all want to abandon the channel – abandon *me*."

Jaydon grunted. "That ain't what this is, bro. We're just

worried, innit? You can't predict crazy. It would be stupid for us to try."

"Call the police," Sadie urged. "Arrange to meet Claypole but send the cops."

Alfie shook his head. It was a comforting idea, that this could be dealt with so easily, but his gut told him not to be so naïve. "Don't you think he has a plan for that? He said we'll regret it if we call the police."

"Because he knows that will be bad for him."

"Maybe. But what if they arrest him and nothing sticks. What ironclad evidence do we have that would see him put away? He could just deny everything."

Ezra pulled at one of his braids and chewed his lip. "We can't trace his messages and we don't have him on camera. The police will release him within the day."

"Still," Sadie said, "no way is Alfie meeting with him. We're not making this worse than it already is by doing something so stupid. We've made enough bad decisions."

"Hey, I'm the one who's taken all the hits," Alfie said, almost growling at her. "Claypole has come after me again and again and again, yet somehow you're acting like I invited it somehow."

"What's the name of the channel, Alfie?" Sadie asked. "Clue is in the title."

"None of us are innocent, Sadie, but we didn't invite this."

Sadie flapped her arms against her sides. "Do you really believe that? Do you not think we deserve to pay for what happened to Henry Stanhope and the others we targeted?"

He shook his head at her. "What is going on with you? We all built the channel, so where is this sudden moral high ground coming from? I'm getting fucking tired of it, to be honest. We all earned money from *Invite the Wolf.* The channel is all of us."

She flinched at his ferocity, but he didn't regret it. She

needed to be straight with him instead of making his muddled mind murkier.

"The channel has always been about *you*, Alfie," she shouted, regaining her confidence. "It's always been about what happened to Daisy and your need for revenge. I... I thought I could help you deal with your loss, but it's only getting worse. We *killed* Henry Stanhope. We've *ruined* people's lives."

"Paedophiles!"

"I'm not talking about them," she shot back. "I'm talking about the families who have to live with the guilt of what we put out on the Internet. The wives and children who had no clue they were living with predators. Because of us, they have to live in shame." She flashed her teeth. "What we do isn't justice, Alfie, it's gross entertainment."

Alfie gawped at her, open-mouthed, for almost a full minute. She stared straight back at him, refusing to look away. Eventually, he turned to face Ezra and Jaydon instead, hoping to find support there. Instead, both of them averted their gaze. Were they unwilling to contradict Sadie? Or did they agree with her?

Traitors. How can you be such cowards? We've been running Invite the Wolf *for three years now, and they bail at the first sign of trouble.*

"This is ridiculous." Alfie stormed over to the small, gloss-white cabinet beside the front door.

"What are you doing?" Ezra called after him. "Dude?"

He yanked open the top drawer and pulled out his car keys.

Sadie's anger ebbed slightly and she took a step towards him. "You're not going to meet with Claypole, are you?"

"What? No. No, I'm just going for a drive. I need to get the fuck out of here before I say something I can't take back."

"Come on, bro, calm down. Don't drive angry."

Alfie glared at Jaydon and then at Sadie. He left without saying another word, but when he was about to jump in his car, he took a moment to reconsider. His heart was racing and his breathing was shallow. As much as he hated to think it, Jaydon was right. It would be a bad idea to drive angry. He put his keys in his pocket and decided to take five before he got behind the wheel. As he did so, he pulled the engagement ring out of his pocket and studied it. The bright gemstones glinted at him almost mockingly, each one like a cheeky wink of an eye. He raised it above his head and prepared to toss it.

He wasn't sure what stopped him, but if it was hope, it was the very last piece of it he had left.

TEN

Alfie decided that instead of driving off, he would hop on one of the quad bikes in the garage and take a spin in the fields. The wind on his face might bring him back down to earth and extinguish the dizzying emotions that clashed inside his head like warring tigers.

He opened up the garage doors and winced at the smell that met him – an astringent, slightly fumey odour which reminded him of fresh paint. It only took a moment to understand where it was coming from. Michael, the security guy, had drilled holes and yanked cabling through several areas of the garage; he had sealed the gaps with wet silicon gel. It clearly hadn't yet fully dried out.

Michael was supposed to come again today, but the guy hadn't turned up. The cameras were up, and a new LCD panel adorned the rear wall of the garage, but Alfie hadn't been shown how to use the system, or even signed any paperwork to accept that the job was done. Henry's suicide and the following police investigation must have prompted Michael to take a day off. Alfie could hardly blame the guy.

But I need those cameras working.

"Jeez, it stinks in here, dude." Alfie turned to see Ezra entering the garage through the open shutter behind him. He wafted a hand in front of his nose and grimaced.

Alfie turned his back. "You been voted to come talk to me, huh? Well save your breath, Ez. I'm not in the mood for any more lectures."

"No one is out to get you, dude. We just don't want you getting hurt again. Sadie wants to call the police, and I agree."

"We've already called them. They can't help. In fact, I don't think they even give a shit. They think we brought this on ourselves. Hell, even Sadie thinks that. It's bullshit."

Ezra strolled across the vacant garage bay, stopping in front of Alfie. "Don't meet up with Claypole, dude. I've seen enough horror movies to know that it won't end well."

"Life isn't a horror movie, Ez. In horror movies, the bad guys lose. In real life, all they do is multiply."

"More reason not to go."

"You think I want to meet with him? Don't you think I know it's insane?" Alfie's anger was fading. He was growing less and less eager to meet with the man who had slashed his face and knifed a pig. But there was something inside him that simply refused to be cowed by a monster who preyed on children.

"He said there'll be consequences, Ez, if I don't meet with him face to face. Maybe he does want an apology."

Ezra tittered. "I don't see you offering one of those."

"Maybe I can, if it means we live to fight another day. Sadie's wrong about *Invite the Wolf*. Sure, we need to make a few changes, but what we do is necessary. Even if it only causes the wolves out there to think twice. We should be growing the channel, not ending it. More money, more staff. The biggest problem is that we're too small and vulnerable. We need to hire security, a legal team, the works."

"Dude, you seriously need to come back down to earth.

It's been a wild ride, but Sadie's right. This has always been about your sister. For the rest of us, it's just a job – and it's time to move on to something else. If you don't recognise that..."

Alfie glared at Ezra in the eye, the sickly smell of fresh silicon irritating the back of his throat and making him nauseous. "I'm tired of being threatened, Ez."

Ezra sighed and took a step back into the space where Alfie's Alfa was usually parked. "Look, you said you wanted to ask Sadie to marry you. Why don't you focus on that? Focus on living a normal life where you can be happy and secure. You gotta let the past go, dude. We're all here for you."

"Doesn't feel like it, *dude*."

"We're not your enemy."

"No, Claypole is my enemy, and the only way I can see a way out of this is to meet with him." He clenched his fists and took a deep breath, looked out of the open garage door towards his vandalised car sitting in the driveway, and then let it out in a forced gust. "But you're right, it's too risky. I won't go."

Ezra exhaled too, his shoulders slumping. "We should do like Jay said and just bunker down some place and hope for things to pass. We have the cameras installed to keep an eye on this place in the meantime."

Alfie turned and walked over to the LCD screen at the back of the space. "If we can figure out how to use them. Michael was meant to come back and finish up."

"The cameras are all up," Ezra said, "so it's probably just the backup drives he needs to come back and install."

"What does that mean?"

"That the cameras are live, but nothing's being recorded."

"So they're useless, then?"

Ezra shrugged. "Not exactly. They might help us to see Claypole coming if he tries anything else. I can probably get the feeds loaded onto our phones. We can take shifts in a hotel or something, each of us checking for Claypole."

"I'm staying here," Alfie said. "I have no place else to go."

"Me either, dude. That's why I said a hotel." He tapped the LCD touchscreen and it came to life, showing six small square boxes – each offering a different view of the old farm: driveway, fields, the hill, the stream.

Only one of the boxes showed movement.

Alfie frowned, at first thinking it was water trickling in the stream.

But it was something else.

"What *is* that?" Alfie tapped the square feed. It expanded to fill the screen, covering the other little boxes behind it. The camera pointed over at the shallow dip beyond the stream.

Ezra made an odd sound in his throat and then attempted to sound nonchalant as he spoke. "Sadie and Jay said they were going for a walk to clear their heads."

Alfie nodded, it being entirely plausible that the two of them might want to do that.

But I didn't see them go, which meant they went out the back door. Why?

In the pit of his stomach, Alfie felt a twinge, like he'd swallowed a bunch of nettles. Sadie and Jay were walking side by side along the stream, chatting back and forth. Were they not worried about him? Did they not care that he had stormed out in an emotional state?

This is from the camera I asked to be raised up high and pointed towards the stream. They don't know I'm watching them. Should I turn it off?

Ezra reached out to close the feed, but Alfie grabbed his hand. "Wait! Don't!"

I need to see this. There's a reason I asked to have the camera adjusted. A gut instinct. It wasn't just about seeing the treeline.

"Dude, we shouldn't spy on them."

"Why not? What's the problem?"

Seeing Jaydon and Sadie alone together wasn't an issue – they were close friends – but they had walked off together instead of checking on Alfie.

We're supposed to have each other's back. We're supposed to be family.

But then Alfie saw who his family really was.

Jaydon grabbed Sadie by the waist and pulled her in. Their faces met and they were kissing. Kissing passionately. Kissing like this wasn't the first time.

Alfie's veins constricted, his nervous system trying to shrivel up and retreat like a snail into its shell. Open-mouthed, he couldn't speak. Couldn't breathe. He fell back, colliding with Jaydon's Range Rover. "Oh, no. Oh God, oh no. No, no, no."

"Jesus Christ, what the hell?" Ezra said, his astonishment clear and genuine. This was as shocking to him as it was to Alfie, and that realisation was the only comfort Alfie could gain from this moment.

At least one of my friends didn't betray me.

Alfie's fists creaked as he clenched them tightly against his retching stomach. Rocket fuel ignited up and down his spine. Fireworks exploded at the edges of his vision.

Silently, he turned around.

Ezra reached out to stop him. "Dude, take a second. Don't blow up."

Alfie shoved his arm away and went over to the garage's workbench – an old chunk of timber, barely used. A few modern tools cluttered its surface. Alfie picked up a hammer and patted it against his hand. The thudding weight against the delicate bones in his palm comforted him.

"Whoa!" Ezra threw up his hands as Alfie moved back in his direction. "I knew nothing about this, Alf, I swear. Dude, I swear!"

"I believe you." Alfie swung the hammer, his jaw tensing with effort.

The passenger-side window of Jaydon's Range Rover imploded. The next blow took off the wing mirror. Alfie completed his assault by whacking a deep divot into the bonnet.

"Alf, calm down, please. You're freaking me out."

He stormed up to Ezra, standing almost nose to nose with him. "Did you just watch the same thing I did? You want me to calm down? Maybe I should go smoke a spliff, huh? Will that make everything better? My best mate and my girlfriend, Ez... I was planning to ask her to marry me."

Ezra swallowed, his Adam's apple bulging. "Ignoring the low key diss to me in that statement, you need to keep your head about you, Alfie. Right now, you're the innocent party, but if you do something crazy... If you hurt one of them..."

Alfie shook his head in disgust. "Who do you think I am, Ez? You think I'm going to go out there and murder them or something? Fuck, you're no different to them. Gaslighting me and trying to make me feel like I'm the bad guy. I made you all rich – dragged you out of your awful goddamn lives and gave you everything you dreamed of. Well, fuck you, Ezra. Fuck you all."

"Come on, dude. We can sort this."

Alfie dropped the hammer on the concrete floor and walked away. "I'm going for a drive. Don't wait up."

He exited the garage and opened up his car on the driveway.

Ezra hurried after him, but didn't dare get too close. "Where are you going? Alfie? Stop!"

Alfie slid in behind the steering wheel. "I have a meeting to get to."

"What? No, dude, don't go. Stay here and we'll talk."

"No, I'm not going to sort things out here. I'm going to

meet with Claypole and put a stop to this one way or another. Then, you, me, and those backstabbing pricks are through." He slammed the door and fastened his seatbelt, put the car in reverse and shot backwards in the gravel, chucking up stones. As he turned around in the driveway, he glared towards the stream, knowing what was happening just out of sight in the ditch beyond.

How could they do this to me?

How could they be so evil?

The answers wouldn't come, but he knew what he needed to do.

I'm going to let my anger out, because I have nothing left to lose and no more fucks left to give.

You're going to be sorry you messed with me, Claypole.

You'll all be sorry.

Alfie put his foot down and sped towards the hill.

———

Alfie hated that the place hadn't changed. It was like stepping back into the past – into the black-and-grey hellscape that had haunted his every night's sleep. Except the black and grey of the past were gone, and the greens and browns of the present were blinding.

Tanning Stanley Fields was a public space about thirty miles out of town, in a leafy borough named Whitebarrow. It was where Alfie had grown up, the same town where his mother had lived and died. The same town where *he* had lived and died – or at least a part of him had.

Claypole knows everything about me. Where does this end for him? What does he want?

Alfie stepped away from his car and clutched his stomach as he realised he was standing in the very same car park where he had last seen Daisy. He stared off towards the far corner, towards the former location of that horrible, dirty white van. Voices echoed inside his head – his sister's confused statement about there being no candyfloss, the stern yells of the concerned teenager. He heard his own sobs, his mother's screams.

I can't do this. I..., I can't.

His phone chimed. He had a text message.

With a shaking hand, he pulled out his phone. The message's content only added to his fear. Claypole had his number. It should've seemed inevitable at this point.

Take a seat with the three little pigs.

Alfie gave the message's meaning some thought. Other than a new set of rugby posts on the field and several tonnes of decorative stones now surrounding the car park, nothing else had changed. His best guess was that Claypole was waiting for him on the benches outside the park's tiny coffee shop which was only a short distance away via a snaking path that cut through a maze of trees and ended in a community garden with sculptures, birdbaths, and six-foot cypress trees.

It's like I was here yesterday.

I hate this place. I don't want to be here.

But if I don't get this over with, I'll never feel safe again. Claypole will invade my dreams right alongside the monster who took Daisy – and I can't let any more devils live inside my head.

Alfie started moving, one foot in front of the other. His heart drummed against his ribs and his mouth had dried up, but he forced himself to continue. The car park was almost empty, but several dog walkers and cyclists dotted the various distant paths that cut around the playing fields. It allowed him to relax a little. Surely Claypole was less likely to try to hurt him with so many members of the public around.

He's just a man. There's no reason to be afraid.

Except that I'm alone and unarmed. I thought I was part of a pack, but really I'm a lone wolf. Always have been.

Alfie felt his torn cheek throb, and the pain was a welcome distraction. He took a deep breath and lengthened his stride, ordering himself to stay strong.

Don't let others hurt you without consequences.

Make them pay.

Alfie hadn't even begun to process what he'd witnessed on the security camera. Trusting people was a mistake – a lesson he'd learned thirteen years ago in this very park. Sadie and Jaydon had tricked him into lowering his defences, but their betrayal reminded him that people always put themselves first. The only person Alfie could rely on was himself.

His phone buzzed again, making him flinch. It could only be Claypole, he assumed, but it turned out to be Ezra.

Dude, I need you to call me ASAP.

Alfie had no intention of calling him, nor did he have any interest in being talked out of what he was doing. Reckless it may be, but at least he was doing something. At least he was trying to put an end to this.

And if something bad happens to me, I hope the guilt eats you up until the day you die, Sadie. You too, Jaydon. I'm here alone because of you both.

Alfie reached the community garden and was shocked by the state of it. As a child it had been a wild, beautiful place, full of vibrant green and flashes of other colours. Now, the concrete bird baths had all cracked and were stained with algae, while weeds and loose pebbles surrounded the aluminium sculptures of a man and woman reaching up to the heavens. Empty beer cans cluttered the parched ground beneath the hedges. The cafe, however, had received a revamp since he'd last seen it, and it now had gleaming full-length windows and Scandinavian-style wooden boards where once there had been drab clay bricks. As before, the small building overlooked a boating pond filled with swans and ducks. To most people, it would have been a pleasant little hang-out spot; for Alfie, it would always be hell.

The cafe was closed. It was eight o'clock in the evening and not long before it started getting dark. Only one person sat at the picnic tables out front: a male in a black leather jacket. When Alfie realised they were wearing a baseball cap, his skin itched.

It can't be him. Not the man who ruined my life thirteen years ago.

But of course it wasn't. It wasn't the same man who had taken Daisy. That tall, craggy-faced man would have been an old man now.

Alfie approached, and he quickly noticed an item lying on the table in front of the stranger. A book. He had to get closer before he could read the title, though.

THREE LITTLE PIGS.

Like Claypole's text message: *Take a seat with the three little pigs.*

Alfie slid his thumbs in his pockets to keep his hands from shaking. He approached the table with a faked, confident stride, taking a seat and staring the other man right in the face. Early thirties. Five o'clock shadow. Short brown sideburns. Distinctly average-looking.

"You're younger than I imagined," Alfie said.

Claypole stared down at the *Three Little Pigs* book, giving no indication he had even heard.

"You picked this place to mess with me. You know what happened to my sister? Predators like to talk to each other, right? Chat rooms on the Dark Web, getting each other off by sharing details about your twisted crimes?" Alfie leant forward, any fear shoved aside by a thirst for raging violence. Maybe he should just beat this man to death, right here and now. "Do you know the man who took my sister thirteen years ago? Tell me, before I stamp it out of you."

Bizarrely, Ezra's voice whispered inside his head. *Easy, Alfie. There might be a better option than violence. Keep your head. Be smart.*

Claypole raised his head to look at Alfie. He held no expression beyond an intense stare, as if his face were a rubber mask and only the eyes were real. "Your sister was abducted? I'm sorry for your loss."

Alfie placed both his hands flat on the table, delicate wooden splinters spiking his palms. "No more games. What do you want from me, Claypole? What will it take to end this thing between us? An apology? A fight? What?"

"I don't know who Claypole is. I'm here because of Henry Stanhope."

"What? What are you talking about? I came here to meet you as you asked, so be straight with me. What does Henry Stanhope have to do with anything?"

"I'm Noah Stanhope. You murdered my father."

Alfie pulled back his hands and placed them in his lap. "Are you being serious? You're Henry Stanhope's son?"

The other man's eyes never left Alfie's. "Henry was my dad – the man who taught me how to ride a bike, kick a ball, and who built a swing set for me in the garden for my fifth birthday. It's still there, you know? Still exactly where he placed it. He bought me my first car, paid for me to study music, took me to Disney World. He was a good man."

"He was a paed—"

Noah struck the table with a fist, teeth bared and spittle spraying through the gaps. "Don't you dare say it!"

Whoa. This guy is on edge. Do I need to be on my guard?

Alfie reared back, a flush of adrenaline soaking his synapses as his body sensed an impeding threat. "Look, whether I say it or not, it's true. Henry tried to meet up with a child for sex. I'm sorry, but that's not my fault."

"He tried to meet up with *you*. You who baited and tricked him. If you hadn't done so, there's a chance my dad might never have hurt anybody."

"Are you really defending him? Seriously?"

Noah looked away, off towards the pond where the swans and ducks glided upon its surface. "Clearly, my father had issues, but I know he never wanted to hurt anyone. If we had known what was going on inside his head – the troubling thoughts he was having – we might've been able to help him. Thanks to you, there'll never be a chance for that."

"What do you want from me, Noah? I didn't plan for Henry to kill himself. I only wanted to—"

"Ruin his life? Make it so he could never get a job or have a family. Why? Why spend your time going after people and destroying them?"

"Because someone needs to protect the children. Children like my sister. She was taken by a predator when I was young. Do you have any idea the types of monsters who are out there, hiding in plain sight? People like your dad."

Noah huffed. "So that's your excuse, is it? A crime was perpetrated against you, so now you're free to do whatever you want in retaliation? Does that give me the right to beat the shit out of you? I mean, vengeance makes it all okay, right?"

"It's not an excuse, Noah, but it is a reason. It's a reason to do something to try to help. Don't you see that I'm—"

"Your pain doesn't make you special, Alfie Everett. All you're doing is spreading your misery around. My mother is suicidal because of you. Her friends won't return her calls. In a matter of days, you've managed to—"

"I can't listen to any more of this." Alfie put his hands to his head, elbows on the table. "I can't let you sit here and act like your dad was... was an innocent victim. He wasn't! Noah, I'm not the villain here, don't you see that?" Removing his hands from his face, he sat back and meditated for a moment, trying to focus on the present moment. When he opened his eyes again, he had a question: "How did you know I would be here, Noah? I came to meet with someone else, not you – someone *dangerous*."

Noah laced his fingers together on the table and stared at his hands. Some of his anger seemed to have drained away. Now he just looked tired, as if he'd been crying non-stop without sleep. "A strange man in a weird hat came to my house and told me he could arrange a meeting with you. I told him I had nothing to say to you, but then he told me he could make you pay for what you've done – as long as I met you here and gave you something." He lifted his gaze again, his expression lifeless. "You need to pay for what you've done, Alfie. It's time for you to look in the mirror."

Alfie tensed up, waiting for the penny to drop. What was Noah Stanhope planning to do?

Does he have a gun? A knife?

Noah lunged – Alfie cowered – but he was merely pushing the *Three Little Pigs* across the table towards him. "The guy told me to give you this. I almost tossed it in a bin, not wanting to get dragged in to anything, but now that I've met you, and seen how little you care, I've changed my mind."

"Of course I care." He let out a sigh, shook his head. "What did the guy look like, the one who gave you this book?"

Noah sneered, his anger quickly returning. "All I know is that he's dangerous." He leant forward, eyes narrowed into slits. "And he's coming for you, Alfie."

Noah Stanhope got up from the bench. Alfie went to grab him, but found his arm swatted away. "Wait, please? Talk to me. I'm not your enemy."

Finally, and for the first time, Noah's expression showed a modicum of pity. "I can't help you now, even if I wanted to. Just open the book. That's what he wants you to do."

"Wait."

"Goodbye, Alfie."

Alfie sat, powerless to stop the man from walking away. He had no right to try to stop him. Noah Stanhope had already suffered enough.

Am I really to blame? Or is Claypole?

Does it even matter any more?

Alfie stared at the copy of the *Three Little Pigs* on the table in front of him. A children's book. Harmless, right?

Alfie opened the front cover.

Oh God.

His stomach filled with molten lead. Written on the book's very first page was a message.

DON'T OPEN YOUR BOOT.

What? What does it mean?

My car? There's something inside my car?

Oh God.

Alfie leapt up and backed away from the table and the book. An innocent children's story, with a message scrawled in blood. He froze for a moment, his mind temporarily unable to compute. Noah Stanhope was still within eyesight, and he wanted to beg the man for help, but he knew he would receive none. Noah Stanhope was already swinging a leg over the saddle of a motorbike parked beside the cafe. He had his phone in his hand, but he slipped it into his jacket pocket now and started up the bike's engine. Then, without looking back, he kicked off the stand and zoomed off down an access road.

Alfie was all alone. The dog walkers and cyclists were nowhere to be seen. The sky was grey, and he felt the lightest drizzle on his naked forearms.

Don't open your boot.

Which meant definitely look inside the boot.

"What the fuck do I do?" Alfie asked the sky, and he prayed to receive an answer.

Just as his friends had warned, this whole thing had been a set-up. Claypole never had any intention of giving an interview or agreeing to a truce. The bastard was playing with him. The game continued.

And Alfie kept on losing.

He wanted to stay where he was – *exactly* where he was – because if he didn't move, nothing else bad could happen. Claypole couldn't mess with him if he just remained standing beside this picnic bench, spattered by the rain and whipped by the breeze. Life would pause, and whatever Claypole planned to do would just have to wait.

But doing nothing never helped. Alfie had done nothing when the tall man had taken his sister away. If he had fought back then, or screamed a moment sooner, then Daisy might still be here.

Doing nothing let the bad guys win.

Alfie finally got moving, racing away from the bench, feet pounding on the pitted grey pavement. Every lunging stride sent a shockwave up his shins, but he couldn't slow down. He sprinted like his life depended on it – or the lives of someone he cared about.

Making it through the neglected garden, he re-entered the near-deserted car park. A red saloon had arrived since he'd left, and there were now three young lads kicking a football around in the adjacent field. Had they seen anything that could help him? Had they seen Claypole messing with his car while he had been talking with Noah Stanhope?

Noah Stanhope... I broke the man. His father might have deserved what happened, but Noah did nothing wrong. Just an innocent victim.

Alfie's car was right where he had left it, still covered in graffiti. He hurried over to the boot and paused in front of it. After a few seconds, his keyless fob triggered the boot hatch to raise automatically. Time seemed to stand still.

Look inside your boot.

The pneumatic lifters made a soft hissing sound as they slid upwards.

Alfie wanted to close his eyes.

A glimpse of a black boot. A bloodstained white sock.

He wanted to run away, he wanted to scream, but his lungs had turned to lead and his feet wouldn't move.

It was Michael, the security guy.

Naked bar underwear, the dead man was covered in blood from a gaping slash wound across his throat. Both his eyes and mouth were only partly open, making him look sleepy and confused. His remains gave off a sickly odour that Alfie realised he had earlier mistaken for silicon paste.

The smell was from a fresh corpse in my boot. How long has it been here?

"G-got to call the police. Got to..." Alfie staggered a few steps, his vision toing and froing. He fought not to pass out. The last thing he needed was someone coming over to revive him and seeing what was lying inside his boot.

Body weak, hands trembling, Alfie struggled to pull out his phone. He needed to report this. It would be moronic to drive around with a corpse in his boot. How could he possibly explain it if he got pulled over? No, he had to be the one to contact the police. He needed to call this in.

He unlocked his phone. It rang in his hand. Startled, he dropped it on the ground where it continued to ring.

"Damn it!" He bent to retrieve it and saw that the call was coming from Sadie. She should probably have been the last person he wanted to speak to, yet she was also the *only* person he wanted to speak to. He loved her. She was his safe place.

Alfie accepted the call.

Sadie's face popped up on the screen. She seemed to be out in the fields, and she was crying – probably out of guilt for being caught red-handed with Jay.

They looked comfortable. It wasn't the first time.

It doesn't matter right now. I need her.

"Sadie? Babe, I need help. This whole thing was a—"

"Alfie, listen! He's here."

"What? Who is?"

A shadow fell across Sadie as a figure stepped behind her – a man wearing a wide-brimmed hat. A broad-bladed knife reflected the meagre light, pressed against her throat – the same knife that had slashed Alfie's face.

"Claypole is here at the Barn," Sadie said, the terror in her voice barely constrained. "He says you need to come home or else he's going to do something very bad."

"Sadie, what the fuck? Are you okay? Is this for real?"

"Alfie, please? You need to come home."

"I... I'll call the police. Hold on."

A laugh broke out, like peanut shells cracking. Sadie tried to speak, but a large, bony hand clamped over her mouth. A face appeared out of the shadows, Claypole leaning over her shoulder. For the first time, Alfie got a good look at the man's face. A spectre, a ghoul. Bony cheeks and an enormous mouth surrounded by a patchy goatee. Dark green eyes like pools of poison.

"Hello, Alfie. Did you get my gift?"

"Why are you doing this?"

"For the same reasons you do, Alfie. We are who we are. We do what we must."

"I want a truce. You said you would give me a truce."

"And still I might, but first you have to come home, Alfie. If you don't, I'll paint the walls of this place with the blood of your friends."

Alfie squeezed the phone tightly, his knuckles creaking. "I'm calling the police. You're a fucking murderer."

"I'm worse than anything you could ever dream up, boy, and if you call the police, I'll end my legacy right here at your home with a joyous massacre."

"You don't have do this. Let them go and I'll do whatever you want."

"If you want to keep your friends alive, you'll return home in the next thirty minutes."

If I go back, he'll kill us all.

But if I refuse, what will he do? He's already proven he's capable of anything.

"You know what, screw it. I'm going straight to the police. Jaydon and Sadie will have to get what's coming to them. They're not even my friends any more."

Sadie sobbed behind Claypole's hand as the tall man laughed. "As you wish, Alfie. Let's hope you're not bluffing." The knife at Sadie's throat moved slowly. She squealed like a mouse as a think vein of blood trickled down her neck. Her eyes bulged out of her skull.

"Stop!" Alfie yelled out loud enough that lads playing football on the field stopped and looked over. "I-I'll come back, okay? I'm coming back right now. Just don't hurt my friends."

"Don't fuck with me, boy. Do you understand what I'll do if you try anything clever?"

Alfie nodded over and over again. "I'll keep my word. I'll come back."

"Good, then you'll get to see your friends alive again. Be quick though, Alfie, because I'm an impatient soul. Drive that fancy car like it was meant to be driven. Don't make me wait."

The call ended. Alfie tried to call straight back, but it went to voicemail. Head in his hands, he tried to keep from screaming.

The lads on the field were now walking towards him, likely coming to check if he was okay.

He was not okay.

I don't even remember what it's like to be okay.

Alfie slammed his boot closed and leapt inside his car. He needed to get home now, and he couldn't let anything get in his way.

Or else that psychopath is going to kill everyone I care about.

He put his foot down and sped out of the car park, just like a dirty white van had thirteen years ago.

Eleven

lfie's Alfa bounced wildly on its springs, bottoming out several times as it sped down the dirt track leading to the Barn. Home swung into view, outlined by the dusky oranges of the sky. Alfie had expected to see Claypole waiting for him, a knife to Sadie's neck, but instead he spotted Jaydon and Ezra sitting out front, drinking beers and chatting.

What the hell are they doing?

When the two of them saw – or heard – Alfie speeding down the driveway, they leapt up in fright. He was driving so fast that he almost failed to brake in time, the car skidding to a diagonal stop. The seatbelt bit into Alfie's collarbone; the flash of pain kept him alert.

Leaping out of the car, he raced towards the house. "Where is she?" he yelled. "Where the fuck is Sadie?"

Jaydon put his hands out in front of him in a supplication of peace. "Alfie, bro, listen, right. What you saw on the cameras, it ain't like it seems."

"Where's Sadie? Where is she?"

"Sh-she went for a walk, bro, but don't lose it with her,

okay? Ez showed me what you did to my fucking car and it's—"

"What are you talking about, you goddamn moron?" Alfie stormed up to Jaydon, causing him to back away in fear. "Just tell me where Sadie is."

"She went to clear her head," Ezra piped in. He was standing nearby, unsteady on his feet, either high or drunk. "She was upset about what happened. Listen, dude, I really need to tell you something. You didn't reply to my text, so I was waiting for you to come ba—"

Alfie flashed his teeth at them both. "Claypole has Sadie, you fucking idiots. You let her walk off by herself and now he has her. What the hell are you both doing?"

Jaydon flinched, the whites of his eyes showing. "Yo, what? Bro, what are you actually saying?"

"I'm telling you Claypole has Sadie, while you two are sitting here drinking and smoking." Alfie clenched his fists. "I should beat the shit out of you both."

"Are you for real, bro?"

"Claypole called me from her phone. He has her. Do you get it?"

Jaydon put his hands on top of his head and started pacing. "We tried to stop her from leaving, man, but she wouldn't listen. She kept saying she wanted to be alone. She's... she's ashamed of what's happened. Alfie, I'm—"

"We need to go find her. Right now."

Jaydon shut his mouth and nodded.

Ezra reached out a hand. "Alf? How do we know this isn't another one of Claypole's tricks?"

"The son of a bitch video called me with a knife to Sadie's throat. Trick or not, she needs us to save her. I-I think she's somewhere in the fields, somewhere close. God, if he's done something to her..."

Jaydon clutched his chest, breathing heavily. "Yo, please

say you're fucking with us, Alf. If this is some twisted act of revenge, then it's too much."

Shaking his head and seething, Alfie march over to his car and opened up the boot. He summoned Ez and Jaydon over and showed them what was inside. They wailed in unison, covering their faces and turning away.

Cowards. They need to face this. They need to accept the reality of what's going on.

Alfie slammed the boot and wafted the smell away. "This isn't a game, okay? Claypole is a certified psychopath who won't stop until he's dead or locked up. We need to rescue Sadie before he cuts her fucking head off."

Ezra scooped back his braids and bent over like he was going to be sick. "It's worse than that, dude. I found something out after you left. That's why I texted you."

Alfie frowned, the sickly-sweet smell of Michael's corpse still stuck inside his nostrils. "What? What the hell is it?"

Ezra straightened back up, and when he looked at Alfie his eyes were bleary. "I made a note of the names graffitied on your car. We never really talked about what they might mean."

"Things have been a bit hectic," Alfie said, flapping his arms. "I was more focused on the threat written on the bonnet than a bunch of random names."

"There're not random. I searched them up on the Internet. Conner, Ivy, Millie, Amira. They're all missing kids, dude. From all around the country, from over the last decade."

Jaydon turned to him. "The fuck? Missing kids?"

Ezra nodded, pale-faced. Clearly, he'd downed a few beers while Alfie had been gone. "Every name I searched brought up a news article or a police statement. Conner Bracken went missing in 2011 after riding his bike in front of his house. Millie Baxter went missing from her family's restaurant while they took in a delivery out back. The most recent abduction was three years ago: Amira Vries. Someone snatched her from her bed while her parents were sleeping. She was four years old."

Alfie collapsed backwards, ending up sitting on the bonnet of his car. "Who the fuck have we messed with?"

There was silence for a moment as they each looked one another in the eye. As they digested what had been spoken.

Ezra finally licked his lips. "I don't think Claypole was coming to get jiggy with a minor that day in the marketplace. He was coming to abduct and murder a child. He's a serial killer, Alfie."

Jaydon almost fell. "Fuck me."

Alfie shrugged. "No shit."

"Dude, please let that sink in a moment. Claypole kills kids. That's an entirely different level of evil."

"We can handle it."

The hell am I saying? Who do I think I am? John Wick?
He's just a man. Killer or not. We can deal with this.

"Your ego is out of control, dude. Sometimes it's okay to run away. This is one of those times."

"Too right." Jaydon set off towards the garages. "I'm getting the fuck out of here. There's no other choice."

Alfie went after him. "Hey, are you forgetting this psycho has Sadie? We need to go save her."

"Save her? From the real-life Freddie Krueger? No way, man. We need to get the feds here pronto. They will know what to do. It's Sadie's best chance."

"I already tried calling them," Ezra said. "Signal's been dead for over an hour now. Don't think it's by accident."

"Great." Jaydon keyed in the code to open the garage doors. "He's a technologically savvy child killer. All the more reason to get the hell out of here."

Alfie grabbed Jaydon by his shoulder and yanked him around. "You're not leaving, man. We have to deal with this."

"I ain't fucking dying here, bro." Jaydon shoved him in the

chest. "You stick around and play hero if you want to, but I'm—"

The punch came before Alfie even made a fist. It came from his gut, an explosion of rage that took over his limbs and demanded violence.

Jaydon spun around like a ballet dancer before collapsing onto his hands and knees with a dazed groan. There he remained for several moments, staring at the concrete and spitting bloody saliva.

Then he launched back to his feet and threw a punch at Alfie.

Alfie ducked and tackled Jaydon around the waist, shoving him backwards. They crashed up against his Range Rover, crumpling the fender and adding to the damage Alfie had caused earlier.

Jaydon landed a short hook, clocking Alfie under the chin and putting stars in his vision. Alfie responded by closing the space between them and grinding his forehead against Jaydon's mouth, trying to crush his lips and nose while wrapping his arms around him to keep him from throwing another punch.

"Stop it! Stop fighting!" Ezra wedged himself between them, a hand on each of their chests. "How is this going to help anything? You want to make it even easier for Claypole?"

Jaydon put his hands up in surrender.

Alfie saw an opening and saw red. He threw another punch, a straight right to his ex-friend's nose. The meaty crunch was followed by a gout of blood dripping from Jaydon's nose.

"The fuck, man?"

Ez shoved Alfie back again, the thud resounding in his chest. "Cheap shot, dude."

Rather than feel ashamed, Alfie glared at Jaydon, desperately wanting to tear him apart. *Needing* to hurt him. It buzzed in his ears, a waspish demon whispering for blood. "He wants to leg it and leave Sadie to die. Why are you defending him?"

"Because he isn't your enemy, Alfie, so stop."

"I don't want her to get hurt any more than you do, bro," Jaydon said. "I just think we should get help rather than play right into this fucker's hands. You're the one who's gonna get her killed."

Alfie prodded his finger in the air. "Claypole said he would kill her if I involve the police. We have to go find her and finish this ourselves. If I have to do it by myself, fine."

"You've lost the plot, bro. This ain't some misfit trying to meet up with a minor. We can't handle this by ourselves. We need the police."

Ezra put both hands on Alfie's chest and forced him to step back another few feet. "He's right, dude. We can't let Claypole control what happens next. We can't play his games."

Alfie continued to glare at Jaydon, but Jaydon looked away, nursing his bloody nose and a swollen lip. The sight of his friend's wounds knocked some of Alfie's anger away, but not all of it, so he turned his attention to Ezra, the only one he wasn't truly mad at. "What if we go for help and Claypole follows through on his threat?"

"And what if he kills her because we have no way of stopping him?" Jaydon said. "Better to have help. Don't you see that? Trust me, bro, I know the kind of person it takes to brutalise a kid. We don't want any part of it. I... I can't face what might happen."

Alfie clenched and unclenched his fists, the anger still flaring in his chest and refusing to leave him.

I'm emotional. Too emotional.

If I get this wrong, Sadie is the one who pays.

Maybe it's time to stop playing vigilante.

Alfie rubbed at his bruised jaw, closed his eyes, and let out a slow, calming breath. "Okay, fine. Jay? Get the hell out of here and call the police as soon as you can get a signal. Ez and me will stay here in case there's something we can do to help Sadie."

"Yeah, man, I'm on it. We'll get Sadie out of this, all right? She's gonna be okay." He hurried over to the driver's side of his Range Rover and hopped inside.

Several moments went by, but the car remained silent. The lights stayed dead.

"What's wrong?" Alfie eventually asked.

Jaydon reopened the door and stepped out. "It won't start. Even the dashboard lights won't come on."

Ezra groaned. "Pop the hood."

Jaydon reached an arm back inside the car, stooping slightly. A metallic *clunk* sounded and the bonnet hopped up an inch. Ezra slid his fingers underneath and hit the latch before lifting the big square bonnet up on its rods. The moan he gave told them all they needed to know.

Jaydon stepped up to inspect his engine, eyes scanning back and forth. "The battery's gone."

"Ignition wire, too. Probably the coils and starter plugs as well. No way will this thing start."

"Then take my car," Alfie said, reaching urgently into his pocket and handing his keys to Jaydon. "Go on. Get going."

The three of them turned as a unit and hurried out of the garage, almost bumping into each other as they moved at differing speeds. Now that they were choosing to get Jaydon out of there to fetch help, Alfie's heart fluttered anxiously, and he had to fight the urge to flee right beside him.

Sadie needs me here. I might have a chance to save her.

Ezra skidded to a halt and Alfie crashed into the back of him, yelling out and swearing. Before he could demand an explanation, though, his eyes drifted off towards the driveway outside.

Claypole stood on the gravel, his machete pointed up at the blood-red sky. An equally blood-red smile stretched his mouth wide.

All the better to eat you with, Alfie thought to himself as he reversed back into the garage.

Alfie's legs almost abandoned him as he faced off against the menace who had turned his life into a nightmare. Images raced through his mind like a cinema reel stuck on high-speed, starting with the sudden glint of a knife in the marketplace and ending with an innocuous chat with a security guy named Michael. "He's been here the whole time."

Jaydon came to a stop beside Alfie, just a couple of feet outside the garage. "What?"

"Claypole was here yesterday, dressed in a Weber-Cooks uniform. We had a conversation. He was messing with me."

I had no idea. He was right in front of me, close enough to slice my neck, and I was oblivious.

The too-small Weber-Cooks uniform Claypole had been wearing must have belonged to Michael.

"This is him, right?" Ezra hopped back and forth like he was preparing to run. "He's come to kill us all."

"He's here to try," Alfie said, but there was a shudder to his voice and he needed the bathroom. His car was tantalisingly close, but Claypole was right next to it, impossible to avoid.

The big hat was gone. In its place was that dented bald head. His voice was low and raspy as he spoke, but it carried easily. "I'm here to blow your house down, Alfie."

"Let Sadie go and stop all this right now. Where is she?"

Claypole grinned wider, his head tilting slightly. His face was stubbled and his eyebrows a pair of thick black tufts. In a crowd, there would have been little to remark upon, but knowing what this man was capable of gave him a deadly aura – like a poisonous weed, innocent until it attacked you.

"Are you asking for mercy? How much mercy have you shown in *your* life, Alfie? Did Henry Stanhope beg you to stop harassing him? Did you give *him* a second chance?"

"He would have hurt a child."

"Ah, children... Your entire life is dedicated to their welfare. An unhealthy fixation, some might say."

"You know why I do what I do, Claypole." Alfie raised his chin, determined not to show fear. He was terrified, of course, but he wouldn't be made to feel ashamed of the things he'd done. "You sent me to Tanning Stanley Park because you know what happened to my sister. Exactly how *much* do you know?"

Claypole took a step closer, an amused twinkle in his eye. "Are you hoping I can shed light on what happened to poor, poor Daisy? You want me to tell you all the terrible things she went through before she finally stopped bleating?"

Alfie couldn't hold back the tears, so he let them fall. Tears made him human. He wondered if Claypole had ever cried in his life, or if the beast was even capable. "Tell me what you know about my sister."

Claypole took a second step forward, his long overcoat flapping around the tops of his boots. "I'm afraid I can't help you, son. Her death had nothing to do with me."

"Bullshit! How did you know to send me to that park?"

"You live your entire life on the Internet, Alfie Christopher Everett. It wasn't difficult to learn what I needed to know about you, to find out where your soft parts are located. Quite the storied history you have. Something we share."

Alfie took a step forward to meet the man, his eyes drawn back and forth between the knife and Claypole's sneering face. "I've made a lot of mistakes in my life, but I'm a good person."

Claypole's grin faded away. "There is no good and bad, Alfie. Just wolves and sheep. Which one are you?"

"I'm the shepherd who's going to put you down if you've done anything to Sadie."

"Your sweet little ewe is fine for now." He looked back and forth between Jaydon and Alfie. "But which one of you will try to save her? To which of you does she belong?"

"Why are you doing this, bro?" Jaydon put a hand on Alfie's shoulder, almost as if to steady himself, but perhaps also showing that they would not be divided so easily. "Why won't you leave us alone?"

"Because you invited me, remember? You invited me long before you ever realised it." He licked his lips. "It's not nice to toy with people. Not nice to tempt their thirsts."

Alfie tried to talk, lost his breath, and had to start again. "D-did you kill those kids? The ones whose names you painted on my car?"

Claypole took yet another step, moving directly in front of Alfie's car now and cutting off any hope of reaching it. "Do you understand what compulsion is? Have you ever experienced a need that puts your teeth on edge and pulls your skin taut around your bones? Have you ever experienced a yearning right down in the bottom of your guts? Alfie, those poor children were fated to die from the moment they were born. Perhaps you are fated to die also. Maybe this very minute. Maybe right here on this driveway. This is more preordained than you realise."

"We've called the police, Claypole. I called them on my way back here."

"They're not here yet."

"Where's Sadie? What have you done to her?"

Claypole had lowered his machete to his side, but he lifted it now and pointed it at Alfie. "You'll be reunited shortly. Right after I yank out your insides."

"Fuck!" Jaydon grabbed Alfie's shoulder and yanked him backwards. Ezra was already racing from the garage towards the main house. Alfie didn't want to run away, but he could do nothing else. And so the three of them rushed for the front door. Alfie reached for the handle, and a spike of terror jabbed his brain – a dreadful certainty that the door would not open and Claypole would slaughter them all – but mercifully the handle turned and they all threw themselves inside.

"Lock it!" Jaydon bellowed. "Lock it."

Alfie slammed the door, pulled up the handle, and twisted the key. Then he put all his weight on the handle to check it was secure. "Okay, it's locked."

"The window." Ezra sprinted into the lounge area and yanked the window shut with a frightened wail.

"Anywhere else?" Jaydon asked, spinning back and forth. "Can he get inside anywhere else?"

Alfie crashed sideways against the kitchen counter, gasping for air. "N-no. No, I think we're okay."

Jaydon put his hands on his head and started pacing. "Bro, we are not okay. That psycho is out there with a machete."

"And we can't call for help," Ezra said.

Alfie leant over the counter, his stomach aching. "We need to find out what he's done with Sadie. I shouldn't have driven off and left."

"This ain't your fault," Jaydon said. "We're all responsible for this. For everything. It ain't on you, Alfie."

Alfie moved away from the counter and went over to the window. Claypole stood on the driveway, inert like a robot who had shut down. "You and me have stuff to deal with, Jay, but right now we need to stick together."

"Deal."

"What is he doing?" Ezra asked, meaning Claypole. He had picked up a crystal ashtray and held it at his side as a weapon. "Is he trying to get in?"

"No, he's just standing there, not moving a muscle."

Claypole stared impassively towards the house, not

seeming to focus on any specific point. Alfie couldn't even see the man breathing.

The lights went out. It was subtle – dusky daylight still spilling in through the windows – but the brightness in the room went down a notch. Alfie turned around and stared up at the spotlights. Then he glanced towards the kitchen – at the blank display on the oven and the microwave. "The electric just went off."

Jaydon tiptoed and peered out the window. "How? He's just standing there. How could he have knocked the power off?"

Ezra moaned. "Dude must have put a blocker on our feed cable or something."

"He was here yesterday," Alfie told them, "pretending to be from Weber-Cooks. He had a uniform on and asked to see the fuse box. That's when he must have done it."

"He has this all planned out," Ezra said. "We're trapped in here with no signal and no power. We can't even send an email."

"He's moving," Jaydon said, rushing up to the window and pointing. "Look, he's doing something."

Alfie turned and watched as Claypole approached the house, the machete swinging in time with his strides. He came right over to the window, putting his face up against the glass and grinning, the straight line of his front teeth like a razor's edge. Slowly, he raised a long-fingered hand, holding a small plastic box with a set of tiny black buttons on it. He pressed it with his thumb and the lights flicked back on. The oven chirped as it came back to life in the kitchen.

He pressed it again and killed the power.

Jaydon moaned and started rushing about without a destination. Alfie flicked repeatedly at the nearest light switch.

"Neat trick," Alfie said, glaring back at Claypole, the air cold on the back of his neck. "I don't see the point, though."

"The point is to make you feel powerless," Claypole hissed, "like every one of the victims you ambushed. You invaded their lives, Alfie, punished them for things they couldn't control – punished them for their immutable natures. What is *your* nature, Alfie? What should your punishment be for your inherent weaknesses? How should you be judged for your greed, your vanity, your wrath? What is the price you should pay? What is the true cost of this fancy house and the life that goes with it?"

"I don't care about any of that," Alfie yelled back through the glass. "Stopping monsters like you is the only thing I'm bothered about. Keeping children like my sister safe is my only mission. But I'm willing to make a truce, Claypole. Let Sadie and my friends go and I swear I won't try to find you. This can all stop right now before it goes any further."

"You want to make a deal?"

"Yes."

"You want to abandon your ideals, your beliefs, to save yourself? Can you really drop this, Alfie? Can you truly move on?"

Alfie turned to look at his terrified friends. Ezra looked ready to pass out. Jaydon had his fists clenched, and he couldn't keep them from.

Alfie turned back to the window. "Not to save myself. To save my friends."

Claypole licked his lips, his tongue pale and slick. "I'll tell you what, kiddo. We can make a deal, but you're not going to like the terms. Want to hear them anyway?"

Alfie swallowed, a lump in his throat. "I'm listening."

"Come outside. Come outside and give yourself to me willingly, and you have my word I'll spare your friends. Sadie and Jaydon can grow old together and have a bunch of kids. Ezra can smoke all the cannabis he wants until he ends up sterile."

"Dude, that's not cool."

Claypole widened his grin. "What do you say, Alfie? Will you come outside and take your medicine in order to save your friends. Are you really the hero you make yourself out to be? Do we have a deal, Alfie?"

Alfie wanted to blink, but he feared what might happen in that split second of darkness. Could he really step outside and let this maniac butcher him. Even if he grabbed a weapon, tried to fight, there was no guarantee he would be successful. He could die right now, right outside.

But Sadie and the others will be safe.

If Claypole keeps his word.

Alfie pressed his forehead against the glass, staring deep into Claypole's acidic green eyes. "No deal." *There has to be a better way out of this.* "No fucking deal."

Claypole's smile melted away, leaving behind a horrid spectre at the window. To Alfie's surprise, Jaydon and Ezra stepped up on either side of him. They each placed a hand upon his shoulder.

For the time being, they were still a wolf pack.

But the wolf outside was rabid.

————

Claypole returned to standing still on the driveway, while Alfie kept trying – and failing – to make a call. The electricity was still off, too, with the light fading more and more with every second, snatching away the colours in the room and turning them grey.

Ezra shimmied back and forth, peeking out a window in the living area. "I can't see him any more. The sun's gone down. It's too dark."

"It's gonna be pitch-black in here before long," Jaydon said, looking up at the dead spotlights. He was sitting in an armchair, foot dancing atop his knee. "Embarrassing confession, but I kinda hate the dark. Ever since the care home. Lights out was a bad time for a kid with no family."

Alfie entered the kitchen and rooted in the cupboards. After a brief search, he procured a pair of citrus-scented candles. He placed them on the counter and lit them with one of Ezra's lighters, then wafted the flickering flame with his hand. "And here's me," he said, "always complaining about how many candles Sadie buys."

Jaydon was visibly relieved as the warm, yellow light spread out from the kitchen. "What do you think Claypole's done to her?"

"I don't want to think about it." Alfie gripped the edge of the cold slab counter. "But the longer we stay in here, the longer she has to suffer."

"I should try to make a run for it. I'm half Nigerian. Gotta be faster than some middle-aged whackjob, don't you reckon?"

"Your knee is still busted up," Alfie said, nodding at his leg. "No, I should be the one to go. Sadie's my girl, not yours, so if anyone is gonna save her, it's me."

"It ain't even like that. We all care about Sadie, not just you."

Alfie rolled his eyes. "Yeah, you clearly care about her more than you ever cared about me."

Jaydon strolled into the kitchen, his limp less pronounced as he obviously tried to disguise it. "I do care about you, bro. You're my best friend."

Ezra groaned. "Never me, huh?"

Jaydon ignored him, keeping his focus on Alfie. "I know what you saw on the camera must have hurt like hell, bro, but I swear nobody meant to betray you."

"Are you kidding me? Seriously? I watched you both; it

wasn't the first time. Don't pretend like it was an accident. You both knew what you were doing."

Jaydon couldn't look Alfie in the eye as he replied. "Look, things have been tense lately. You've been spinning out over Claypole and the channel, and then Henry Stanhope... did what he did. Say and me just grew closer, you know? Over our concern for you."

Alfie blinked slowly. "Wow, I'm so lucky to have good friends. So concerned about my welfare."

"Sadie loves you, bro, but shit's been tough on her."

"So you moved in to comfort her, huh? How fucking noble." He clapped his hands right in Jaydon's face. "What a guy."

Jaydon couldn't disguise his irritation, but he seemed to push it away. "You and me have stuff to talk about, for real, but this ain't about not caring about you, Alfie. Shit's just complicated. It don't mean I ain't got your back."

"Got my back? You broke my fucking heart, *bro*."

"I'll go," Ezra said suddenly. He moved away from the window and joined them at the kitchen counter. "Jaydon's knee is busted, and Alfie, you can't run for shit."

Alfie made an *uh-huh* sound. "No way, Ez. We can't let you do that."

"Why? Because I'm not an alpha male like you? That's exactly why I'm the one who should go. Do you know how many bullies I had to outrun in high school? Turns out, I can run pretty fast when I need to." He looked towards the front door and swallowed, clearly not relishing the thought of going outside, but willing to do so. "I can make it past the hill and head for that newsagent a couple miles down the road, or just get far enough away to make a call."

Alfie studied him. "Claypole is out there. Aren't you afraid he'll catch you?"

"I'm a thimbleful of water away from pissing myself, but if

we stay here, Claypole is going to pick us off one by one. Everything he's done up until now has been planned out and calculated. He *wants* us trapped inside this house, barely able to see. If we don't find help soon, bad things are going to happen. I'm the quickest. I should go."

Jaydon squeezed Ezra's bony shoulder. "We can't let you do that. It's suicide."

Ezra shrugged him away. "I'm not asking your permission, Jay. This is our only option. I'm not waiting around here for Claypole to turn this place into the *Texas Chainsaw Massacre*. Let me do this, please."

Alfie chewed his bottom lip for a moment. "Ez, are you sure?"

"I'm trying to think about this logically, okay? It's barely nine o'clock, and we don't have a neighbour for miles. If we don't find help, then help ain't coming. One of us needs to make a run for it. I'm the only choice."

Alfie felt a headache coming on. *He's right. Claypole has a plan, and right now he wants us stuck inside. The best thing we can do is refuse to play ball. One of us needs to get the hell out of here.*

"All right, Ez, you can make a run for it, but you're not going out there unarmed. We have to find something to defend yourself with."

Ez frowned. "Like what? A bread knife?"

"How about one of the tripods in the office?" Jaydon said. "They collapse down."

It was worth exploring, so the three of them headed into the Barn's large backroom studio. When they found it too gloomy to see, Alfie went and fetched one of the candles. Its flame cast flickering shadows on the wall.

One side of the studio had a backdrop with three mounted cameras pointed at it. Ezra removed one camera from its tripod and collapsed the stand. Weighing it up in his hands, he said: "Too heavy. Hold on."

They waited while Ezra further collapsed the tripod, removing some of the struts and tossing them away. Once he was done, he had a compact length of black-painted steel.

"Take a swing at me, bro," Jaydon said. "Test it out."

Ezra held the metal tripod like a baseball bat and swung it meekly, making sure Jaydon had enough time to duck out the way. A smooth, even stroke that cut through the air easily.

"Capable of cracking a skull, I reckon," Ezra said, propping the makeshift baton over his shoulder.

"You ready?" Alfie asked him.

Ezra sighed, shook himself, then blew air out of his cheeks. "Yep. Let's get into starting positions."

Alfie shared a look with Jaydon and wondered if he too had a bad feeling about this.

TWELVE

"You don't have to do this." Alfie peered out of the glass pane at the top of the front door and searched for Claypole. But night had landed, and their enemy was nowhere to be seen. The full moon added enough light to make out the shape of Alfie's car on the driveway, but it was impossible to make out any details. Something seemed to move in the gloom, a shifting of the shadows that was difficult to pinpoint.

"I do have to do this, dude. Unless you can think of a better way out of this trippy nightmare. Seriously, dude, do you have something? Because I really don't want to go out there. It doesn't even have to be a good idea, I'll take it."

Jaydon grabbed him by the shoulders and looked at him. "No one is making you do this, bro. We can reconsider."

Ezra's pale cheeks highlighted his freckles as he sucked in air. He scooped back his braids and swore underneath his breath. "No, I've thought this through. It's our best chance, and being scared isn't a reason not to do it. Sometimes you got to step out from behind the camera, right? Time to stop watching while others take all the risks."

"Do not slow down or look back, okay?" Jaydon patted him on the back. "Whatever happens, you get the hell out of here and don't stop."

Ezra tittered. "No heroics, then? Roger that. I'm just gonna imagine the world's longest spliff waiting for me at the end of the road and run as if a maniac is chasing me – because there will be."

Jaydon glanced out of the window. "What about your car, Alfie? It's right there on the driveway. Should Ez make a run for it?"

"What if Claypole messed with it like he did your Range Rover? Ez could jump inside only to find himself trapped."

Ezra grimaced. "Think I'll stick with running for my life. Simple. Effective. Classic."

Alfie grabbed his friend and pulled him into a hug. "It's gonna be okay, man. You got this."

"Yeah," Jaydon said. "You got platinum balls, man."

Ezra turned to the front door and stood stiffly with the folded metal tripod in his arms. "Let's hope they don't slow me down. Open the door."

Alfie unlocked the bolt as quietly as he could and placed his hand around the handle. "After three, okay? One... two... three!"

He yanked the door open and hopped out of the way.

Ezra lowered his head and bolted forward like a rifleman racing for the safety of a trench, but instead of a rifle he had a short length of metal and no helmet. The night yawned, ready to swallow him whole. Somewhere distant, an owl hooted – an excited spectator.

Jaydon and Alfie stood in the doorway, shoulder to shoulder, and watched Ezra risk his life for them.

It should be me. Alfie thought. *I should be the one to get us out of this.*

"I don't see Claypole anyway," Jaydon said. "I think Ez is gonna make it."

Alfie tentatively agreed. Ezra was already twenty metres from the house, almost at Alfie's car. Freedom lay right ahead.

"Get in, lad!" Alfie clenched a fist triumphantly. "Go, go, go."

Ezra tossed the tripod aside, obviously feeling safe enough to lose it in exchange for extra speed. His hands formed blades, cutting through the air like a T2000 as he faded more and more into the beckoning night.

The owl hooted once again, cheering him on.

Ezra fell.

It wasn't a stumble or a pratfall; he went straight down on his face, legs arching up behind his back like a scorpion's tail. For one dreadful, icy second, Alfie feared his friend had been shot. But there had been no sound of gunfire, and even a silenced weapon made a noise.

Jaydon gripped the doorframe. "No, no, no. Get up, bro. Get up!"

Ezra was dazed for a moment, but then he tried getting to his feet. He quickly collapsed and grabbed his leg.

Alfie's stomach dropped to the floor. *What happened? Why did he fall?*

Jaydon gripped the door frame and cursed. "Come on, bro. You got to get up."

Alfie stepped forward, balancing on the doorstep. "He's hurt. He can't get up."

Claypole appeared out of the darkness like a summoned spirit. He started towards Ezra, less than twenty metres away.

Ezra tried to get up again, but still couldn't manage it. He yelled for help – for his friends to come and save him. Yelling for Alfie.

Jaydon danced back and forth. "What do we do? What do we do?"

Alfie was already out the door, unable to stand by and watch while Ezra begged for help. But Claypole had a head start on him.

"EZ! Ez, you need to get up. He's coming."

"Alfie? Alfie, I'm hurt. My leg."

I know you're hurt, buddy, but you got to get up. Claypole is right behind you.

"You need to get up. Get up now!"

Claypole had put his hat back on and, along with his long black coat, he looked like the Grim Reaper coming to collect a victim.

Alfie sprinted as fast as his legs would allow, but rushing through the darkness was perilous, and he gambled on twisting an ankle or breaking a leg with every patch of uneven ground. "Stay away from him," he yelled impotently. "Leave him alone. Fuck. Please!"

Alfie saw a silvery thread glinting in the moonlight, razor-sharp like the edge of a page. Claypole had set up a tripwire, and Ezra had run straight into it, slicing open his leg. Alfie leapt it, praying to God there were no other traps.

Ezra dragged himself along the ground like a stepped-on slug. Alfie was still ten metres away, powerless to act as Claypole grabbed his friend by his braids and yanked him to his feet. Ezra hopped on one leg, screaming, and tried to pull away. Claypole manhandled him like a child.

"Let him go!" Alfie cried, skidding to a halt and putting his hands out pleadingly. "Please don't hurt him."

Claypole positioned Ezra in front of him and placed the cruel edge of his machete against his windpipe.

"Don't do this, dude," Ezra begged. "You got us, okay? You scared the shit out of us and showed us who's boss. We're sorry, okay? We're so fucking sorry."

Claypole looked over Ezra's shoulder at Alfie. His eyes caught the moonlight like the glittering gems of a jaguar. "Are *you* sorry, Alfie? Sorry enough to take my earlier offer? Your life for your friends?"

"Nobody needs to die, Claypole. We can work something out. Just let him go and we can talk all you want."

"The wolf is hungry."

Ezra twisted back and forth. "Let me go. Let me go. I'm begging you, man. Please."

Alfie shook his head, unable to take his eyes away from the blade pressed against Ezra's throat. "He's just our cameraman. You don't need to punish him."

Claypole's eyes darkened. "Guilty is the spectator. Damned is the witness."

Before Alfie could even digest the words, his head filled with the most awful sound; a keening screech that rattled his skull. The sound of Ezra wailing as the sharp metal tip of Claypole's knife leapt up and plunged into his left eyeball.

"Stop!" Alfie screamed, covering his ears. "Stop, stop, stop!" He wanted to race to the rescue, and beat Claypole away in a flurry of fists and headbutts, but he couldn't move his feet. His knees had calcified. Vomit leapt into his throat and ejected from his mouth. It made a pathetic *pitter-patter* sound as it landed in the grass.

Claypole clamped a fist around Ezra's screaming mouth, holding him upright as if he were a doll filled with weightless feathers. "You can save him, Alfie. You can exchange places with him and be the hero."

"I... I can't."

I don't want to die.

Ezra was quivering and convulsing. His throat bulged, screams trapped in his throat. His left eye looked like a crushed cherry tomato, gooey insides leaking down his cheek.

Claypole moved the blade back to Ezra's windpipe. "Are you watching, Alfie? Do you see the consequences of your actions?"

Tears fell down Alfie's cheeks. "Have mercy."

"As you wish." Claypole yanked his arm to one side, the machete skimming across Ezra's neck.

Ezra's remaining eye bulged in its socket. His mouth opened and closed like a suffocating fish. Without a word, Claypole released his braids and let him collapse to his knees. He teetered back and forth, clutching at his gushing throat.

Alfie threw himself to the ground and grabbed Ezra in his arms just as he flopped sideways. He tried to get his friend to focus, but he wouldn't keep still. Dark, glistening blood bubbled at his throat and spurted weakly in time to his heartbeat.

"Ez! Ez, it's all right. I got you, man. I got you, dude. Just hold on."

Jaydon was yelling something from the house, but Alfie couldn't make out the words. He was stranded in a void, floating on a patch of moonlit grass where only he and Ezra existed. Soon, Ezra would be gone and Alfie would be all alone.

The light faded from Ezra's eyes. The bloody bubbles ceased along with his attempts to breathe. Finally, he went still and focused his one eye on Alfie. There was a calmness to his expression that no cannabis leaf had ever given him.

"Ez..."

Then he was gone, an empty dead thing in Alfie's arms.

A soft, wolflike howl drifted through the air, and when Alfie looked up, he saw Claypole walking backwards into the shadows, his bloody machete pointed up at the moon.

———

Alfie didn't know what to do. Ezra was dead, but it felt wrong to leave him out there covered in blood. At the same time, Claypole was still near, skulking somewhere in the shadows.

Ez would be alive if I had offered to take his place.

Am I a coward for not wanting to die?

"Ez, man, I'm so sorry." Alfie placed his friend down on his back, positioned his limp, lifeless hands over his chest, and leant down and kissed his clammy forehead. Then he rose to his feet and stumbled back towards the house, hoping to get there before Claypole reappeared. As he put one foot in front of the other, he drifted away from his body, watching himself like the spectator of a horror movie, screaming at himself to run.

Run for your life, you idiot. Claypole is coming.

No, not Claypole. That's not his real name. Who is he really? And why do I feel like I should know?

Who cares, just run for your life.

But Ezra had already tried running. And now he was dead.

Jaydon had closed the front door, but he reopened it as soon as Alfie got closer. "Get in, bro, get in." He grabbed Alfie and yanked him inside, relocking the door behind them and placing his back against it with a *thud*. "Ezra? Is he... is he...?"

"Claypole cut his throat." Alfie staggered into the candle-lit kitchen and threw up in the sink. The fumes of his own stomach acid stung his eyes and added to his misery. After he was done, he wiped his mouth and turned around. "I watched him die, Jay. I saw the fear in his eyes as he tried to hold on."

"Fuck, fuck, fuck. We are so screwed, bro. We're gonna fucking die." Jaydon put his hands on his head and started pacing. "This can't be real. We're actually gonna get murdered."

Alfie wished he could argue, but it seemed like a reasonable assumption. It was a puzzle that he himself wasn't panicking. All he could put it down to was the shock of watching Ezra die. It kept replaying in his mind, keeping him from thinking about anything else.

Jaydon went into the living area and sat down on the sofa,

staring at the floor tiles with an unblinking stare. "Jesus Christ... What do we do? What do we do? Ezra..."

Alfie went over to the window and tried to see Claypole. His gut told him that the danger was over for now, and when he failed to see the man outside, he became more sure of it.

He wants us to stew in here for a while. He has all the time in the world to play with us, to drag things out.

Alfie sat in an armchair opposite the sofa and lowered his face into his hands. "If Claypole can butcher Ezra like it's nothing, what has he done to Sadie? What if he's killed her, Jay? What if she and Ezra are both dead?"

"Nah, nah, don't think on that, bro. If Claypole was gonna kill Say, he'd want us to see it happen, right? He'd want to torment us as much as possible. Sadie's alive. I know it. I know it."

Alfie nodded, a slight weight lifting. "What the hell do we do, Jay? Claypole's out there, waiting for us in the dark, and we have no way of calling for help. We can barely even see."

"We're fucked – for real, bro – but... but shit ain't over till it's over, right? We just need to make a plan and do everything we can to get out of this. That's all we can do. We have to fight to stay alive."

Alfie tutted. "How?"

"No fucking clue, bro, but how hard can it be? You're Alfie Everett; you take down bad guys for a living. Nothing scares you."

"Bullshit. I might have convinced myself that what we were doing was a good thing – and maybe at some point it even was – but all I've been doing is letting my anger control me. Every wolf we've hunted and exposed was an attempt to make up for what happened to me when I was a kid."

Jay ran his fingernails down the sides of his face, raking himself slightly. "What are you saying, bro? This don't sound like you."

"I'm saying Claypole is my punishment for refusing to let go of the past. He's my anger reflected back at me, the consequences of my obsession." He reached into his pocket and pulled out the engagement ring, showing it to Jay. "Can you believe I thought Sadie would want to marry me? I was so convinced I was the hero and that I deserved it all. Maybe I should have opened my eyes and seen all the damage I was causing."

"Christ. Give yourself a break, bro." Jaydon leant forward on his knees, his hands clasped together in prayer. "What happened to you as a kid was rough – something no one should have to have gone through – and it's not your fault if it left a wound."

"You were *abused*, Jay. You have as much right to screw up as I do, but you've managed to let go of the past and be at peace. It's because you're stronger than me."

Jay pulled a face, clearly disagreeing with the statement. "What I have here with you guys... Shit, there're the only relationships I've had that have lasted longer than a few months. Getting close to people – actually trusting them..." He flared his nostrils and snorted. "Trust me, bro, I'm as fucked up as you are. If I wasn't, I would never have stabbed you in the back by kissing Sadie."

Alfie tried to look him in the eye, but failed, so he lowered his gaze to the floor tiles instead. "Why did you? There are so many other girls out there."

"I dunno, man. Maybe because I've jeopardised every friendship I've ever had. I wreck things before people get a chance to abandon me like my parents – or the fuckers who were supposed to keep me safe in the care home. Everyone I've ever cared about has hurt me. Except for you guys."

"And what's Sadie's excuse? It took both of you to stab me in the back."

"You'll have to ask Say about her side of things, but I'm

the one who pushed it – I made it happen – so blame *me*, okay? For what it's worth, I'm sorry, bro. More than you know."

"It's too late for that." Alfie didn't say it with malice, just an acceptance of what was. He put the engagement ring back in his pocket and sat up straight. "You have trust issues? Well, join the club. I'll never be able to move past what I saw on that camera."

Jaydon slumped back against the sofa cushions and groaned. "You don't learn, do you? Holding on to shit is your biggest problem – you said it yourself – so don't decide not to forgive me without even trying."

Alfie rolled his eyes. He hated to admit that he saw his friend's point, so rather than address it, he stood up and went back over to the window. "There'll be no chance to forgive anyone for anything if we don't get the hell out of here. What are we gonna do, Jay?"

Jay got up too. "We gotta out-think this son of a bitch. He's got a plan; we make one of our own."

"His plan is to kill us."

"But why? Alfie, why has this fucker got such a hard on for us?"

"Because he's a serial killer with a bunch of screws loose. He killed those kids, the ones whose names were written on my car."

"If he's a child murderer, then why come after us, a group of adults?"

Alfie left the window and went into the kitchen to pour himself a glass of water. He gulped the contents down in one swig and then placed the empty glass down in the sink. An errant water droplet slid towards the plughole and he watched it. He saw himself swirling towards his doom.

"Bro, what are you thinking? Don't go quiet on me. I'm barely keeping my shit together as it is."

Alfie turned away from the sink. "When Claypole tricked me, pretending to work for Weber-Cooks Security, he said his name was Brent. Not a very common first name, is it?"

Jay shrugged. "I guess not."

"In fact, in my entire life I've only ever met one other person with the first name, Brent."

Jay frowned, not understanding. Alfie waited for it to dawn on him, and slowly it did. "Oh snap! No way. No way."

Alfie leant back against the sink, the cogs in his brain whirring as it all started to make sense. "This whole time, right from the beginning, Claypole has been hunting us."

———

Sadie's head was an overinflated balloon, threatening to drag her up into the sky. Alfie, Jay, and Ezra waved to her in the distance, desperate to reach her before she left the ground and floated away forever. Meanwhile, her head kept on swelling. Bigger and bigger and bigger.

I'm going to pop.

My friends are going to watch me die.

Sadie awoke with a gasp, followed by a groan as she fingered an almighty lump on the back of her head. It was like lifting her face from a bathtub full of water, her senses confused and all mixed together... yet slowly clearing.

She remembered...

I was walking in the fields, trying to clear my head and figure out what to do next. My heart was beating fast. I was sweating. A panic attack.

Alfie saw me and Jay kissing.

That was all that came back to her: a dreadful portion of memory abruptly sliced off and replaced with a long frame of blackness before eventually resuming at this precise moment.

Looking around, Sadie tried to figure out the part of the movie she was missing.

She was lying in the back of what appeared to be a dimly lit van, one side of it stacked with blinking technical equipment that even Ezra might not understand. Cables, screens, antennas, and dials. There was a pair of tool cabinets, too, secured to the side panels and fitted with low-light LED bulbs. So much equipment that she could barely move. When she tried, she realised her ankles were roped together and attached to a hook in the ceiling.

She struggled. "Oh no, oh no, oh no."

Still failing to fill in the blank section of her memory, Sadie came to a dreadful conclusion. Claypole had knocked her unconscious and thrown her in the back of this van. She was caught in a spider's web. But where was the spider?

I need to get out of here. I need to escape before Claypole comes back.

She continued struggling but couldn't get her feet on the floor, the rope around her ankles keeping them elevated. She tried clawing at the knot to free herself, but it was tight and intricately woven. Desperately seeking something to help her, she probed the cramped space with both hands – grabbing at loose cables and yanking on spindly antennas – but nothing would pull free. Gasping for breath, she placed her elbows on the floor and shuffled her body around to face the other way. Her head bashed up against one of the tool cabinets, causing her to hiss in pain and fear. Was Claypole near enough to hear the noise?

She started to hyperventilate, her world a shadow-black and red-LED nightmare. She found herself desperate to be in Alfie's arms. Despite his trauma and obsession, he was her safe place, and she needed him more than ever.

But I cheated on him. He'll never forgive me.

"No time to think about that now," she told herself. "I'm not dying in the back of some psychopath's van."

She continued to search for a solution to her deadly predicament, and when she struck her head on the tool chest again, she knocked one of its drawers loose. Hands shaking, she yanked it open all the way and reached inside. A groan rumbled in her throat as she found nothing but a stack of technical manuals and a plastic tub full of 3A fuses. There was nothing to help her.

The last thing she found sitting in the drawer was a paperback-sized picture frame with a photograph inside. It took only a moment for her to recognise the two men staring back at her.

The first was clearly Claypole – a tall, dark-eyed skeleton wearing a stupid black hat. The other man was smaller, bright-eyed and smiling. It was Brent Busey. Invite the Wolf's very first target and the star of episode one. The first person they had ever ambushed on camera.

A new movie played in her head, one where a friendly oddball of a man failed to realise the severity of the crime he had attempted to commit. By the end of the episode, Brent Busey had been howling like a baby and claiming to be frightened of Alfie.

But Alfie hadn't cared. He focused only on the fact Brent had attempted to meet up with a twelve-year-old boy named... named...

"Fuck!" she whispered to herself, unable to keep her shock silent. "Are Brent Busey and Claypole related?"

Sadie dropped the picture frame back in the drawer and clawed at the knot around her ankles. If she didn't free herself soon, the inside of this van might be the last thing she ever saw.

Alfie. Alfie, I need you.

THIRTEEN

Alfie found more candles, illuminating the Barn's interior with a warm tangerine glow. Outside was as pitch-black as tar.

Jay stood at the window, Alfie in the kitchen. Neither had spoken for the last twenty minutes.

"Do you see him?" Alfie finally asked, carrying a candle over on a saucer. The hot wax gave off an oddly comforting odour, reminding Alfie of his childhood when his mum would sometimes forget to top up the electricity meter and the lights would go out. They would light candles and read *Beano* comics together until bedtime.

"What do you suppose he's up to?" Alfie asked, staring out the window but seeing nothing but a lonely moon.

"Waiting to kill us, bro. What d'you think?"

"I was hoping he might have gone on a break."

Jaydon chuckled, but it was a weak sound.

Alfie licked his lips and squinted, trying to see a little better. "What if he's doing something awful to Sadie? We can't just stay here and do nothing. It could be days before anyone drops by, and even then it's only likely to be the bloody postman."

Jay turned to him. "I can't even think straight, Alfie. I feel like a frikkin' mouse, and there's a cat watching us and waiting for us to break cover. Just like Ez did."

"I let him die," Alfie said evenly. "I stood there and let it happen."

"At least you were out there. I didn't even make it past the doorway." He put his hands on his head and arched his back, letting out a muffled groan. His eyes were bloodshot, his cheeks sallow. "We'll grieve later. After we find a way out of this."

Alfie peered around the empty kitchen and then up at the vaulted ceiling with its thick wooden beams. "There's got to be a way. I keep telling myself that Claypole is just a man, and if he's just a man, we can find a way to beat him. We just need to get our heads sorted and—"

A thud at the window made them both jump.

What the hell?

Claypole appeared behind the window, his pale face pressed flat against the glass.

"Fuck you, you freak!" Jaydon yelled as he backed up against the kitchen counter. "Get the hell out of here."

Alfie didn't react. This was about instinct now. Animal behaviour. Wolf vs wolf. Flight vs fight.

And I choose to fight. It's the only option left when you're backed into a corner.

Claypole pulled away from the window, his pale face darkening in the shadows.

The window thudded again. A second face pressed up against the glass.

Jaydon recoiled. "Oh shit, bro!"

Ezra's gormless dead face stared in at them through the window, his punctured left eye like a crushed black olive. His lips were papery and flat, while tangles of bloody spaghetti dangled from his ragged neck hole.

Alfie turned his head and puked on the tiles, but forced himself to immediately straighten back up. He refused to look away. Claypole wouldn't make him run this time.

Claypole pressed Ezra's face against the glass and dragged his head around by its ginger braids. His nose flared like a pig's snout against the glass, his squashed lips like two pale worms.

Then Ezra's head fell from sight, dropped in the dirt like a piece of rubbish.

Alfie clutched his windpipe, trying to keep his gorge from rising. *He's the Devil. He's evil.*

Something else struck the window.

Alfie might've puked a second time if not for the fact his stomach was empty.

Claypole wiped a hand back and forth across the window as if he were cleaning it, but instead of suds, he smeared a fistful of intestines over the glass. Ezra's insides.

"The fuck, bro." Jaydon began retching. "F-fucker ain't human. How can he be?"

Blood and gore coated the window, caked on from corner to corner.

Once Claypole was done, he reappeared at another window, smearing a fresh batch of offal over the glass.

"He's blinding us," Alfie said. "He's covering up the windows so we can't see out. "We need to escape."

"How bro? How do we get out of here without him seeing us? Or without us falling into one of his traps like Ez did?"

"We need to get inside the garage. If we can get to the quad bikes, we might be able to ride out of here."

Jaydon's eyes widened manically. "Yeah, yeah, or we could get the power back on and send an email or something. B-but how can we get in there? We can't go outside."

Alfie glanced at the central ceiling beam and followed it to where it terminated against the end wall.

No, they go through *the wall. Right through into the loft space of the garage.*

Alfie spat a mouthful of bile on the kitchen tiles, unable to keep his stomach from rebelling any longer. Ezra's intestines were still sliding down each of the windows. Once he got a hold of himself, he grabbed Jaydon by the shoulder. "I have an idea. How's your leg?"

Jaydon put a bit of weight on his knee and immediately winced. "Just tell me what the hell I have to do to get the hell out of here."

Alfie told him what he was thinking.

———

Sadie gasped when she found a long-shafted screwdriver sitting inside another of the tool cabinet's drawers. Not as good as a blade, but it was at least something she could defend herself with or...

Immediately, she started hacking at the ropes around her ankles. The screwdriver was ill-suited to the task, and she had to use both hands to keep it steady, but little by little, the fibres began to fray. All she needed was time. Time to cut the rope and get the hell out of there.

But where is here? *Am I still at the farm, or did Claypole take me someplace else? Why has he left me here alone?*

"Come on, come on." Sadie cursed at the rope, wishing for it to magically disintegrate, wishing that it wasn't so slow. She had no way of knowing when Claypole would be back. But, with no other option, she continued hacking away, slicing at the ropey fibres.

Where is Claypole right now? Has he hurt Alfie? Jaydon and Ezra?

What was the maniac capable of? Kidnap and assault, clearly, but what about murder? How far did he intend to take this madness?

Please be all right, guys.

Still working the screwdriver, Sadie studied the technical equipment around her inside the dimly lit space. Were the contraptions part of Claypole's job, or did he use them to stalk and molest people regularly? Maybe this kind of thing was his hobby.

Were we right to go after him? Or stupid?

Ice flowed through Sadie's veins, the onset of anger. She always imagined rage to be hot, but the opposite was true. Anger was a chilly thing.

Time passed by like a lover's touch, lingering yet fleeting. After a while, Sadie didn't know if minutes or hours had gone by. Eventually, blessedly, the rope fibres snapped apart and she was able to untie her ankles.

Her feet hit the floor with a thud. The blood rushed back into her ankles and brought an ache. But then came relief – the relief of a wolf gnawing off its own paw to escape a trap. The pain was a victory.

The relief was short-lived, for she wasn't out of the woods yet. No longer tied up, sure, but still trapped.

She rooted amongst the equipment, searching for something besides straight metal edges and plastic knobs – something that might allow her to send an email or make a call. Like a naïve child, she tried willing a mobile phone into existence. It left her flabbergasted when she actually found one – or at least something resembling one.

The handset she had pulled from the drawer of the second tool cabinet was an old-fashioned thing, with rubber number keys and a green LCD panel, and it reminded Sadie of the old Nokia her dad had always kept in the kitchen junk drawer.

She pressed a key and the LCD screen lit up, showing the

time to be 11:09. There was a tiny image of a satellite spinning in the lower right corner.

"It's a sat phone," she surmised. "Why would Claypole need one of these?"

Sadie had never used a sat phone before, and she prayed it wasn't complicated. Calling 999 would be the obvious thing to do, but they might ask her endless questions and take up time she might not have. She also didn't know exactly where she was and assumed they would be unable to trace a sat phone.

The little satellite stopped spinning. A small black tick appeared beside it. Did that mean it was connected? Could she make a call?

Officer Kilmani gave me her card. Do I still have it?

After receiving the officer's business card, Sadie had put it in her card wallet that she almost always kept with her. Reaching inside her jeans pocket, she felt the small leather wallet inside. "Yes! Thank you, thank you."

She found Kilmani's card and quickly keyed in the number. But when she pressed the small green telephone button to make the call, nothing happened.

"No. No. Please. Why isn't it working?"

She wracked her brain until a possible solution came to her.

The country code.

If the phone connected to a satellite instead of a cell tower, she was essentially making an international call rather than a local one. The satellite needed to know where on earth she wanted to call.

She typed in Officer Kilmani's number, but replaced the first number – 0 – with the UK's country code – 44.

The phone made a beeping sound, then clicked repeatedly. Sadie squeezed the handset so tightly her knuckled bulged.

Her senses were so heightened that she could smell the oily residue on the bolts keeping the van's panels together.

"H-hello? This is Police Sergeant Kilmani? Who is this?" The voice sounded tired, as if the woman had just been woken up. Sadie didn't care about the inconvenience.

"Officer Kilmani! It's Sadie. Sadie Chase from the Barn. I need help. Claypole came back and—"

The floor tilted backwards. The van's rear springs squeaked.

"Oh no. No, he's here. He's coming."

The van's back doors swung open. The air turned colder.

A shadow leapt inside. Rushed towards her.

The floor bounced like a trampoline.

Sadie could say nothing else as a bony hand swatted the phone out of her grasp. A heavy boot struck her in the stomach and sent her crashing against the rear wall. She collapsed in a breathless scream, her palms flat against the wooden floor panels.

Claypole glared down at Sadie with the Devil's eyes. Naked from the waist up, his chest and arms were stained almost black with some kind of thick crud.

Blood. He's covered in blood.

Claypole stamped on the sat phone, causing it to come apart. "Wrong number," he growled, and then grabbed Sadie, screaming, by her hair.

———

"Just jump." Alfie reached out a hand. "You're almost there."

Jaydon perched atop the living room sofa, which they had placed on its end against the Barn's western wall, creating a sort of ladder. On the other side of the wall was the garage – and possible freedom if the quad bikes were still in working order. Alfie had already climbed up onto the roof beam, but Jaydon, with his injured leg, was struggling to join him there.

Their plan was to cut, bash, or stomp their way through the upper wall into the garage. Old photographs Alfie remembered seeing of the Barn before the conversion had shown a vaulted ceiling with supporting walls at each of the far ends. That meant the barrier between the house and the garage was likely little more than an insulated stud wall or partition.

"My leg," Jaydon said with pain in his voice. "Damn thing won't let me jump."

"Just... force yourself."

Alfie reached down as far as he could, his fingertips tickling against Jay's and making him think, unhelpfully, about that famous painting of God and man.

"All right, bro. Get ready to hoist me up. One... two... three!"

Jaydon's jump was pitiful, but the momentum allowed Alfie to grab his wrist and yank him upwards, high enough for him to hook both elbows over the ceiling beam. From there, he managed to place his hands flat and press himself up and over, straddling the wood like the back of a stallion.

Alfie steadied Jaydon as he tensed his thighs against the beam. The wood was strangely cold, as if the dark brown paint had sealed off its ability to absorb heat.

"What do we do now?" Jaydon asked, looking down anxiously. "Other than try not to break our damned necks."

"We spoon." Alfie pulled out the stainless steel tablespoon he'd taken from the kitchen and started scraping at the plaster. It chipped away easily, turning chalkier once he got through the paint. Dust filled the air, and he had to turn his head to avoid breathing it in. Jaydon straddled the beam closely behind him and reached out to get at another patch of wall with a separate spoon. It was a strangely intimate moment, and one that might have made Alfie uncomfortable if not for their absolute need to do this.

I could throw Jay off right now and watch his head splat on the tiles below. After what he did, he deserves it.

And then it would be me left alone to face Claypole.

They scraped and scraped and scraped until they had dug a dinner-plate-sized hole in the wall. When Alfie bashed his fist against the divot, it felt brittle. They might even break through sooner than he'd hoped. Then, it would be a short yet precarious climb down the other side into the garage, where they would try to get the power back on or escape on the quad bikes.

Jaydon wiped his forehead with the back of his forearm. "I'm getting hot, bro. This shit is hard work."

Alfie put a palm against the wall, tilting his head and concentrating. "The wall's warm."

"What you mean, bro? The wall is warm?"

"I might be imagining it, but the plaster feels like it's giving off heat."

"Maybe Claypole's whacked the heating up to smoke us out, like they do with hostage takers and shit."

Alfie shook his head. "No, that's not it. Oh... Oh, shit."

"What, bro? What is it? Don't freak me out."

There was a faint crackling sound coming from the other side of the wall.

Dread filling his chest, Alfie lashed out and punched the plasterboard as hard as he could. Tiny fissures appeared around where his fist had landed, so he struck the same spot again. And again. And again.

By the time his fist broke through the wall, his knuckles were torn and bleeding, but it was just another wound to add to the list. His forearm had lodged in the plaster, and his hand dangled in the warm air beyond. For a moment, he feared he was stuck, and that Claypole would suddenly slice off his hand unseen. He ended up yanking his arm back so forcefully that he almost went tumbling backwards off the beam. Jaydon had to steady him.

He could have let me fall. Have Sadie all to himself...

"Thanks."

Wispy grey smoke billowed through the hole in the wall, catching both of them in the face and making them splutter. The heat was now obvious.

"He's set fire to the garage," Jaydon said, scooting backwards on the beam. "We need to get the hell out."

Alfie turned and grabbed his friend's thigh. "Wait! That's what he's planning on. We can't see out the windows, and now he's set a fire next door. He wants us panicking in here like rats, until we eventually have no choice but to run blindly outside."

"I ain't burning, bro." Jaydon scooted back further and flattened his chest against the wood, ready to get down. "So if that's his plan, it worked."

"Just hold on a sec."

"No way, bro. That smoke is gonna choke us unconscious if we don't—" He slid off the beam and tried to catch himself in order to dangle and drop, but he only got a partial grip and barely slowed himself at all before he landed on the tiles below. The screaming was immediate.

"Ah, my knee. Shit! Oh God."

Alfie tried to see through the hole in the wall, but there was too much heat and smoke billowing through. His home was about to go up in flames. The only question was whether he went up with it.

Jay's right. We have to go outside.

Alfie carefully lowered himself from the beam and dropped down onto the tiles with only a brief shock to his ankles. But Jaydon was clutching his knee and hissing, his crash landing having done his injured knee no favours.

"I think it's broken, bro. I broke my knee."

"Can you break a knee?" Alfie shook himself. "You gotta suck it up, Jay. We got to get out of here before we burn."

Jaydon's face was a picture of misery, but he nodded.

The flames had started to lick through the hole in the eaves, seeking fresh oxygen.

"Let's get you up, Jay."

"Yeah, just..." He wrapped his arm around Alfie's neck while Alfie hoisted him up like a deadweight.

"Jesus, mate, how much have you been eating?"

"Screw you, bro. It's all muscle. Fuck, my leg hurts."

"I know, man. Just focus on getting out of here."

Together, they stumbled towards the front door.

"S-shouldn't we go out the back, bro?"

"Claypole's probably planned for us coming out of either door."

"What do we do once we get outside? I can't run, Alfie."

"Running isn't going to help us. Right now, all I can think to do is beg." He pulled the tablespoon from his pocket, now sharp around the edges from scraping it against the wall. Perhaps if he was lucky he might manage to slice Claypole's neck.

A spoon versus a machete.

As they reached the front door, a strobe of light caused them both to stumble and shield their eyes. The windows were still crusted with Ezra's insides, but they didn't block everything. Alfie leant forward, tilting his head to try to see through the gaps. "Are those... are those headlights?"

Jaydon's eyes went wide. "You think someone's coming? Someone good?"

"It has to be a trick. Claypole's messing with us."

"Maybe someone saw the fire in the garage."

"No. No, you can't see the Barn from the road. Our nearest neighbour is a mile away."

Jaydon shook his head at Alfie as if he were an idiot. "It's night, bro. Fire lights up the sky. Someone must have seen it from far away."

Alfie looked up at the flames coming through the wall. His sweat-damp T-shirt suggested the garage blaze was fierce. Perhaps Jay was right and someone had seen the flames lighting up the sky.

The strobe became a static, glaring light, and over the cracking and popping of the ravenous fire, Alfie could hear a car engine idle to a stop.

Then came the most welcome sound in the world.

Officer Kilmani's voice.

"Sadie Chase? It's Sergeant Kilmani. You called my number. Where are you? Sadie? Are you in danger?"

Jaydon and Alfie looked at each other, and a spark of hope passed between them.

Sadie managed to call for help. She escaped.

"Sadie, I'm going to get the fire brigade out here right now, but call out to me first, okay? Let me hear that you're okay."

Jaydon threw himself forward, almost falling as he seemed to forget he only had one good leg. He unlocked the front door and yanked it open with a desperate squeal. Alfie had to lunge to keep him from falling. "Yo, calm down. We don't even know—"

"Officer Kilmani! We need help."

Kilmani shielded her brow, trying to see them in the flickering glow of the fire that made the night seem more like dawn.

"Over here, over here." Jaydon stepped out of the doorway, forcing Alfie to do the same as he had both arms wrapped around his waist.

Kilmani had a radio up near her mouth, but she lowered it when she saw them both staggering out the doorway. "What's going on? You two need to get away from there right now. The entire building is about to go up in flames."

Alfie shielded his face from the burning air that was spreading out from the garage. The night sky was orange, and thousands of fairy-like embers floated in the air.

Kilmani shouted again. "Over here. Quickly!"

"Wait!" Alfie's stomach turned. "Are you alone? Is it just you?"

Kilmani took a step forward, moving in front of her car that she had parked a few metres behind Alfie's Stelvio. It wasn't a squad car, it was her personal car. She wasn't in uniform either. Where's Sadie?" she yelled out. "Is she hurt?"

"Call for backup," Alfie cried. "Claypole killed Ezra and set fire to the Barn."

Kilmani froze. She stared at them blankly for a moment, her face flame-lit, but then she nodded urgently and put the radio back to her mouth. "Okay, kids. Just stay calm. I'm calling for backup."

But instead of calling it in, she proceeded to drop the radio and stumble sideways – an odd, unnecessary movement that was made even stranger by the contorted expression on her face. Her eyes turned into mirrors, reflecting the flames above the house.

Alfie couldn't bear the heat from the garage any longer – it was cooking him alive – so he grabbed a hold of Jay and started forward, fleeing the only sanctuary they had left.

Kilmani dropped to her knees. Her stare was vacant, as if she'd downed a bottle of vodka and washed it down with sleeping pills. It was too far away to hear, but she seemed to be muttering something under her breath.

"O-Officer?" Alfie asked. "Are you okay?"

Kilmani collapsed face down in the gravel in front of her car.

In the near darkness, someone softly howled.

Alfie dragged Jaydon along as quickly as he could, not having a plan other than to not stand still.

"Get her car keys," Jaydon said, pointing to Kilmani's prone body. "Her car keys, bro!"

"She's too far."

"You think we can just limp our way out of this?"

Alfie ground his teeth. "Damn it!"

He left Jaydon balancing on one foot and raced for Kilmani. Claypole hadn't yet revealed himself. Perhaps he was far enough away that Alfie could make it to Kilmani's keys before getting butchered and killed. Then it would only be the simple matter of hopping in Kilmani's car and speeding the hell out of there.

But what about Jaydon? No way will I have time to go back for him.

Alfie peered left and right into the darkness that fought with the glow from the fire. Still no sign of Claypole, but the wolflike howling had stopped.

He made it to Kilmani.

He dropped to his knees, panting, and rolled the woman onto her back. He gave her a shake, but she didn't respond. There was a coin-sized dent between her eyes leaking blood. Alfie reached into her pockets and rummaged around. When he found her car keys, he leapt up triumphantly and jangled them in the air to show Jay. "Jay, I got 'em. I—"

Something bit the back of his hand, striking bone. He dropped the keys and grabbed his fist, hissing in pain.

One of the windows of Kilmani's car shattered. Glass shards rained down onto the gravel.

Alfie tried to pick up the keys, but something struck the

ground mere inches from his fingertips and forced him to recoil.

Another projectile struck Kilmani's car bonnet with a loud *bonk!*

"He's shooting at us." Alfie backed off, not knowing where the danger was coming from. He ducked down between Kilmani's car and his.

Jaydon hopped on one leg, trying to escape the growing blaze behind him. "Your car? Do you have your keys?"

"Yeah. In my pocket. But it's blocked in."

"It's our only chance, bro. Come on."

Alfie raced back towards the Barn and gathered Jaydon around the waist. Then the two of them made for the Stelvio as quickly as they could manage, projectiles pinging and hitting the driveway all around them.

"What the fuck is going on?" Jaydon screamed.

Claypole appeared out of the shadows, further down the driveway, beyond Kilmani's car. He was topless, his pale chest glistening. He swung something over his head in a tight circle, over and over again – around and around. Then he suddenly flicked his arm in their direction.

Alfie got bitten again, this time on the collarbone. He howled in agony, but kept on moving.

Claypole was at least thirty metres away. Still a chance to make it to Alfie's car.

"He's slinging rocks at us," Jaydon said.

Claypole reached into a bag at his hip and loaded something into a strap hanging over his arm. Then he began that swinging motion again. Around and around his head.

"Shit!" Alfie said. "Duck."

They stooped, and a stone sailed over their heads, disappearing into the night behind them. Alfie lunged for his car and grabbed the driver's side door handle. It unlocked automatically, lights flashing and the wing mirror unfolding. "Jay, get in!"

Both of them dived inside the car and slammed the doors behind them, Alfie in the driver's seat, Jaydon a passenger behind him.

Silence.

Alfie ducked behind the steering wheel, peering up at the windows and waiting for one of them to shatter. His hand was on fire and his collarbone felt snapped in two.

Jaydon was wheezing in the back seat. "Who the fuck uses a sling?"

"He's stopped firing. Do you think he's out of ammo?"

"You mean stones? That he can pick up off the ground. Get us out of here, bro. Come on!"

Alfie tossed his keys into the central cup holder, put his foot on the brake and thumbed the START button. They both cheered as the V6 engine grumbled awake and the automatic headlights switched on. For whatever reason, Claypole had neglected to tamper with the battery.

Alfie put the car in drive and put his foot on the accelerator. The vehicle lurched forward.

He stamped on the brake.

In the back, Jaydon fell into the footwell. "What the hell?"

Alfie stared through the windscreen. "Sadie?"

Jaydon struggled to right himself, groaning. "Bro, why'd you stop?"

"We can't leave," was all he could say.

Claypole dragged Sadie along behind him by a rope attached to his ankles. Slowly, he positioned her on the driveway in front of Alfie's car. The Barn, burning behind him, was like a portal to Hell, and Claypole was a demon spilled from it. He dropped the rope and let Sadie's legs flop in front of her, and then he reached down and grabbed her by her hair, forcing her to sit up like a floppy teddy bear. His naked chest was so caked in blood that he looked like some kind of feral tribesman.

Jaydon pushed himself into the gap between the front seats. When he saw what was happening, he reached out and grabbed Alfie's arm. "No. Please..."

Alfie tried to swallow but couldn't, nor could he take a breath.

Claypole raised a bloody hand.

And slapped Sadie across the face so hard that her head spun.

FOURTEEN

Alfie didn't think twice. He tumbled out of the car and staggered forward. "You win," he yelled. "I give up. Just let Sadie go. You said we could make a deal, right?"

Sadie was out cold from the meaty, open-palmed slap, and when Claypole let go of her hair she flopped lifelessly onto her back. He then turned to face Alfie, his body framed by the raging inferno behind him. "I changed my mind. No deals."

"This is between you and me, Claypole. You blame me for putting your brother in prison. You want revenge."

Claypole, for the first time, appeared close to human. His vengeance ebbed, and a flash of sadness appeared in his eyes. "You act like you care about justice, but really it's about the power, isn't it? The destruction you cause, you revel in it, gleefully stretching out your victim's misery in the name of *content*." He said the last word like he was trying to pass a tonsil stone. "On the night two thugs stabbed my brother to death in his cell, you were probably screwing your sweet little girlfriend here on a bed on money and thinking about whose life to destroy next."

A roof timber snapped like a giant's fingers. The Barn's roof slanted inwards and released a legion of fresh embers into the throbbing sky.

Alfie blinked as the heat dried out his eyes. "I didn't know Brent had died." He let his hands drop to his side. "And you're right, it was never about justice; I wanted to destroy your brother."

"Brent was little more than a child himself." Claypole looked Alfie in the eye, the machete rotating back and forth at his side. "He didn't understand a lot of things, didn't always understand right from wrong."

"That doesn't make him innocent."

"Nor does it make you."

Alfie was short of breath, so his words came out rapidly. "It's not my fault a pair of fourteen-year-old girls came forward after seeing my video online. Brent would barely have got a slap on the wrist if not for crimes I didn't even know about. Brent only had himself to blame."

"Amanda Clay and Jess Pole. Children posing as whores."

"Children all the same." Alfie curled his lip in disgust. "So that's where the name's from, huh? Clay-Pole. Must have taken you all day to come up with that."

"So simple, and yet you didn't see it. Guess you're not so smart either."

"Smart enough to trick your brother and expose him for the monster he was."

Claypole raised his machete and pointed it at Alfie. Embers descended upon him, landing on his bony shoulders and fizzing out. "Brent had goodness inside him. He was no monster."

Alfie chose to stay quiet.

Claypole's face darkened as he continued. "He was my little brother."

Alfie finally saw it. The reason for everything. "You blame yourself."

"Of course I do! Of course I blame myself. But I blame you more, Alfie Everett. I blame you for profiting from my brother's misery and ruining his life for entertainment. You're as much a predator as those you go after."

Alfie took a step forward. "Bullshit. All I do is expose people for what they are."

"How has it felt these last few days, hmm? Having your darkest secrets dug up and broadcast over the Internet?"

"Pretty awful, I admit. You've ruined my reputation, destroyed my livelihood, and killed my best friend. What fucking more do you want? Let Sadie and Jaydon go and we can finish this." He looked up at the almost-but-not-quite full moon, then back at Claypole. "You've won. Let this be the end of it."

Sadie rolled onto her side, leaking blood from her mouth. "A-Alfie?"

Alfie reached out to her, but didn't step any closer. "Sadie? It's okay. Everything is going to be all right. You're going to get up and join Jaydon in my car, understand? Go now."

Claypole waved his machete. "No, they can walk. Should take them, what, an hour or so to reach the nearest neighbour? Jaydon's leg doesn't look he'll be running, so that leaves plenty of time for you and me to have some fun, Alfie."

Alfie clutched his wounded hand and tried to keep from trembling. The pain in his body was already too much to bear; how much more awaited him? He'd already given up on the thought of trying to defend himself with a sharpened spoon.

"Just let them go."

"But where's the fun in that?" Claypole whirled around and did the unthinkable: he slashed his machete at Sadie's face. She screamed in pain and grabbed her ear, but her anguish clearly meant nothing to him. "Get up and go," he growled. "Before I slice you apart, girl."

Alfie motioned with his hand. "Sadie, quickly."

For a moment, she clutched her face and sobbed on her knees, but then she climbed to her feet and stumbled towards Alfie like a zombie.

"A-Alfie, I..."

He shushed her. "It's okay. Just go."

Jaydon was standing outside the car. He motioned at Sadie to come to him and then glanced at the open driver's-side door. Claypole took three steps forward and pointed his machete. "I'll have both your hands before you can even grip the wheel, boy. Now get walking."

Alfie looked back at Jay and nodded. "Find help. Maybe it'll get here in time."

"Bro..."

"Get Sadie someplace safe."

Jaydon bent forward, as if he were about to vomit. He then gathered Sadie in his arms and led her gently away, limping with every step. Alfie wasn't even sure Sadie knew what was happening from the dazed way she was walking.

"Get down on your knees, boy. It's time for you to repent."

Alfie glanced back one last time, making sure Sadie and Jaydon were well on their way. They had already made it to the end of the driveway and were starting up the dirt path towards the hill.

As demanded, Alfie dropped to his knees. "You don't need to do this, Claypole. Haven't you hurt enough innocent people?"

"Innocent people perhaps, but there's one guilty person left to punish before I call it a night." He shoved the machete's tip into Alfie's collarbone and twisted.

Instead of screaming, which every cell of his body begged

him to do, Alfie bit down on his lip and moaned low down in his belly. If Jaydon and Sadie heard him, they might turn around and come back to save him, which would be a fatal mistake. The only thing left to salvage from this nightmare was his last two friends in the world escaping with their lives.

"You're trying to be brave," Claypole said, smirking. "Like your friend, Ezra, right before I sliced his throat."

Despite the whizzing sparks of agony racing up and down his collarbone, Alfie managed to glare. "You're no different from me. This isn't justice, it's vengeance. You enjoy other people's pain. You murdered those children!"

Claypole removed his machete and frowned. "What kids? Oh, you mean the ones whose names are now written all over your car?" A twinkle in his eye. "They all went missing, yes, but not because of me. They were taken by the same man who took your sister."

"W-what?"

"You thought she was the only one, Alfie? You thought he took one child and stopped? Ha! The police might not have connected the dots, but it's obvious when you look at them. Those children met the same fate as your sweet little sister, Daisy."

Alfie's world spun. He teetered back and forth on his knees. "W-why did you write their names on my car?"

Claypole bent at the middle and stared Alfie right in the eye. "To torture you. To let you know that the man who destroyed your life continued preying on innocent victims for years after he left you alone in that car park. But instead of going after *him*, you wasted your time on pathetic, bleating lambs like my brother. Because you were afraid."

Alfie was afraid. He was afraid right now, but tried not to give in to it. "You think your brother was pathetic?"

"He was an embarrassment to me. I joined the army as soon as I was old enough just to get away from him." He raised his machete and licked his lips. "But he was still my little brother, the same little kid I used to push on the swings. I still remember the sound of his laughing. It echoes in my head when I try to sleep. Maybe after this, your screams will be the echo I hear."

Claypole pushed the machete back into Alfie's collarbone, wrenching out more misery. More pain.

Fifty metres beyond, his home collapsed into fiery rubble. The air grew hotter and hotter.

He was in Hell.

———

During their clumsy attempts to flee along the dirt path, Sadie and Jaydon fell upon an unexpected survivor.

Kilmani was crawling aimlessly through weeds, a hundred metres from her car. Blood covered her face, and when they approached her, she couldn't seem to properly focus her eyes. But she was conscious. So Sadie and Jaydon did their best to drag her along with them, a trio of shell-shocked survivors trying to find cover.

"Are you okay?" Sadie asked the women when they stopped to catch their breath. Her mind had been muddy since waking up, but it was gradually righting itself, which made the horror of the situation increasingly real and less dreamlike.

"W-what's happening?" Kilmani murmured. "Who... who..."

"It's Claypole," Jaydon said, his voice fraught – desperate and tired. "He killed Ezra and the security guy who installed our cameras. Probably more. We need to get the police here. Lots of police."

Sadie fell backwards on her backside. The grass was cold,

but dry, the sky overhead a mixture of dark blues and oranges. "What? Ez is... He's...?"

Jaydon looked her in the eye. "He's gone, Say. There was nothing we could do."

Crying was a useless thing, but something she was powerless to fight as hot tears spilled from the corners of her eyes. She collapsed onto her back and covered her face with her hands. "No. No, no, no."

Ez can't be dead. He can't be dead.

Please no.

Jay sat on the grass beside her and rubbed her arm. His touch was both welcome and annoying. It offered comfort, but reminded her of her shame.

I'm a bad person. I deserve everything that's happening.

Kilmani alerted them with a groan. The woman lifted her radio to her mouth and called for backup. Nothing came back in response. She tried again, and again, but each time they were met with nothing more than silence.

Jaydon put a hand on Kilmani's wrist, indicating she should stop trying the radio. "Claypole's done something to jam everything. Phones ain't working – radios neither, by the looks of it."

She winced, closing her eyes and gritting her teeth. "I-I probably have concussion. I'm too dizzy to stand. If my brain is swelling, I... You two need to go get help."

Jaydon flopped backwards in the grass and took a deep breath. He lifted his straight leg a few inches from the ground. Even in the near-dark, Sadie could see how ballooned his knee was. "My leg is completely wrecked. I can't make it any further."

Kilmani turned her head dozily towards Sadie. "Can you make it? Can you walk?"

Sadie rolled up onto her knees, then rubbed at her tear-streaked face, trying to regain the last morsels of her senses.

"Yes, but what about Alfie? We left him back there. I... I can't go without him. I won't."

"We go back there, we die," Jaydon said. "Alfie wanted us to get to safety and bring help. It's the only chance he's got."

Sadie shook her head, then looked towards the Barn blazing in the near distance. "No. We can't abandon him."

"You need to leave here." Kilmani sounded half-asleep, and her left eye didn't quite match the right, but she was adamant in her tone. "I'll keep trying the radio until I find a frequency that works."

And what if you never find one? Sadie thought. *Alfie could die.* She stared at the officer's thick black belt, full of pouches and gizmos. Then she grabbed at it with both hands.

"Hey, what are you doing? Stop!"

She batted away Kilmani's hands and stripped her of the things she wanted – a canister of what must have been CS gas and a collapsible steel baton. "I'm going back. I can't leave Alfie behind with that psychopath."

"You can't take those," Kilmani said, reaching out both hands like a baby. "Give them back."

Sadie got to her feet, which were finally stable beneath her. "You can have them back later when I'm done with them. Keep trying your radio."

Jaydon leapt up onto one leg and nearly fell back down again. "Don't be stupid, Say. Our only chance is getting help."

"And Alfie's only chance is if we go back and save him."

"Save him? Claypole will just kill us all. What good will that do?"

"We started this together, Jay – the channel, living here at the Barn..."

He reached out and grabbed her arm. "Say, I can't let you do this. I-I love you."

She shrugged him off and shook her head in disgust. "Alfie

needs us, and I can't betray him again, Jay. I'm going back, even if it kills me."

Everything about his expression suggested he was going to tackle her to the ground and prevent her from leaving, but instead he nodded. "You're right. We started this together. It ain't on Alfie. It's on all of us."

"Split up the weapons," Kilmani said. "The pepper spray and the baton, one each."

Sadie frowned. "Huh?"

Kilmani sat up a little straighter. "You kids need to get the hell out of here, but if you're stupid enough to go the other way, at least be smart about it. Divide up the weapons, approach that psycho from opposite sides, and make sure you keep him at arm's length while you attack. He's bigger than you, so if he grabs you, you're screwed. You're probably screwed anyway, and that means I am too, seeing as I can't get out of here by myself."

Sadie looked at the officer and realised she was part of this mess as well. Because she had called the woman for help.

And she came.

Without a partner. The idiot.

"If you were able to stand, would you go back to help Alfie?"

"It's my job."

"Well, Alfie is my family. Don't you think that's an even stronger reason for going back?"

Kilmani sighed. "I guess it's duty either way."

Sadie reached out an arm and allowed Jaydon to take it. They nodded a goodbye to Kilmani, who raised her radio and went back to trying to get a call through. Then the two of them hobbled back towards their burning home. Where Claypole was probably going to kill them both.

Duty? Family? Or stupidity? Sadie didn't know which, only that she didn't have a choice.

———

The last remaining sections of the Barn's roof collapsed, birthing a thousand fresh embers and spitting them into the sky. It was impossible to take a clean breath, the air sullied by smoke and ash.

Blood soaked Alfie's face, dripped from his chin and stained his clothing. He held no more delusions that a scar or two would improve his image. This wasn't about clicks and views any more. Only pain and death.

Claypole booted Alfie in the chest, sending him sprawling into the biting gravel. Something hard and irregular dug into his thigh as he landed, and he quickly reached into his hip pocket to remove the source of his pain. He thought it might have been the box with the engagement ring, but that was in his other pocket. It was something else: his phone.

A phone that can't make a call.

Claypole appeared in no rush to kill him. He stood three feet away on the driveway, his face a shadow. "How does it feel, Alfie?" he almost whispered. "Do you think it hurts as much as it did for Brent, when they stabbed and beat him to death?"

"Ask me when you're done." Alfie rolled onto his stomach, a defenceless position but one that somehow felt safe. It allowed him to secretly unlock his phone by shielding it beneath his body.

"How much pain will it take, Alfie? How much suffering until your ego finally shatters and you beg me? Are you even capable of remorse? Humility?"

Alfie remained on his belly, but crawled away slowly to disguise what he was doing. "Y-your vendetta is with a character I play. That's not who I really am."

Claypole's footsteps crunched in the gravel behind him. "We are the characters we play. The faces we wear. The choices we make."

Alfie pushed himself up onto his knees and pivoted one hundred and eighty degrees. He hit *record* on his phone and pointed the lens at Claypole.

Claypole grunted, taken by surprise. "What are you doing?"

Alfie's entire body trembled, but he thrust himself onto his feet with barely enough strength remaining. "A-Alfie Everett here, guys, and this is the final episode of *Invite the Wolf*. Here with me tonight is Claypole83, the biggest, most delusional degenerate we've ever had on the show. He's been trying to avenge his child-molesting brother, Brent Busey, who you might remember from episode one, but he hasn't succeeded in anything but—"

"Quiet!" Claypole's lips curled back like a theatre curtain. He lunged at Alfie, raising the machete above his head – leaving himself exposed.

Alfie ducked and threw a punch. His knuckles thudded against Claypole's ribs, and the sound of air escaping the man in a pained gasp was like a song from the gods. He immediately threw a second gut-punch and bellowed at the top of his lungs. "Motherfucker!"

Claypole clutched his side and staggered backwards, wheezing and raising his machete defensively to keep Alfie at bay.

Alfie shambled after him, his heart thudding like a piston, fuelled by white-hot oil. "I'm not afraid of you, Claypole. The whole Michael Myers act is nothing but a way for you to convince yourself that you're powerful. But you're not powerful, Claypole, you're pathetic and worthless and lonely. If you had any life at all, you wouldn't be doing any of th—"

Claypole let out a demonic roar and swung at Alfie with his machete. The flat, silver blade cut through the air like a guillotine – too rapid to avoid.

Alfie felt cold air against his wrist, but no pain. He stepped back, a little light-headed, but grinning victoriously as he realised the swing had missed. "I'll never beg you, Claypole. Do you know why? Because I don't regret what I did to your brother. Brent got what he deserved. Catching his tears on camera was one of the greatest moments of my life. I pointed the camera right in his face, just like this!" Alfie attempted to raise his phone again, but it was no longer in his hand. Four glistening stumps spurted blood where his fingers had once been. "M-my fingers. W-where are my..."

His stomach churned, his mouth filling with bile that simply sat there, unexpelled. His soul turned cold as the understanding that he had been irreparably changed dawned on him.

He's sliced off my fingers.

Claypole grinned. "Looks like you dropped something there, Sonny Jim."

Alfie couldn't breathe, couldn't even scream. His gaze lowered until he spotted his phone lying face down in the gravel, its red recording light still on and the glinting camera lens pointing up at his face and capturing his misery. Scattered nearby were four chubby white grubs. His fingers.

Don't worry, Sonny Jim. You're next.

Alfie collapsed to his knees. "W-what did you just say?"

Claypole got down on his knees as well. The two of them could have been praying together, close enough to hold hands. "Don't you see the resemblance, Alfie? Haven't you looked into my eyes? Look now."

Alfie studied Claypole's face. Dark, sunken eyes. Crowded teeth. Tall, skeletal frame. "No..."

Fear wrapped his heart, a boa constrictor inside his chest. The last of the fight left him. In fact, he had never truly even been in the fight.

"My uncle went to the grave thinking about you, Alfie. *The one who got away*. Do you know he came for you several times – tried to take you – but you were never alone? A fearful little boy at first, too wary to catch, and then you found your friends and clung to them like a life raft. As time went by, Uncle Mitch got older, and you remained his greatest failure. He was at peace with that for a while, but then..." Claypole shook and tittered, like they were two friends sharing a joke. "Small world, eh?"

Alfie teetered back and forth on his knees. He could still feel his missing fingers, but when he tried to move them, fireworks ignited in his vision. "B-Brent...?"

"Yes, Alfie. Brent and I are the nephews of the man who took your sister. Mitchell spent his final years plagued with gout and a failing heart, watching you on the Internet, powerless to do anything when you destroyed Brent's life. You made my uncle feel powerless. Weak."

Alfie gave an ill-tempered laugh. The heat from the fire wrenched sweat from his every pore now, soaking his back and shoulders. Its loud roar was now a guttural purr, like a well-fed lion returning to sleep. "Your uncle was a monster. I hoped he died soaking in his own piss."

Claypole placed the machete's sharp point against Alfie's Adam's apple and twisted it gently. "My uncle was a great man, the one who taught me how to fish and hunt and kill without hesitation. A wolf amongst lambs." He turned away momentarily, his coal-chunk eyes glistening. "The last time I saw him before he died, he told me about you and your sister. He told me how he kept her alive for weeks."

Alfie groaned. "Stop. Please."

"Stop? But don't you want to know what happened to her? Don't you want to hear how she quietly sobbed at night, bloody and sore? How she called out your name every time it hurt?"

Alfie could feel nothing but the sharp metal at his throat. "You're evil. A demon."

"No, no, Alfie. I'm no demon. Before my uncle died, I was a sergeant in the Royal Signals. Men are alive today because of my actions. I'm a goddamn hero, a veteran of a dozen successful missions, but when you ruined my family, I found a new mission. A new kind of duty." He removed the machete from Alfie's throat and placed it on the ground beside him. Then he moved his hands to his thighs like a kneeling samurai. "I've been waiting a long time for this, boy. Finally putting an end to *the one who got away*."

Alfie couldn't keep his eyes focused. They kept rolling around in their sockets, trying to get away from him. He tried to speak, but his mouth was dry, filled with blood and ashes. Tears evaporated on his cheeks.

Claypole reached up with both hands and removed his hat from his bald, dented head, placing it upside down on the gravel. Something was stuffed inside, something Alfie slowly recognised.

"No..." was all he could say.

Claypole lifted the folded baseball cap and placed it on his head. The last time Alfie had seen the thing was thirteen years ago in the car park of Tanning Stanley Fields. The howling wolf was exactly how he pictured it in his nightmares.

"Are you ready to join your sister, Alfie?"

Alfie nodded. His adrenaline was all burnt out. Even standing seemed impossible now, so why fight? For so long, he had carried this gnawing fear in his stomach, while a clock ticked constantly in his head, counting down to some life-changing tragedy that he had always known was coming. No matter how high he built his life, it had always been destined to come crashing back down. Alfie was ready for the tragedy of his existence to be over.

"I'll make it quick," Claypole said, and then smiled. "Or perhaps I won't."

Alfie didn't look away. He refused to give Claypole that.

I won't beg. I won't scream.

Claypole rose to his feet, his boots crunching in the gravel, seeming to unfold endlessly until he was towering over Alfie like a giant. Even his machete seemed longer, more like a sword than a knife. The sky swirled blood-red above them, as if the heavens were really Hell.

"Get it over with, bitch."

"You had a good run, kid. You should've died thirteen years ago."

The machete rose in the air, displacing swirling embers. The air was so hot that it felt like the earth might begin to boil.

Alfie couldn't help it. He closed his eyes.

Daisy. Will you be there? Will you have forgiven me?

"Fuck you, you crazy motherfucker!"

"Get back!"

Alfie reopened his eyes and saw Claypole inexplicably flailing, wheeling his arms and twisting back and forth. Something was wrong with his face. His eyes were wet, and his dark eyelashes were beaded with liquid.

Sadie appeared on the driveway, thrusting out an arm and spraying something from a canister. Jaydon was there, too; he walloped Claypole around the back of the head with a long black rod. The giant became a man, cowering and trying to cover up as Jaydon whacked him again on the back of the neck. The wolf baseball cap fell from Claypole's head and landed in the gravel. A moment later, Claypole landed in the gravel too.

Alfie struggled to remain on his knees, his body having already accepted death.

What's happening? I told them both to run.

But they came back.

His vision flashing with colours and his ears overwhelmed by sound, Alfie collapsed onto his side and wriggled along like a worm. He found his phone lying nearby and grabbed it, not knowing why, but finding comfort in something that was his.

Need to call help. Need to find a way.

He dialled 999 and begged for the call to go through. When it failed, he rolled onto his back and groaned in defeat. *Can't fight any more. I just want it to end.* He slid his phone into his pocket and lifted his wounded hand up in front of the moon. The bloody stumps glistened silver.

Sadie grabbed Alfie by his T-shirt and fought to get him up. "Alfie! We're getting the hell out of here. Together."

"I told you to leave."

"And I ignored you. Now get up."

Alfie tried to rise, his mind dangling by a thread above a dizzying vortex. Claypole was related to the monster who had taken Daisy. Everything that happened was because of that day at the fair. The past had never been behind him, it had always been spying on him from the shadows.

I'll never be free. It will never not hurt.

Jay continued to brutalise Claypole with the baton, clubbing him over again and again, teeth bared like an enraged barbarian.

Claypole screamed in agony.

It was glorious.

But Alfie wondered what it meant that he could so enjoy someone else's pain. He wondered what it meant for his soul.

Sadie fought to get him to his feet, but he was sure he had enough strength left to keep on living. Strength or desire.

FIFTEEN

Alfie struggled to put one foot in front of the other. He felt empty, light-headed and nauseous. Sadie and Jay weren't in much better shape, with Jay hardly able to place any weight on his bad knee at all and Sadie dizzy from being knocked unconscious. They held on to each other as they shuffled alongside the stream and headed towards the hill, main road, and blessed rescue.

"We need to get Kilmani," Sadie said, pulling them off their current course. "She's injured."

Alfie gasped. "She's alive? I saw her die. Claypole struck her right between the eyes."

"It turned her lights out," Jaydon said, "but she woke up. She's trying to radio for help but can't get a call through because of whatever Claypole did to block everything."

"He's ex-army. A signalman or something, he said. Those are the tech guys, right?"

Jaydon shrugged. "No clue."

"I was in Claypole's van," Sadie said. "There's all of this equipment in the back, stuff that even Ezra would struggle to understand."

Jaydon said, "So our enemy is Rambo with an IT certification? You can't make this sh— ah! Goddamn it..." He suddenly grabbed his knee and forced everyone to stop.

Alfie didn't like delaying and risking Claypole catching up. Jaydon had beaten the son of a bitch unconscious, but unconscious wasn't the same as dead.

Alfie stared back towards the Barn. The blaze had lost none of its gusto, but the flames had dropped several feet and the roof was non-existent. The stone walls were black, the windows all melted to slag. By morning, only scorched earth would remain.

Their empire was gone.

Was it ever even real?

While he waited for Jaydon to finish taking a breather, Alfie's gaze drifted off towards the stream. The lower section reflected the fire, turning the water tangerine. It was the exact spot he had seen Jaydon and Sadie kissing. The memory of it was like a hot coal in his throat.

How did I miss it? How did I not see it happening right under my nose? Do they love each other?

Sadie reached out and took Alfie's arm. "Can you help us?"

Us?

Alfie froze for a moment, but then he shook himself back into the present. Sadie was struggling to hold Jaydon's weight, his arm around her neck and dragging her down. He quickly helped her, grabbing Jaydon underneath his other arm and lifting him back up. Then the three of them got going again, searching for Kilmani.

A featureless black void met them, crimson hellfire at their backs. An additional light appeared to their left, sweeping across the fields and lighting up the near side of the hill. With it came the rising grumble of an engine.

"What is that?" Jaydon stood on one leg and cupped his eyebrows. "Did Kilmani manage to get help?"

The noise and lights were coming from the wrong direction, from the fields and not from the road. "I don't think it's help."

"Oh no," Sadie said, her eyes sparkling white. "It Claypole's van. He's coming."

Alfie gave them both a shove with his injured hand, the stabbing pain almost dropping him. "Hurry."

They hobbled in the direction of the hill, hoping to reach it before Claypole could reach them. It wasn't steep enough to prevent a vehicle traversing it, but it might be enough to slow one down – or maybe even cause it to tip over if driven erratically by a lunatic driver. There was nowhere else to go, regardless.

The van bounced heavily on its springs, the headlights whipping up and down. If what Sadie had said about it being full of tech equipment was true, then it was a charging bull picking up speed.

Maybe it will be slow to turn. Maybe that's our chance.

They reached the bottom of the hill just as Claypole's zigzagging van came into view. Old and white and dirty. A family heirloom.

Just hop on up and get whatever you want.

Candyfloss.

Alfie's legs turned to stone. His escape faltered. He could do nothing as the van that had once sped away with his sister inside now sped towards him.

"We need to move, bro." Jaydon grabbed him.

Alfie tried to shift himself, but his foot struck a rock and he fell without resistance, his muscles seizing up on him and refusing to take any more. Jaydon and Sadie tried to help him, but he batted away their attempts before vomiting into the grass. "G-go! Get out of here."

"Together," Sadie said. "We're getting out of here together."

He waved her away again. "If we stay together, he'll run us all down. Get up the hill. Head for the road." He reached down into the grass and picked up the fist-sized boulder that had tripped him so easily. "I'll... I'll do my best to get away, but I need a minute."

"You have five seconds, bro," Jaydon said, staring off towards the approaching headlights. Demon eyes.

"Then give me that. Don't let him knock us down like bowling pins."

After a short pause, Jaydon and Sadie nodded and carried on up the hill.

Alfie lay panting on the ground, praying for a solution that would finally put an end to this.

Movement occurred near the stream.

Was it Kilmani? Could she possibly help them now? She *was* a police officer, after all.

She can't deal with Claypole by herself.

The best I can hope for is that she gets through on her radio.

The van made a beeline for Alfie. He managed to clamber to his feet, his vision untethered and swaying to and fro like a boat on the ocean. To his right, Jaydon and Sadie hobbled up the hill.

"That's it..." Alfie glared right towards at the incoming van, trying to see Claypole through the windscreen. "I'm the one you want. Come right at me."

The van wasn't particularly fast – and it was ill-suited for the uneven terrain – but it had a weightiness to it that kept it hurtling along. That was good. It gave Alfie a chance. A chance to leap aside at the last possible moment. The van would need time to slow down and turn.

The growling engine got closer and closer. Claypole came

into view, glaring over the steering wheel. A bald psychopath from a family of psychopaths.

Brent, Mitchell, Claypole – how can one bloodline be so tainted?

Seconds left before the van splattered him across the grass.

Need to wait until the last breath.

Can't give him a chance to change course.

Five... four... three... two...

The van careened to the left, suddenly turning and heading up the hill. The rashness of the manoeuvre caused it to tilt precariously on its springs, but the sheer weight of its cargo kept it grounded. Suddenly, Claypole was driving away from Alfie...

...and towards Sadie and Jaydon.

"No, you bastard." Alfie waved his hands like he was trying to flag down a ride. "Over here, over here."

He's going to mow them down in front of me. Hasn't he tortured me enough?

Alfie clambered up the hill on all fours, too weak to sprint.

Jaydon and Sadie realised what was happening and panicked. Quickly realising he had no hope of escape with his dodgy leg, Jaydon pushed Sadie ahead and turned to face the van.

Alfie kept on up the hill, desperate to reach them, wishing he could fly. Wishing he could *run*.

Jaydon balanced on one leg and made a beckoning gesture with both hands. *Bring it on.* The headlights made his eyes glow.

Sadie screamed his name.

Jaydon.

The van's stumpy bonnet struck Jaydon with an awful *clonk* that launched him sideways into an airborne pirouette. He made no sound as he flew, perhaps already dead.

The van lost no speed at all. It carried on up the hill, heading after Sadie.

"You bastard!" Alfie yelled, barely able to get the words out. There was nothing left in his tank. He was cold and dizzy and heavy. Sleep beckoned him absurdly, as if he could simply choose to lie down and close his eyes.

But he couldn't stand by and watch Sadie get hurt. He couldn't stand by and do nothing.

Not again.

In his left hand, he still held the rock. From somewhere deep, he found the strength to stand.

The van careened back and forth, its wheels skidding on the grassy incline. Its hungry bonnet quickly ate up the distance between it and Sadie's tiny frame. Seconds left.

Alfie cried out his entire lung capacity, knowing he was about to see the woman he loved – the woman he had wanted to marry – mown down right in front of him.

I'm going to fail again. You can't stop monsters from feeding. It's stupid to try.

The van skidded, a quarter turn.

Sadie stumbled.

Claypole slammed on the brakes. The van skidded to a stop and he immediately hopped out. Sadie screamed and tried to escape him, but she was too out of breath and her attacker too fast. He wrapped a long arm around her waist and plucked her off her feet, while using his other arm to yank open the van's side panel.

Alfie's heart threatened to burst.

"No. Not again."

Sadie yelled out for Alfie, begging for help. She clawed at Claypole's arm and kicked out with her legs. When he tried to throw her into the back of the van, she grabbed the doorframe and fought with everything she had. But it was only a matter of time before her strength gave out and the beast got her inside.

Alfie broke into a loping sprint. He was still too far away to save Sadie in time, but he could do nothing else but try. He squeezed the rock in his hand so tightly that his fingernails splintered, but the pain only helped him run faster.

"NOT. AGAIN!" Alfie launched himself off his back foot and landed on his front. At the same time, he whipped his arm through the air and released the smooth round boulder from his hand. He was usually right-handed, but he was going to have to learn fast how to use his left.

The boulder skimmed through the air like a flying saucer, the moon a spotlight keeping track of it. Something in Alfie's gut told him it was a good throw – a pure throw – and with every microsecond that passed, he became ever more sure.

The boulder fell out of the sky and pelted Claypole right on the back of his bald, dented skull. The crack echoed across the hill.

Alfie almost cheered.

Claypole released Sadie and staggered sideways, clutching his head with both hands. The blow had clearly knocked him loopy, because his legs crossed over themselves and he strode around in a dizzy circle.

Sadie looked towards Alfie and raced towards him. Claypole swiped at her and missed. Three seconds later she made it halfway down the hill and threw herself against Alfie. Miraculously, he managed to stay standing and catch her. "It's okay," he said. "I've got you."

She turned and pointed. "Jay. He's hurt."

"I know. We need to get down from this hill. I have a plan."

"What? No, we need to make it to the road."

"We'll never make it. We're too badly injured."

Sadie panicked, shaking in his arms and moaning to herself. He grabbed her chin and made her look at him.

"Trust me," he said. "I won't let Claypole hurt you."

"Alfie, I..."

"Babe, can you trust me?"

She got a hold of herself and nodded. "Yes. Yes, I trust you."

He took her hand and led her down the hill. As he did so, he looked back towards Claypole and shouted, "You lose, motherfucker! Just like dear old Uncle Mitch and your pathetic brother, Brent."

Claypole was still clutching his head and staggering around, but this seemed to wake him up. He lowered his hands and glared back and forth until he spotted Alfie and Sadie hurrying down the hill. Predictably, he leapt back inside his van and gunned the engine, waking up the beast.

He came for them again.

"He's right behind us," Sadie moaned. "He's going to catch us."

"No." Alfie clutched her hand and pulled her along, letting gravity toss them into a sprint.

But the van was faster.

"Keep going," Alfie yelled. "Almost there."

"He's going to get us."

Alfie glanced back, but was only able to grab a sense of the van rushing up behind them. Ten metres away, going full pelt. Headlights blinding.

Too fast to stop.

"When I say, jump to your right as far as you can manage."

"What?"

"Jump to your right."

"When?"

"Now!"

Still holding hands, Alfie and Sadie threw themselves

aside. For a second they were flying, the declining ground and their uncontrollable speed helping them achieve an impressive distance before crashing down and tumbling painfully in a tangle of limbs and the *clonking* of heads.

The van hurtled right past them, its large wheels missing their trailing ankles by inches and making the ground vibrate.

Alfie rolled onto Sadie and covered her with his body. "Are you okay? Are you hurt?"

"Alfie, I can't go on. I can't do this."

Alfie lifted his head and watched the van bounce erratically down the hill.

Claypole didn't even see the stream directly ahead.

The van hopped the shallow bank at an awkward angle, clearing the water but not the opposite rise of land. The left front wheel hit the rocky earth first, but the right stayed airborne. With an almighty *crunch*, the van bounced upwards and rotated as the impact tore off part of the fender. Claypole could do nothing as the van flipped sideways and came crashing down on its left, where it proceeded to skid through the dirt like a wounded bull, coming to a stop twenty metres away with its rear wheels still spinning.

Alfie collapsed on top of Sadie, hugging her. "Let it be over," he said. "God, please, let it be over."

———

The van was a mess. Its rear doors had flapped open and an array of shattered equipment littered the grass like the innards of some slain beast. Was Claypole's signal jammer amongst the wreckage?

Alfie reached inside his pocket with his left hand and pulled out his phone. The screen had cracked in the top left corner, and the battery was in its death throes, but it was still working. And it had a signal.

He dialled 999 with his thumb.

The call connected.

Thank God.

Alfie shuffled over to Sadie and handed her the phone. "It's working. Get the police."

She took the phone, almost dropping it, but then she frowned at him. "What are *you* going to do?"

Alfie got to his feet with great effort. "I'm going to finish this."

"Alfie, no."

"Just get the police here, Sadie. Get them *all* here."

As he limped towards the stream, Alfie stared up at the starless sky. He had no idea of the time, but night still reigned supreme. This wasn't over, and his gut told him that Claypole was merely licking his wounds. The crash had been violent, but the driver's side appeared mostly undamaged.

Rather than hop across the stream, Alfie stepped right into the water. Its cold kiss put steel in his stride and added to the numbness of exhaustion.

As he climbed out onto the opposite bank, the van's driver's side door opened towards the sky and Claypole's bald head rose through the gap. He failed, several times, to hoist himself up, before finally managing to extricate himself fully. He slid off the top of the wreckage and landed with a *thump* on the grass.

He's hurt, Alfie realised. *The crash knocked him about worse than I thought.*

Alfie found a second wind that he knew was an illusion. His body was close to giving up, capable only of this one last push. His fingerless right hand and was stiff and swollen. His collarbone throbbed and burned – most likely fractured. Whatever survival instinct his body possessed had put his pain inside a locker at the back of his mind, but it was kicking at the door and would soon get out.

I need to finish this.

The man who took my sister is dead. Brent Busey is dead. Claypole is the last wolf left in a rotten pack.

This is what I do. I invite the wolf.

And then I put it down.

Alfie stopped short of the overturned van. He could have rushed, tried to beat Claypole down before he got to his feet, but that wasn't how he wanted this to go down. He wanted to face Claypole dead on, let the fucker see there was no more fear or shame left inside him to exploit. Whatever decisions Alfie had made in life, they were a part of him now. He could live with the past, because he intended to fight for his future.

Splashing sounds made Alfie turn around. It was Sadie, crossing the stream and staggering towards him. She had his phone up in front of her with the recording light on.

"Sadie, what are you doing?"

"The police are on their way, Alfie. You're live on the channel. Whatever happens now, we're going to show our viewers the truth. This is the final episode."

"It doesn't matter. The channel is finished."

"On our terms. We end this properly."

Alfie stared at the solid red light. If nothing else, streaming the next moments live would provide a record for whatever happened next.

Let people see Claypole in the flesh.

"Keep your distance," he said. "Claypole's hurt, but he's still a psychopath. Anything happens to me, you run, okay?"

Sadie lifted the phone a little higher. "Just make him pay, babe. Make him regret ever messing with us."

Alfie had never seen Sadie be vengeful, and honestly, he didn't hate it. "I love you, babe."

"I... love you too."

Alfie turned and made his way towards Claypole.

The man was on his feet, but his left arm hung limply at

his side and a bone jutted out of his wrist. A ragged gash dissected his forehead.

Alfie spat a mouthful of blood from a slice inside his lip, then let out a chuckle. "Looks like you've been in the wars, Sonny Jim."

Claypole nodded, almost respectfully. "You've got a few injuries yourself, lad. Not such a pretty face any more."

"Ah, plastic surgery don't cost that much. I'll just spend some of the money I made ambushing your brother."

"You've learned nothing."

"You're finished, Claypole."

"Oliver."

"What?"

"Oliver Busey. You should know my name before I kill you."

"I'll put it on your obituary."

"I lost my machete." Claypole pulled something from his belt – another knife, but shorter and less curved. "Now it's going to take longer to gut you."

Alfie was done with words. He looked up at the moon and howled, then raced forward with his head down. Claypole swiped at him with the knife, but he dodged inside and tackled him around the waist. He couldn't get the taller man off his feet, but the impact was enough to knock the wind out of him. Taking the advantage, Alfie whipped his head back and caught Claypole underneath the chin.

Claypole snarled and tried to toss Alfie aside, but they were locked together, dancing back and forth while both trying to lead. Alfie started to gain the upper hand – until Claypole jammed a thumb into his torn cheek and forced him to recoil. A fatal mistake.

Alfie felt a punch under his ribs. He let out a gasp, but couldn't take a breath in again. Stars erupted in his vision and a coldness washed over him.

Claypole pulled back his arm, revealing the bloody knife in his hand. Blood covered his face as he snarled at Alfie. "You're not big enough to take on this dog." His breath was like rotten meat. "You don't have the bite for it."

"Y-you're... wrong." Alfie wrapped his arms around Claypole tightly and squeezed, trapping their bodies together in a bear hug. Then he bit down on Claypole's neck like a flesh-hungry zombie, clamping his teeth together with all the strength his jowls could muster. Skin, fat, and then gristle gave way. Tiny bones crunched. Alfie's mouth filled with blood, but rather than disgust him, it awoke a pit bull inside him that refused to let go. He bit deeper and harder, deeper and harder, wrenching gargling screams from Claypole's throat as hot, metallic blood gushed from his jugular. Some of the hot liquid made it down Alfie's throat, like bitter tea.

Alfie felt another punch, this time in his thigh. The pain made him gasp and release his bite. He stumbled backwards, his leg threatening to give out.

Claypole held his neck, blood spurting through his fingers. "Y-you animal."

Alfie spat blood, feeling it coat his teeth. The bloody knife now jutted out of his leg. He yanked it free and tossed it aside, opened his arms wide. "Let's finish this."

Claypole charged, throwing himself at Alfie and forcing him backwards. Alfie fought to stay on his feet, beating at his enemy's back and grabbing him in a headlock. Sadie called out his name fearfully, but he could do nothing to comfort her, only try to ensure she survived this dreadful, endless night.

The floor disappeared beneath Alfie's feet. He fell backwards through the air, twisting sideways right before he hit the stream. Claypole landed beside him.

Icy water covered Alfie's face, snaking inside his ears and nostrils and filling him up. He choked out a bubble of oxygen, his chest tightening with panic. Sharp rocks and sticky gravel scratched at his arms as he tried to find the stream bed.

He exploded from the water, gasping.

Claypole was beside him, face down beneath the water. Alfie leapt on top of him, trying to hold him underneath. When he failed to win that physical battle, he resorted to using his teeth again, clamping down on Claypole's cheek and ripping away fat and tendon – a final reply to Claypole's first obscene attack back in the old market square.

Claypole screamed and shoved Alfie away. He then tried to roll on top of Alfie, but Alfie reached out with his wounded hand and shoved his thumb – his right hand's only remaining digit – into his eye, pushing and probing until he felt tissue pop and fluids leak. Claypole's body shuddered, and the fight left him in an instant. He dived backwards into the stream, splashing in the water and screeching.

I've changed you. Changed you forever.

No matter what happens now, you'll never be free of me.

Alfie lay half in and half out of the stream, panting and moaning and bleeding. Water lapped at his thigh, collecting blood from his wounds and taking it away. His breathing was shallow, a great pain growing in his side.

I might be dying.

In the distance came the squeal of sirens.

The only thing louder was Sadie's tears.

———

Alfie kicked his legs and pushed himself up out of the water until he was halfway up the bank. Sadie was several feet higher, calling out to him. "Alfie? Alfie, are you okay? You're bleeding really bad. Oh, God."

Alfie tried to examine himself, but the water in his eyes, along with the darkness, made it too hard to see. His body was leaking all over, rusty fishhooks tugging at his insides and drawing out his fluids. His cheek, his hand, his ribs, his thigh... Which was bleeding worse? How much could a person bleed?

"Alfie? Can you move?"

"I-I'm okay. Just let me lie here."

"The police are coming. They're almost here. Hold on."

He shuffled up another few feet on his elbows before collapsing breathlessly. "I-it's all over now, babe," he muttered. "It's... over."

I blinded that son of a bitch, tore out his throat with my teeth.

Am I an animal or a man? Is there a difference?

"Just hold on, Alfie." She dropped down beside him, putting a warm hand against his wet chest. "Stay with me, okay?"

"D-did you get it on film? Me being a total badass?" He let out a wheezing laugh, tasted blood.

Sadie returned his laughter, but it sounded like a glass breaking. She kept rubbing at his chest, as if to keep him from falling asleep. "I got it all, babe. Don't worry about that now."

Alfie heard the first police car skid to a stop on the dirt road, its blue flashing lights bouncing off the stream.

The cavalry finally arrived.

Car doors opened and closed. Footsteps hurried through the grass and pebbles. "West Mercia Police. Everyone remain where they are."

"W-will do," Alfie muttered.

"I-I'm Sadie Chase. I called you. The man who attacked us is right over..." She hopped backwards and ended up splashing into the middle of the stream. The alarm in her voice was clear. "He was lying right over there. You need to arrest him. He's dangerous. Please!"

"Ma'am, everything will be fine, but we need to ensure your safety. Walk over to me, both hands in clear sight."

Alfie rolled onto his side with a groan and craned his neck to see. A male police officer stood several metres away, holding a gun confidently in both hands.

But where's Claypole? I don't see him.

The armed police officer was quickly joined by four other officers, each holding bright yellow devices that must have been Tasers.

The armed officer put out a hand out towards Alfie. "Sir, medical assistance is incoming. Try to remain still until it arrives."

Alfie was a nodding dog, unable to raise himself even onto his hands and knees. "Claypole. You need to stop him."

The officer turned his head, looking at Sadie. "Miss, come to me now, please. We'll get you safe inside a police car. Your friend will be fine."

Sadie murmured assent, but instead of moving towards the officers, she turned towards Alfie. "Babe, can you get up? Can you try? I don't want to leave you."

His feet were dangling in the water, and when he tried, he was able to pull them up beneath his chest. "I'm not sure. I... I can't feel anything. It doesn't even hurt."

She reached out to help him, but he shook his head. Chances were, she would prod a wound and cause him pain. Either that or pull him off balance.

"Sir, please stay where you are until we can tend to your injuries."

Alfie ignored the officer's demands. He had got there way too late to be making them.

Need to get up. Something doesn't feel right.

Where's Claypole? He can't get away.

Alfie made it up onto his knees like a slow-growing weed, every minute muscle contraction a battle he could barely win. The absence of pain was not a blessing. In fact, he yearned for it to come back and remind him he was alive.

The numbness made him feel like he was blowing away with the breeze.

"Sir, please."

Sadie waded back a step in the water to give Alfie some space.

The water seemed to rise up behind her.

Alfie tried to get to his feet, but his balance betrayed him and he spilled back down into the stream. "Sadie. Sadie, get out of the water."

Claypole emerged from the water like a dripping-wet sea creature. The knife was still in his hand.

The armed police officer yelled with authority. "Get down now! On your knees."

But, just like Alfie, Claypole didn't take orders. He rushed through the water, his body a tapestry of wounds, his left eye missing. He was no longer human – just a wraith of agony and rage.

"Get down!" the police officer yelled again. "Now!"

Claypole raised his knife over his shoulder and snarled, his square teeth like the keys of a piano.

Alfie tried to find his centre, to locate his feet and get up.

He's not coming for me. He's heading for Sadie.

Sadie half turned, with only enough time to scream.

Alfie put a hand on the bank and gritted his teeth, biting through his lip and finding his pain. The white-hot flash brought his body back to life.

The police officers yelled.

Claypole roared.

The knife swung at Sadie's neck.

Alfie threw himself out of the water.

He collided with Sadie and barged her onto the bank so hard that she cartwheeled. With her out of the way, Claypole barrelled into Alfie instead, the knife thudding against his chest.

The two of them stood eye to eye in the middle of the stream, their bodies propping each other up. Claypole's face was a mess of ruination. His one eye closed up and swollen. His cheek hanging off like tobacco-stained wallpaper.

"You got me." Alfie panted, feeling the steel blade between his ribs. "The one who got away."

Claypole pushed the blade in deeper. "It was always going to be this way. It's fate."

The police bellowed a barrage of indiscernible noise that sounded far away.

"You're going to die," Alfie spat through bloodstained teeth. "I got you too." He began to laugh, spraying blood.

Claypole sneered and wiped his face. While he was distracted, Alfie placed both hands on his chest and shoved the man away. Claypole still had a firm grip on the knife. It slid out of Alfie's chest with a sucking *plop*.

Claypole caught his balance in the middle of the stream and raised the knife again.

Alfie smiled. *It's over.*

The gunshot was a hundred times louder than anything Alfie had ever heard. Two more followed and left the world ringing. Claypole's body danced in time to the beat, his arms flopping up and down. A thick mist exploded in the air behind him. For a moment, it looked like he might remain standing, but then, like a puppet whose strings had been cut, he fell and disappeared beneath the shallow water.

Alfie collapsed in much the same way, flat on his back on the muddy bank. Sadie raced to his side, screaming out his name.

He concentrated on breathing. On staying alive.

But his pain had once more gone away.

Sixteen

Alfie didn't try to get up; he knew it was impossible. His lower body was gone, but his upper body tingled as if he were touching a loose lamp wire. He moved his tongue but couldn't feel his teeth. The only thing he *could* feel was Sadie's arms around him as he lay across her lap. All he could see was her face.

"You're shivering," she said. "You're so wet."

"Am I?"

"You're so cold."

"Yes. Cold."

Police officers scurried along the bank, barking into radio handsets or calling out to one another. In the distance, the sirens of an ambulance sounded.

"Help's here," Sadie said with a smile that wasn't happy. "Just a few minutes, babe."

"Okay. It's okay. We got him, yeah?"

She shook him softly, and he felt the rattle in his bones. "*You* got him, babe. He can't hurt anyone else because of you."

"I... I'm sorry for not... for not being better."

She shushed him and wiped his cheek with her thumb. "Hey, stop that. I'm the one who's sorry."

"Things got on top of me and... and..."

She shushed him again. "Help is coming."

"Will you stay with me?"

"Of course. I'm not going anywhere. I won't leave you."

He smiled, everything suddenly seeming okay. The nightmare was over. Only the future now.

"I love you... Daisy."

She kissed his lips. "I love you too."

"I'm sorry." Alfie closed his eyes and waited for help to come.

————

Sadie didn't know the exact second Alfie died in her arms, but at some point she became aware of a subtle change. The body in her arms suddenly felt heavier and less real, and a loneliness washed over her as if her soul could sense that Alfie's had departed.

Perhaps she should have screamed and howled and cursed God Himself for allowing this to happen, but all she did was sit in silence, rocking Alfie's body in her arms. She even shushed him gently, hoping his spirit would gain comfort if it hadn't yet left.

Alfie's gone.

Everyone I care about is dead.

Her arms grew tired. She adjusted her grip and felt something hard and angular in Alfie's pocket. It wasn't his phone because she still had that. She shuffled her hand into the pocket of his soaking wet jeans to find out what it was.

She pulled out a small black box.

Is this what I think it is?

Sadie flipped the box open with her thumb and gasped as a

glittery gem revealed itself, seeming to capture the meagre light of the moon and amplify it. A whopper of an engagement ring.

He was going to ask me to marry him.

Would I have said yes?

I... don't know.

After everything that had happened, with Claypole and with Jay, Sadie could barely put her thoughts in order. It was difficult to remember how she had truly felt about anything. Even with Alfie dead in her arms, she had no tears left to cry.

So she kissed his cold forehead and said goodbye. "I don't know what the future held for us, Alfie, but thank you for loving me, and for allowing me to love you."

"Ma'am, I need you to step away now. The paramedics are here and they need to take a look at your friend."

She lowered Alfie's head to the bank and slipped her knees out from underneath him. "It's too late," she said, sliding the engagement ring onto her widow finger. "He's already gone."

Sadie walked past the officer and headed towards the flashing lights of a police car. A pair of paramedics rushed over to the stream with their bags, but they were wasting their time.

There was never any help for us. We were always on our own.

Broken kids trying to fix each other. Family.

A couple of officers checked on her, but she refused to be taken anywhere. She needed to walk a short distance and feel the cold air on her face. She needed to convince herself that she had survived this nightmare and was not dead or dreaming.

"Say? Say, thank God."

Sadie turned, the Barn still burning in the distance. No doubt the fire brigade was on its way, but like Alfie, it would be too late to do anything. But it wasn't the fire that caught her eye.

She gasped. "Jay?"

Jaydon limped towards her, half-bent at the middle, and so pale he almost looked like a white guy. Helping him along was Kilmani, who also looked worse for wear. It was hard to tell who was leaning on who.

Sadie didn't speak. She just went over and wrapped her arms around Jay, both of them trembling with shock and exertion – and blessed relief.

"I thought Claypole killed you," she said.

"I thought the same about you. Where's Alfie?"

She eased back from him and tried to communicate without having to say it. It worked, because Jay started shaking his head and his face contorted with anguish.

"No," he said. "Nah, he can't be gone, Say. Not him *and* Ezra. Is it really just us? Is there any chance that—"

"Alfie lost too much blood. He couldn't hold on. He tried, but..."

Kilmani groaned. Her frizzy hair was half-caked to her head and flattened with mud. "I'm sorry."

Sadie considered the woman's apology and whether it was an insult. They had called the police about Claypole several times, and yet the psycho had gone on to terrorise and murder them.

But she came here in the middle of the night to help me. She got hurt trying to rescue us.

"It's not your fault," Sadie said. "No one could have expected this. No one."

Kilmani gave her a thin-lipped smile, but the sadness is her eyes was clear. "We need to get you both seen to. Let's head on over to that ambulance. With any luck, they can put us back together again."

Sadie looked back towards the stream, where the paramedics were doing everything they could to achieve nothing. Then she looked up at the sky, which was slowly turning blue. Alfie had gone up with the dawn.

Are you a star or a cloud?

Whatever you are, I hope you find Daisy. I hope she's waiting for you.

All three of them made it to safety, but no amount of glue would ever fully put them together again.

EPILOGUE

Sadie activated her webcam and gave a wave. She had a clump of yellowish flour on the back of her index finger so she sucked it off and gave a wave. "Hey, Jay! It's been too long."

Jay gave her a bright big smile, as handsome as ever with his hair now grown out in an afro and retro-style moustache. "Couple months at least," he said. "How you doing? And when's this new channel of yours launching? I can't wait to watch."

"*Sadie Bakes* will be launching in approximately forty-eight hours," she said, looking back at the chaotic mess of pans and ingredients littering the compact modern kitchen behind her. "I just put an Oreo fudge cake in the oven that's gonna be to die for. Need to keep an eye on my figure."

Jay was wearing an open-collared white shirt with a name badge on the breast. "I'm gonna have to swing by the city and taste one of these masterpieces soon, girl. Who knew you were destined to be the next Mary Berry? As for your figure..." He waggled his eyebrows at her.

She blushed. "I just hope the channel does well, so I can keep on doing it. Baking relaxes me. It's simple, you know? Pure, even."

"And nobody gets hurt. I get it. How are you doing, Say? It's been a year."

She looked down at her laptop's keyboard, not wanting to look him in the eye as she spoke. After Ezra and Alfie's death, they had slowly drifted apart, unable to put the trauma aside and go on with life together. As much as it had pained Sadie, there had been no choice but to build new lives separately – leading her to a swanky flat in the city that was paid off in full thanks to the proceeds of *Invite the Wolf*.

At least something good came of it all. A chance to use the money to do something that makes me happy.

"I miss them," she said. "Every day in fact. I miss Ezra's stupid sense of humour and Alfie's... I miss the belief he always had in us all. In me."

Jay sighed. "Guy had a way of making anything seem possible, huh. Had enough self-esteem for the whole lot of us. Never have another friend like him."

"Alfie helped us believe in ourselves, Jay, but we have to take it from here." She looked back at the screen, pushing a smile onto her face. It really was good to see him. "So, how are things in the world of social care?"

He threw back his head and laughed. "Exhausting. As part of my course, I have to spend Fridays at an old people's home. It's rough, Say, seriously. I wipe a lot of butts and listen to so many sad stories that it's hard to sleep at night. There're a couple folks with pretty bad dementia and things like that. They should really have better care, but I do my best to help and be useful. Me and the other nurses all hold each other up."

"You're a good man, Jay. They're lucky to have you."

"Maybe." He shrugged. "It will all be worth it once I'm

working with kids and giving them the support I never had when I was in the system. *Invite the Wolf* was an attempt at doing good – I truly believe that, even after what happened – but it never quite sat right, you know? It was always this candle burning out, melting us away instead of adding to us. This... this feels like what I'm meant to do. It's building me, making me more whole. Like you and your baking."

She nodded, amazed at how at peace he seemed. Jay wore the past like a badge, something he accepted and displayed proudly. Sadie wasn't so strong, and some nights she still cried against her pillow, but she was getting there. Every morning she woke up a little more hopeful than the last.

She barely even thought about Claypole any more.

Oliver Busey. Ex-army psychopath and multiple murderer.

"Hey, do you still keep in touch with Kilmani?" she asked, knowing that Jaydon had remained in town and that the officer had helped him with a reference when he had applied for university.

"She's good. I see her every few weeks for a chat. I think she feels guilty about what happened, but she's already made up for it as far as I'm concerned. She's good people."

"I'm glad she's doing well."

"We're all doing well, Say. That's the only way it can be. Can't let life grind us down, can we? There's plenty of evil in this world, but there's also us. We fight back in whatever ways we can, spread a little happiness in whichever way we see fit."

A timer went off in the background, the cookies she was baking now ready. "Oh, I forgot I had something in. I'd, um, better get it or else they might burn. Text me, okay? We should meet up soon and have a drink."

"Make it a coffee and it's a deal. Gone teetotal since starting uni. Not going to do anything that might hold me back. I... I owe it to Alfie and Ez, you know?"

She smiled. "I do. They'll always be with us, Jay. Part of our history. A piece of who we are."

"True that. Anyway, I'll let you get back to it, chef. You need me, I'm here, okay? Always."

She rolled back on her chair slightly. "Same. Take care, Jay."

"You too."

Sadie closed her laptop and went over to the oven. When she pulled out the cookies, they were perfect: large, round, and smelling of heaven itself. For the first time in her life, she was in control of her world. Her destiny was her own. She was finally strong enough to walk alone.

"But I miss you, Alfie. I miss you so much."

She had worn his engagement ring for a few weeks before placing it in a drawer. It had never been on the cards for them, she knew that now, but that was okay, because it meant the true love of her life was still out there someplace, walking around and dealing with his own tribulations. He didn't even know she existed yet, but one day he would.

And by then I'll be whole and he can love me in full.

Sadie went over to the window and opened it, wanting to let the cookies cool. Their sugary smell was like hope itself: a mix of ingredients entering an unbearable heat before coming out warm, soft, and beautiful. The sky outside was overcast and grey, but the future was a whirlwind of bright lights.

One year. One year since the terrible murders that had dominated the news. One year since the interviews and inter-rogations. Three hundred and sixty-five days ago Alfie had died in her arms, killed by a monster named Claypole83.

Life was a fairground, but she was done with the scary rides.

She placed the cookies on the window ledge and looked out at the city, full of people good and bad. She was pretty certain she was one of the good ones, and that was all the peace she needed.

Looking up at the sky, she smiled. "Kick some ass up there, Alfie. The angels won't know what hit 'em."

DEAR SISTER

Chlodah took off her police cap and placed it down on her desk at home. Her husband, Steven, had gone for a pint with the lads, which suited her just fine. She had work to do–family business.

She opened up her laptop and loaded the virtual computer that she used for all her personal pursuits. It ran off a server in Moldova–completely private. Currently, the desktop displayed a single folder named: **TWO LITTLE PIGS LEFT SQUEALING.**

She opened the folder and loaded up some of the images she had placed there. One had been taken by a National Highways speed camera. It showed the image of a silver Porsche and its driver: Jaydon Truman, twenty-three years of age.

From what Chlodagh gathered, the kid was well underway on a new career path–health and social work. Noble. Rewarding.

Underserved.

Then there was another image of a fresh-faced young woman beaming in a kitchen as she kneaded a ball of dough. It was a screen capture from a popular online video channel:

SADIE BAKES. A lucrative and empowering business on the rise.

Underserved.

Chlodagh pressed her fingernails into her palms, letting the pain filled her veins. A cold, seething fury flowed around her, and she imagined it fanning out and filling the room like a dark phoenix.

The next picture she opened was from her native desktop, her computer's photo album. A family photograph taken ten years ago at a medal ceremony.

Her brother, Oliver, was receiving a commendation for valor. The whole family had been there to see him rewarded— the Busey clan's hero and figurehead. Their brother, Brent, was there too, beaming proudly. Beloved uncle Mitch sat in his wheelchair, prouder than she'd ever seen him.

Now, all three of them were gone and only Chlodagh remained. The last sibling. The last Busey.

Because of four little pigs that were now two. Oliver had taken care of half the problem, but there was still blood left to spill.

Two more pigs left to butcher.

Sadie Wilson and Jaydon Truman.

"I'm coming to blow your houses down." She seethed, staring at the smiling faces of her dead family. "I'm going to teach you about pain and suffering and things you won't believe."

Her work phone rang. She pulled it out of her blazer pocket and answered the call. "This is Chief Inspector Busey. Make it quick because I've got things to do."

WANT FREE BOOKS?

Don't miss out on your FREE Iain Rob Wright horror pack. Six terrifying books sent straight to your inbox.

No strings attached & signing up is a doddle.

Just Visit IainRobWright.com